REBORN

"I've gone from editing Stephanie's Ellis's books to blurbing them, and if I can tell you anything about Ellis's fiction, it's that she is one of those writers who works tirelessly to improve their craft. I relate to that. I respect that. And she's got this wonderful way of opening that eye in your mind and giving you something new and different. An unexpected surprise. That alone makes Ellis a force to be reckoned with in the horror community. And that's why her fiction is so anxiously met with praise. *Reborn* is no different. Long live the Weald."

– Kenneth W. Cain, author of *Storm Shadows*
and editor of *Blood in the Soil, Terror on the Wind*

The world building is sensational, the imagery magical, the characters alive with nuance.

– Coy Hall, author of *Grimoire of the Four Imposters*
and *The Hangman Feeds the Jackal.*

A Novel by
Stephanie Ellis

REBORN

Edited by MJ Pankey.

Cover illustration and design by Elizabeth Leggett.
www.archwayportico.com

Formatted by Kenneth W. Cain

First Edition: October 2022

ISBN (paperback): 978-1-957537-24-5
ISBN (Kindle ebook): 978-1-957537-25-2
Library of Congress Control Number: 2022937443

BRIGIDS GATE PRESS
Bucyrus, Kansas
www.brigidsgatepress.com

Printed in the United States of America

Content warnings are provided at the end of this book.

To the farmers and landscape of Shropshire, the inspiration behind the Weald.

ACKNOWLEDGEMENTS

Reborn was the book I wrote for myself. To me it told the story I wanted, but as always, I needed to make sure that it worked as a tale and that it was a worthy follow-up to *The Five Turns of the Wheel*. Thanks must go to Coy Hall, an excellent author and wordsmith, and one who, having read *Five Turns*, I trusted to take a first look at *Reborn*. His subsequent comments shored up my own faith in this work. To anyone who hasn't read Coy's work, go now and remedy that!

To Steve and Heather Vassallo of Brigids Gate Press. Thank you for continuing to publish and promote my work. *The Five Turns of the Wheel* and *Reborn* have, I think, found their spiritual world with you.

Thanks also to Elizabeth Leggett for her fantastic cover and MJ for her timely edits!

And finally, thanks as always to my husband Geraint, for giving me the time and space to write and for being up for the excursions for research purposes when I need them! We will be visiting Lancashire soon …

PROLOGUE

BECOMING

He could remember nothing before this moment. The woman in front of him said she was his mother, but he did not understand the word. Nor could he remember seeing her before—or the boys either side of him who proclaimed themselves his brothers. Yet they were his family.

These people were using words he had never heard, although something inside him told him what they meant. Mother. Family. Brothers. The words tugged at him, made him feel connected to those who spoke. It was a pull in his blood, a sense the rhythm of their heartbeats was the same. They belonged together.

"It's nearly time," said Mother. She was smiling down at him, holding something in her arms. "First, you'll need to eat. On a night such as this, we—you—deserve a feast."

His brothers took a hand each and led him to the table.

"Look, brother. So much meat! Father killed the best calf for you!"

"Father?" He looked around. There was nobody else there.

"Hweol will see you after you've eaten," said Mother. "When I have dressed you and I take you to him to receive your name."

He perched on a stool. His stool. So much he knew.

"You did well," said Mother. "Reborn in fire, you'll live long beyond the normal span. With your brothers you will carry our name and honour Hweol, and through him, Cernunnos, the Father of all."

At the word fire, a flame burst across his vision. Bright and searing, he could remember its heat, how it had washed over him. Behind his mother, the fireplace blazed. Something else he was connected to.

"Tommy," said his mother, "give your brother the heart. Fiddler, pass him the lungs."

His brothers took the organs and put them on his plate, added other cuts of meat. A thick, crimson sauce was poured over it. His stomach rumbled its hunger, saliva dribbled down his chin.

"You have the heart and lungs of Nature's beasts," said his mother. "Eat their gift and reinforce your bond with the land and its animals."

A knife and fork sat next to the plate, he made to pick them up, understanding they helped in some way.

"No," said his mother, "eat with your hands. We are of the land. We must touch what we have killed to eat. Understand what it is we have taken from life. It is the only honesty."

He plunged his hands into the mix and felt the slippery texture of offal, the velvet of beef. The heart intrigued him. He scooped it up into his palm and studied its shape.

"The heart is the centre of our world," said Mother.

"It is our force," said Tommy.

"It is our music," said Fiddler.

"It is life," he said, with a sudden clarity. The words were stacking up now. Forming images and ideas in his mind, creating a new knowledge. Words. Useful things, but they would not be his primary understanding. For him, the senses were his main experience—his guide.

"You dine first with your eyes," said Mother. "Take in every part of it. Look at the colour, the shape, the fine lines."

He looked. Oval and veined, parts were smooth, deep red, almost brown, with fine traceries running through. Around the upper part was a wrapping of fat, reaching around the sides like fungus. A short stalk was at the top, which on closer inspection was merely a cut tube. It gave the heart the appearance of an apple. The fruit offered by the serpent in the garden. A fruit to be plucked and eaten, for with its devouring, the gift of knowledge would be imparted.

"Then touch," said Mother.

He obeyed and refocussed on its texture, its weight, the compactness of all that gave life to another in this small organ. Its beat, its music was gone, yet still it spoke to him, of the blood rushing through it every minute, every second; of the focus of the whole of the body in this power station. The brain was the electricity, the impulse, but the heart was the centre of this creature's universe. Its rhythm directed all.

He slipped his fingers into the openings. Prised the organ apart to reveal four chambers. He allowed his fingers to keep breaking the heart down, peeling off slivers with ease, filaments showing veins and patches of fat. Clots of blood remained in parts, a piped decoration.

"Now taste."

He placed a slice on his tongue, let it sit there as he analysed it. Meaty, metallic, bliss. This was not something to be devoured, but a delicacy to be savoured. He started to chew, his teeth compressing and breaking the matter into silky morsels which he swallowed with ease. He repeated with each part of the heart until the whole had vanished and he had taken the beast into himself.

The remainder of his meal was eaten at a swifter pace. He understood this was the fuel of the body, it was needed to burn, and already he sensed a fire in him begin to rage, reflecting that earliest memory lurking in the corner of his mind.

"There will be times when you eat with haste, when hunger and desire drive you," said Mother. "But when it comes to the heart, that alone you must honour."

Tommy and Fiddler had already emptied their own plates and sat waiting for him.

"Time to get ready for your Becoming," said Mother, beckoning him over. In the light of the fire, she pulled off his shirt and slipped the dress she had been holding over his head. Soft and silky, it flowed over him like water, finishing barely below his knees. It was black, shot with silver.

"For the moon, and for night. For the darkness of the world in which we live. It is your baptismal gown."

He raised his bloodied hands to her, knowing his face too would be smeared with the juices from his meal.

She shook her head. "Sacrifice, voluntary or not, is always honoured with blood. You pay tribute to Hweol by wearing its paint."

He glanced at his brothers. They too wore the remains of their meal on their skin.

"What will I become, Mother?" he asked, as she guided her sons out into the darkness.

"What you already are," she said. "All that is left is to give you a name."

As they stepped outside, he felt the cool chill of air on his face. It was a sharp contrast to the warmth of his home but no less welcome. He revelled in its sharpness, the alertness it transmitted to him. They were in a clearing of trees. Huge specimens towered above them, creating a canopy which did not quite hide the sky from view. He gazed up at the stars glittering on the black curtain.

"Pretty," he whispered.

"Sing it louder," said Fiddler, taking an object—a fiddle—from a bag he carried.

He watched as his brother took the bow and pulled it across the strings on his instrument. The sound was like nothing he had ever experienced before. The melody seeped into him, coated his body as if he wore another dress. Already it dictated his movements, and as he swayed, he saw his brother play the stars down. Glittery motes danced around them all, a sparkling confetti twirling in time to the song Fiddler sang into the darkness.

He clapped his hands and tried to catch the darts of gold. "Pretty," he cried, louder this time. The word sounded right, felt right. "Pretty." He was laughing now as were Tommy, Fiddler and Mother. They were all happy.

On the family danced, along paths lined with fern and holly, moss and ivy. Through gaps in the trees, he could see other lights. They were all heading in the same direction, wherever that was. So many different shapes. Some small, silver, giggling and darting about; others huge, lumbering and sedate; yet more shrouded in cowls and hiding their faces. With them were hounds and horses, hawks and falcons. Hunters all, they too were family.

Through the forest they continued, and he knew they were going into its heart. Always the heart. The beating centre. Gradually, the trees fell back and the forest opened up. They were in a grove over which twisted boughs arched and interweaved. The trees reached out to each other, contorted themselves to look down on the throng gathering at its edges. In the midst was a pit lined with wood around its rim.

By the pit stood a creature he knew instinctively was Hweol, Lord of Umbra. This antlered figure, clad in animal pelts, was his father.

"Go," said his mother. "Go and claim your name."

He walked forward, could see Tommy and Fiddler following from the corner of his eye. He noted how they were young in comparison to those around them, yet no one laughed at their youth. The excitement fizzed and buzzed through the air. He understood his naming, his Becoming, was important to them all. He was important.

"Sons," said Hweol, placing a cold, skeletal hand on each as he spoke. "The Three are finally together. A Trinity to lead us in our song and bring others to us. People of Umbra, here are the true Wheelborn, the blood born."

He felt the ownership in that touch and accepted it. Then he was guided to the pit, stepped down, and took his place at its centre. Beneath his feet, warmth seeped up from a huge log at its base. It simmered there, part of this and yet separate.

"The log is the spirit of Winter. It carries the fire of the year and all the years before. This fire is the baptism of my son."

As Hweol spoke these words, flames started to lick up the sides of the pit, jumped on to his dress to add their amber to the silver already there. Twirling around his body, the fire grew, gaining strength until it became an inferno. At its cold centre however, he could feel little. It did not burn him, in fact added another layer like the blood had done. Another coating of the paint which made him. He was being shaded in many colours.

Through the orange curtain he could see Hweol, his mother and his brothers, and many Umbran folk. They were dancing to whatever tune Fiddler was playing for them. He couldn't hear it above the roar of the fire, but he could feel it. Notes escaped and sank into the flames, settled on his skin, their melody seeping into his spirit. He started to dance and spin inside the fire, whipping the flames higher. On and on he danced to this unheard music until gradually he could feel it slow, saw Fiddler ease his bow away from the instrument, come to a stop.

At this, the flames vanished but the warmth remained. Heat occupied every part of his body. This was what he had been born for. To be—and to burn.

He stepped out of the pit and stood before Hweol. He sensed he had grown in some way and as he looked around at those gathered, he realised he had become a giant.

"You have Become who you are," said Hweol. "The energy gifted by this rite will carry you for many years until you need to be Reborn again. All you need is a name! Friends, call out the names of your mothers, for that is how we will revere such a son as this!"

The crowd gathered, tankards were passed around and drinks poured. The murmurs became vocal. He cocked his head to one side and listened.

"Eawynn."

"Mildritha."

"Sweterun."

"Wynflaed."

"Beorhtwen."

Beorhtwen. The name caught his attention and he turned towards the person who had spoken. Their eyes met and the name was repeated.

"Beorhtwen."

He smiled, allowed himself to taste the feel of it in his mouth. He played with the letters, not quite getting it right, became impatient until he cried, "Betty, Betty!" *His* name.

"Beorhtwen, *Betty*," said Hweol, coming over to him and embracing him, pulling him close to his corpse body which still felt as though it had the strength of kingdoms in it.

"Betty," said his mother, hugging her son when Hweol had released him.

"Betty," repeated Tommy and Fiddler in unison. These too, appeared to have grown and aged as if they had merely been wearing a disguise before. Fiddler began to play again. This was a different tune, a new tune, one written for their newly-named brother. This was his tune. It was a violent, frantic song which made him want to tear across the landscape and rip things apart, feed and devour, feast on the hearts of the world.

CHAPTER ONE

MEGAN

Hweol's voice whispered in her ear. *Another day, Megan. What will you do with yourself? I can tell you.*

A year had passed, filled with his murmurings and his silences, mind games slowly sending her mad.

The voice which had sent her here in the first place, that of the Mother, had faded.

Did she ever really speak to you? asked Hweol. *Are you sure you didn't imagine it? Are you sure you're not imagining me?*

The pressure was becoming too much, his voice pushing at her from the darkness of her mind and then fading away for long periods of time. It added to the doubts about her sanity which had built to such a pitch she could barely contemplate any sort of future for herself. The only thing which kept her going was the need to make amends to her husband, or at least that element of him which remained.

Or is that another figment of your imagination?

Maybe I should just kill myself, she responded. *Silence all these voices, these imaginings, as you call them.*

It was a threat which usually caused Hweol to withdraw for a while, or at least reduce his attacks on her grasp of reality. Such an action would be the worst possible outcome for him. It was the one hold she held over him—if he existed.

"Good morning, daughter." Tommy's voice broke into her thoughts.

She raised her eyes to his, his stormy grey matching her own. He no longer called her by her name. Took every opportunity to refer to their relationship, a connection which filled her with loathing. He had destroyed her mother, Liza, had been party to the murder of the man she had believed to be her father. She kept quiet.

He grinned. "Hweol got your tongue?"

Megan stood and began to walk away, but Tommy remained at her side, a leech determined to drain her.

"An early morning walk is good for the soul," he continued. "Clears the mind."

Her hand rested on the sword, wrapped in cloth and hanging at her hip. The bundle—the last of the swords Tommy used in the Dance—had never left her since her arrival in Umbra. Nobody was allowed to touch it. Her fingers twitched, eager to free the blade and use it on Tommy. The steel was crying out for blood. It was thirsty. John was thirsty.

"You could always give it to me," said Tommy, seeing the movement.

"I wish I could," she said. Both knew exactly what she meant. He laughed, appreciating her joke at his expense. It was something she would never do. A contamination of her husband she couldn't bear. By her actions, his spirit remained trapped in the blade of the knives they had tried to destroy and which in the end, had destroyed them. Her actions? No, it had been Hweol asserting control over her body, forcing her to push John into the forge's inferno where he burned, freeing his soul to become one with the blade at her side. Her sleep had been destroyed by that memory of seeing him fall into fire, the puzzled expression on his face, replaced by horror and agony as the flames ate him. She dreaded the moment her eyes would close.

"You should thank Betty, you know," said Tommy. "If he hadn't retrieved the swords, your John would most definitely be a goner. He's over there if you want to have a little chat."

Megan had already spotted the giant, had smelt him first. She had no intention of talking to him ever again if she could help it. She was only speaking to Tommy because he was forcing her into it. "I think I'll pass."

"Fair enough. Thought you might like to discuss fashion, his dress for the coming autumn."

"He can make do with what he's got," she growled. Betty's dresses meant ritual and death. By now, they were stepping onto the hidden path which allowed the Folk to travel between Umbra and the Weald—the human world, her world—unseen. Her old home was calling her. Tommy halted. Whenever any of the Umbrans had tried to cross the threshold into the Weald, fires had blazed up to stop them, a visible reminder of the Mother's anger. Lately, however, those flames had weakened, become a mere flicker. Megan's way was clear, whilst only a thin glow appeared in front of Tommy. Megan sensed change was upon them and the Umbrans would be free, their sentence served. *What had been the point?* she wondered. What had she achieved?

Nothing, came that voice in the corner of her mind. *Nothing at all.*

"Soon," called Tommy, as she walked away from him and into the village of Cropsoe. "The Mother will free us soon." His laughter followed her, echoed by that in her head.

Megan couldn't help but think he was right. Her sense of failure overwhelmed her. Ahead, at the end of the lane stood The Five Turns, closed up and silent.

"Megan!"

She jumped at the sound of her name. On the few visits she had made, most pretended not to see her, easier than awkward platitudes on the loss of her family, their complicity. It was her uncle, George Wheelborn: her father's—her assumed father's—brother, so … not really her uncle.

"I've been watching out for you," he said. "Hoped to catch you one day."

"Just passing through," she said. She didn't add it wasn't safe for her to stay too long, Hweol could take over her body at any moment. Cause pain to some other innocent soul. She didn't want to be responsible for that as well.

"Fair enough," said George, "though you know you've got a home with me and the missus if you ever want it."

Her uncle was looking at her awkwardly, his grey eyes concerned, kind. It had been a long time since anyone had looked at her like that. She smiled but shook her head.

"Here," he said, pulling her into his arms, "take a hug at least."

Megan allowed herself to be buried in the big man's embrace. It had been so long since another person had held her. She lost herself in his warmth, the steady beating of his heart. She pulled back, reluctant to maintain a connection which would end up being destroyed like so much else.

"You'll always be Simon's daughter, my niece," he said, taking her hand. "You do know that, don't you? We're still family."

They were words she needed to hear, and she smiled at him, grateful. She tried to fight back the tears as the resemblance to her father became more pronounced until, for one glorious moment, she felt as if she was walking beside Simon Wheelborn—a little girl holding her father's hand as they continued towards The Five Turns.

"I've been dropping in here when I can," said George. "I open the windows, air the place, keep it clean. I took the barrels over to The Yew Tree. Hope you don't mind."

"Ale and cider are the last things I want to think about," she said. "You may as well get something out of selling it. How is life in Soulsbury?"

"Quiet," said George. "Folk aren't quite certain what they can and can't do. Some, the youngsters mainly, have packed up and left for the city. The old 'uns are scared. Think they'll be punished if they don't carry on as they always have. It's the same across the Weald."

Escape. She and John had tried and been thwarted. She hoped those who'd got out were left free to enjoy their new lives.

"The Cropsoe folk grumble quite a bit about having to walk all the way over to The Yew Tree to get a drink," said George. "They think me being a Wheelborn gives them some protection if the three come back." He snorted. "They should realise by now the Wheelborn name is the worst thing to have."

Her uncle was right. Folk such as they were usually the ones who gave the most. It was why no one could ever look her in the eye when she came back.

"Will you open it again?" he asked.

They had arrived at The Five Turns. It looked no different than it had when she had lived there. The small grass beer garden was neat and tidy, the windows shone, the door sported a new coat of paint.

George saw her looking. "I've tried to keep it right for you. Just in case."

Despite everything, this was still her home. Megan blinked back tears. "Thank you."

Apart from the visits when she had slipped down the lane in the twilight hours to gather up a few belongings, she had often stood at the end of the lane from Umbra and looked on the village, on her home. She tortured herself with the memories, believed she deserved the punishment.

So, we're agreed then, murmured a voice.

Megan closed him out, took in the nearby cottages where a few faces appeared in the windows, vanishing when they saw she'd spotted them. The green opposite the pub had been returned to its pristine state. There was no sign of the remnants of the night of the Sixth Turn, the blood-soaked soil, the ravaged corpses, the barbaric maypole—even though it had been October. The Umbrans had their own ritual calendar, distorted and vicious.

"It was like everyone wanted to forget," said George, following her gaze. "They all mucked in and cleared it up. Out of sight, out of mind, I suppose. Can you blame them?"

Blame them? Yes, she could. They'd rather pretend nothing had happened, even if they had lost someone, turning that loss to a mere gap in memory.

He pulled out a key and leaned across her to unlock the door. Her dad had given him that key years ago, in case of emergencies. They stepped into the cool and silent building, leaving the curious stares behind.

"Sit yourself down a minute," he said, making his way to the bar and taking down a bottle of whisky and a couple of glasses. He hadn't taken everything, only the stuff that would spoil. He pushed a filled tumbler towards her. "Drink. Then talk."

Talk. She hadn't talked properly to anyone about anything since she'd left. There was no one amongst the Umbrans she could talk to, and those who spoke to her were voices she didn't want to hear. What could she tell her uncle that wouldn't make him think she was mad?

George refilled their glasses.

"Don't blame yourself for what happened," he said. "Your mum and dad, they made their own decisions. They understood the consequences. And you and John. You tried. It was more than any of us have ever done. More than I could even contemplate. That took guts."

Tears threatened again. "I was stupid," she whispered. "Why did I think I could ever make a difference?"

"But you did. Yes, it's all a bit uncertain, but it's the chance to change and we've never had that before. You gave us that."

"Perhaps." She thought of the worm in her brain. Hweol was biding his time as he waited for the opportunity—the body—to step out from her shadow and reclaim his rightful place. How could she tell her uncle that when he seemed so hopeful? And the lessening of the Mother's fires? It all spoke of a return to the old ways.

"And if they return," he said, as if sensing something of her thoughts, "perhaps we'll be more prepared, more able to stand up to them."

"Would you?" she asked. "Would you stand up to them?"

He paused, the glass at his lips, then swallowed quickly. "I think I would. I'd like to think I would, after what you all did." Another swallow. "I hope I would."

There it was. In his voice, in his eyes. The fear. The doubt. The shame.

Megan poured herself another drink. She was beginning to feel light-headed, but it felt good to be able to let go for once, cast her troubles aside.

"How are you?" he asked, changing the focus back to her. "Truly?"

"I'm fine," she said. "Apart from being widowed, childless, and haunted."

George reached over and squeezed her hand. "Not alone though."

No, you're not, are you? chuckled the voice. *Are you going to tell him—or shall I?*

He glanced at his watch. "I have to get back," he said. "Opening time. Unless you need me here—or you could come with me?"

She shook her head, thankful for his distraction. She didn't want Hweol to appear, to destroy George's illusion his niece was recovering. "No, thanks. I just need a bit of time on my own. Get my head straight."

"Decision time?" he asked, shrewdly.

She laughed. "You were always the one who knew exactly what everyone in the family was thinking."

"Not everything," said George, a slight sadness tinging his voice. "If I did, I would maybe have stopped a few things happening."

It was her turn to reach across and squeeze his hand. "It's not your fault either."

They smiled at each other with mutual sadness and affection, then George rose and gave her a peck on the cheek.

"You know where I am," said George. "My home is your home. Always."

The door closed behind him and Megan was left on her own.

Didn't want to tell him about me, eh? Didn't want him thinking you were mad?

She had known Hweol would start up again, that there would be no respite.

And what of your poor old husband, eh? Been a bit neglectful there, haven't you? Not let that sword see the light of day. Not talked to him.

It was true. Megan no longer looked at the blade whose shifting surface showed the presence of her husband's spirit, allowed his voice to speak. Guilt consumed her. A tiny part had hoped one day she would look at the sword and he would've faded away. She despised herself for such thoughts, but it would make life so much easier. Hweol's laugh echoed around the bar.

The sound made her look up, expecting to see the creature. Then she saw herself in the mirror opposite, mouth wide open. The laughter was coming from her. It was becoming unbearable. She picked up her empty tumbler and hurled it at the mirror. The glass shattered but didn't break. Instead, it distorted her image, made both sight and sound a hundred times worse. Coming back here hadn't solved anything, hadn't given her any ideas. She stood and made her way to the door. George would clear up the glass. She felt slightly guilty about leaving it, but she couldn't bear another minute in the pub. She made herself a promise. For as long as Hweol resided within her, she would remain as far from Cropsoe as possible.

Megan didn't mind. It was best the villagers put the past behind them, tried to become part of the modern world. As she left, she could feel the eyes watching her from behind net curtains, following her progress out of the village and back to Umbra.

There is a way to rid yourself of me, said Hweol, as they walked. *You don't want to spend the rest of your life listening to me, do you?*

They had reached the lane boundary again. Megan stopped and sat down, pulled the bundle onto her lap and unwrapped the sword. Its surface shifted, but it was very faint. If John was there, she couldn't see or hear him.

I can think of a way, she said, feeling the edge of the blade with her finger. The fire had blunted it somewhat, but it could still cut. She allowed the edge to hover at her throat before drifting down to her wrists. *Which would you prefer?* she asked. *The quick death, or the slow bleed out. There's no one around to help you. They can't hear you. There's only me.*

CHAPTER TWO

TOMMY

Tommy had watched her tear the pelts and tapestries from the walls of Hweol's dwelling, had heard her prohibit the hunt. *His* daughter. Telling *him* what he could or couldn't do. *His* daughter had stopped the Wheel from turning, had tried to destroy Hweol, would have brought about his own—and his brothers'—end. Except she hadn't.

A malicious little grin appeared as he pondered the state of affairs. Yes, the Mother had given Umbra and its people to Megan to command, but she had not been honest with his Wheelborn offspring, failing to tell her of one important aspect of his—and Hweol's—origins. Nature was cruel whatever face she wore, pitting species against species. Skin Walkers were one of the oldest of those who walked the face of the earth. Organisms who could shape shift according to desire, who could slough off their physical form if they so wished, who could bury themselves like a worm into the consciousness of another. This was the clan to which Hweol, Tommy, and their kind belonged—except Betty. Betty was different.

The Mother had told Megan nothing of this and allowed her to believe Hweol could be destroyed. Why? He had an idea, one he needed to ponder further. It afforded him some amusement however, to see Megan's discomfort at being a home to a parasite. Knowing she would be hearing the creature's voice, always in her ear, whispering.

There was also the matter of that other little lie. Her husband, John, was dead. There would be no reincarnation for him, regardless of the story spun to Megan. Yes, his spirit resided in the blade of the sword at her side, but there was nowhere for it to go but up in flames. One day the sword would return to *his* side and then the Dance would begin again. His daughter was truly haunted.

Despite the year of abstinence from ritual and the hunger that had created, little had changed, a mere blip in the rhythm of life. Mothers would always punish their sons and then forgive them. The lowering of the fiery boundaries around Umbra was sufficient indication. Their sentence was almost up. It still rankled however, that with his brothers, Fiddler and Betty, Tommy had been relegated to the sidelines, or if summoned to his daughter's presence, he was challenged on every aspect of the way of the Mother.

"She is the one who guided us," Tommy had said. "It is she who created our laws and traditions. Undermine them and you undermine Her."

Megan had looked at him. "If she was so happy with *you*, then why did she send *me* here, set me above you all."

Tommy had remained silent. He knew some of the answers, perhaps their rituals had developed a cruel edge. The rites the Mother had commanded they obey, had, after all, been born in blood. Blood these days was an element most definitely lacking and he was suffering its absence. A year had passed, and he found himself desperate to hunt, to tear something limb from limb. Megan knew what he wanted but refused permission. *It's the Mother's punishment*, she had said, with an annoying smirk on her face.

The three had taken to living in a corner of the forest some distance from Hweol's old hall and the hovels of the creatures who'd paid court to him. It gave a small illusion of freedom, and he knew it irritated his daughter. Added to her impression that he was continually plotting and scheming against her—and she was right.

Tommy poked at the small fire in front of them, trying to stir the flames. He didn't need the heat, that was for Betty. But he needed the flames, their movement, their dance. Betty and Fiddler were sat at his side, equally unhappy.

"I can't live like this," said Fiddler.

Betty grunted his agreement.

"We can't challenge her here. We're no longer as strong as we once were. It is near our time. We need to hunt to be reborn, to return to our beginning. We need food, real food. We need blood."

"Hunt," said Betty, poking at a worm wriggling through the dead leaves with his finger before picking it up and popping it in his mouth.

"Yes," sighed Tommy. "Hunt. We need to get away, become strong again. Then we can return and put this place to rights." He had been unable to rid himself of the riddle of the Mother's punishment, the feeling the answer was almost within his grasp.

"There is nowhere in Umbra we can go," said Fiddler. "She would be able to track us anywhere."

Tommy had given the matter much thought. Sent his eye roving over the Weald and their own Umbran shadow world. A smudge of grey on its border caught his eye. It hovered there briefly and then blinked out. Hiding? No. Sister was blocking him.

He grinned. Time to pay the brat a visit. "There is a place," he said, looking at Fiddler and then at Betty. "It's a place we've not visited for many a year. Centuries if truth be told."

Fiddler stared at him, surprise crossing his face. "The Layerings? Do you dare? We didn't leave it on the best of terms."

"I think I do," said Tommy. "There's nothing for us here at present and the Layerings—well, I've heard Sister has become quite inventive."

Fiddler's smile matched his own. "It would be interesting. Perhaps yes, it is time for a reunion, see if she's forgiven you. Betty?"

Betty looked confused.

"The Layerings," said Tommy, "are amongst the oldest lands of this island nation, older than Umbra. It is where we all come from, including you, though you probably have little memory."

It had been the same as the Weald in so many ways—valleys and meadows, hills and dales. A beautiful land. Until they'd taken more than it could give, turned it into a barren wasteland to the fury of the Mother. It was she who had expelled them from that world, demanded they keep their new world 'sustainable' whilst haranguing Cernunnos, the Father, and imprisoning him at the edges of the Layerings, where he remained, hidden by Sister.

As the Creator of Life, the Mother had always been the strongest in that particular partnership. Even the Father of All, the Destroyer, depended on her for his existence—but now? As a family fallout it had been pretty spectacular. The idea that had taken hold in his head, the reason for Hweol's treatment, their punishment, blossomed into a certainty—the Mother had planned this! She was sending them on a pilgrimage of sorts, a journey back to the beginning, to make amends, be born anew. His spirits rose.

Another realisation dawned. The Mother *needed* them. The modern world had changed so much. Somehow, man, that hopeless little creature—no more than food and drink for his kind—had shown they could tame her, destroy her. The Mother needed her family to bring back the balance, and Tommy was more than happy to oblige, especially if she allowed him to do it on his own terms. The Mother was still needed to give life. In her need, he saw a chance to check her power, take a little of it for himself. Well, perhaps a bit more than that. His mood lightened as he saw a new future appear, one which spread further than the Weald.

He needed to track down Tobias. A Skin Walker like them, he had been part of that initial migration but had left them and settled on the borderland between the Layerings and Umbra. An area amongst humans unaware of his true nature. Sometimes Tommy would visit, the need to see for himself overriding his vulnerability in the modern world. It was not the humans themselves but the shields, the weapons and technology in which they had wrapped themselves which caused him his anxiety. They had removed themselves from the Mother and so were harder to read.

Tobias served both Sister and Hweol, and over the years had travelled back and forth between Umbra and his home, telling Tommy how Sister had formed her world, how she had rebuilt and fashioned the Layerings. What form Sister herself had taken was something Tommy was still unsure about. Tobias had said she had taken many shapes, tried many diets and would often change, just as you got used to her. *Typical female*, thought Tommy, disregarding the part he had played in this aspect of her, the reason for their falling out.

Tobias was the key to the return of the Father and with that, their own rebirth.

"They are dark lands," said Tommy, "but Sister has been feeding them. Tobias has told me of her hunts. It is time we dined at her table. And it will be far enough from Megan to come up with a plan to Turn again and to return us all to what we should be, what we were made at the First Turn."

Betty perked up at the mention of travel, of hunting. "We're going? Together?"

There was a lost air hanging over Betty, one which had increased as the year had worn on. It brought home to Tommy how much he would miss his brother should anything happen to him. He put an arm around Betty and allowed the giant to pull him into an embrace. Brotherly hugs weren't normally their thing, but in this instance, it felt right. Fiddler was smiling and nodding at the two, then allowed himself to be pulled into their fraternal embrace. The three becoming one.

If Fiddler had been able to play, he would've been able to command a tune, allow his notes to guide Betty. Something else that needed to be put right. Perhaps the first thing. Tommy took in their surroundings.

The forest was still shrouded in gloom, shadows looming up and fading back. Dense branches cradling each other to block out the sky in parts, hide those who lived beneath. Tracks appeared and disappeared beneath their feet; they knew every path, every twist and turn of this ancient woodland. Winter, spring, and summer had passed since their interment within its bounds. That they would be escaping as autumn arrived filled Tommy with hope. This was his time as much as any other. It was when he was most powerful. *His* time.

As they walked, they occasionally heard the giggle of an Imp or saw a shrouded Wyve lurking in the foliage. Their escape was being watched and noted by all who wanted the old ways to return. He sniffed the air, felt a sudden lightness, a tang that spoke of open skies. The trees thinned, a sweep of hill and vale came into view. Behind them, Tommy could feel a presence build, a wall of shadows, of his brothers and sisters, of his Umbran family.

He turned and spoke into the darkness. "We will return. We will be Reborn. We will bring the Crow Folk and the Whipping Boy. We will bring the Skin Walkers and our Cousins of the Wyrd. We will bring back new blood. The Wheel will turn again. So tell me," he stepped closer to the hidden crowd, spread out his arms as if to embrace them all. "What is the First Turn?"

"The First Turn is the Wheel that burns, the Maid who is wed to the land of the dead. The Dance claims us all."

"We bow to the Maid who will show her love," said Tommy, relishing the taste of the old, familiar words on his tongue.

"We bow to the Maid," came the response, muted, no doubt worried Megan might hear and they would be punished.

"What is the Second Turn?" he pushed on.

"The Second Turn is the Wheel that crushes. When the son of the soil is ploughed into the land. The Dance claims us all." Their voices were a little louder this time.

"What is the Third Turn?"

"The Third Turn is the Wheel that flies. When the crone rides the night and old bones are crumbled. The Dance claims us all."

The chant and response warmed him, strengthened his resolve. As his family gave voice in their turn, he could tell they too had been affected, were revitalised.

"What is the Fourth Turn?"

"The Fourth Turn is the Wheel that freezes. When the Whelp walks in the forest. The Dance claims us all."

"Brothers! Sisters! Tell me. What is the Fifth Turn?"

"The Fifth Turn is the Wheel that bleeds. When the unborn are taken into the womb of Nature, their blood the right of the OtherWorld. The Fifth Night is the night of the Wheelborn. The Dance claims us all."

"The Dance claims us all." This final line roared defiantly out into the world.

"And we will Dance again," said Tommy quietly, smiling at them all. "We will have our Sixth Turn. Have no doubt, all will become as it should."

Betty had already gone ahead, stepped out beneath the growing light, sniffing the air, hungry. Fiddler moved after him, ready to restrain him if need be.

"Smells different," said Fiddler, as they walked.

"The boundaries are weak, the world is encroaching," said Tommy. How easy would it be to push back against such a place? He refused to let future problems worry him. He lived for challenge. Relished the solution.

"Where do we go first?" asked Fiddler, as the three stood surveying the familiar landscape.

"To the city," said Tommy, rubbing his hands. "To visit old friends." He was curious to see how the Master fared in the world of concrete and steel, electricity and oil; although the man's home was ancient. They had not met for a long time but would occasionally exchange messages via Tobias. Was there another power there he could tap into? He had promised to return to Umbra, and he would, but that did not mean he would pass up new opportunities or the chance to renew old acquaintances.

"Don't worry," he continued, noticing Fiddler's worried glance. "We stay on the edges, find the underbelly. There's always a seam of misery hiding in plain sight. We'll sniff it out, use it. At least restring your fiddle!"

Fiddler laughed. "It'll make our lives easier once that's done."

The power of Fiddler's music could not be underestimated. It turned people's minds, controlled their monstrous brother, directed events. Though he didn't like to admit it, Tommy worried that without Fiddler's restraining music, Betty would be beyond his control. His brother had a strength greater than any of them, yet to a large part remained unaware. He had always been kept in check. He could not be Reborn without the music ready for him. If that happened, even Tommy and Fiddler would be at risk.

Fiddler nodded. "To the city then. Strings don't make themselves!"

His words were like a starting pistol to Betty who loped off ahead of them.

Tommy's heart quickened as he spoke, felt a spike of excitement. "I sense new opportunities, brothers, but we must move quickly. Our friends will hinder Megan for as long as they can, but knowing my daughter, she will be on our tails eventually."

He caught up with Betty and gently gripped the man's shoulder, slowing him down. The giant felt less solid than usual and there was a pallor to the little amount of skin visible beneath his hair-shrouded face. They would have to move quickly.

"Come on, Betty," he said. "It's time for us to bring back the music."

The sun dipped behind the trees and he shivered. It was the chill of an approaching winter, although autumn had only recently begun. The next season would certainly be a harsh one. He felt the urgency thrumming up through the soil, urging him to get up and get moving. Regroup and bring back the Weald to Hweol.

CHAPTER THREE

BETTY

Betty took in the landscape, it wore the colours he adored—deep reds, slashes of orange, yellow, burnt ochre, and emerald. He wistfully imagined a dress of these colours, melding him with the seasons and their change. As Fiddler had been denied his music, he had been denied his robing. Unable to mirror the soft silence of winter, the vibrancy of spring, the hum of summer, he felt he had lost a vital connection and it saddened him.

He knew they were being punished but that too puzzled him. His was a nature moulded by the Mother. She had called him the heart, the representation of all her creations. It stung to think she considered he had failed her. Sometimes he'd look at Tommy and Fiddler and feel his anger rise, it was *their* fault, he had only ever done what he'd been told. Then Tommy would bring him some extra carrion, would try and take him somewhere to hunt quietly, taking on Megan's ire when she inevitably found out. Fiddler would sing him to sleep, soft lullabies without his instrument, songs Megan banned as soon as she heard them. Whatever she did, they continued to try and look after him. No, he couldn't be angry at them, but he could be angry at her—at Megan.

Something brushed his cheek, a breeze caused by movement nearby. He looked around and spotted a hawk swooping down to spear some unsuspecting prey with its talons. A kindred spirit. They were not quite out of Umbra but they weren't far from the border lands, that much he could sense. Any thought of Megan's disapproval was shrugged off as he started to scan land and sky for predators. He wanted to join them, if only for a short while, experience that strength, the sheer power, which coursed through him as he ran with the pack. The electricity of the hunt was as vital to him as blood. They were leaving and she couldn't stop them. He grinned and cast another hopeful look at his brothers.

"No, Betty," called Tommy. "Not here, not yet. It isn't safe for you. Soon, I promise."

Betty stamped his foot and a startled rabbit shot out from a nearby hedge. He reached down and grabbed it, turned towards his brothers, holding it up defiantly in front of them. Tommy and Fiddler caught him up as he stood there with the animal struggling in his hand.

"You need to stay close to us," admonished Tommy.

More words telling him what he could and couldn't do, but the look in Tommy's eye told him so much more, that his brothers loved him and didn't want to see him come to any harm.

"Pretty rabbit, though," offered Fiddler, eyeing the petrified animal.

"Pretty," agreed Betty, cupping the animal in his palm and stroking the fur. He loved their softness, the fluffy powderpuff tail was an especial favourite. He ripped it off and tossed it into his mouth. "Tasty," he added, and devoured the rest of creature to the amusement of his brothers. Trees edged the field and he followed his brothers reluctantly. He preferred the open where he could run. The pulse beneath the ground pulled at him, an invisible cord binding him to the Mother.

CHAPTER FOUR

MEGAN

No, no. The words spun round in her head. The Dance claims us all. The Dance. The old nightmare which had never gone away had taken on a new strength. Her eyes flew open. No, not a dream. The old words were being shouted at her. Tommy stirring up the Folk to torment her, taunt her. The words continued to roar at her.

"Brothers! Sisters! Tell me. What is the Fifth Turn?"

"The Fifth Turn is the Wheel that bleeds. When the unborn are taken into the womb of Nature, their blood the right of the OtherWorld. The Fifth Night is the night of the Wheelborn. The Dance claims us all."

The Fifth Turn stabbed its words into her, daggered her heart. Hweol remained silent in her head. The words and memory enough to continue her destruction. She curled up on her rough bed, a blanket thrown on a pile of dead fern inside a small cave. Foetal. Cried anew for her mother, her baby, her husband. As she sobbed, the memories of the pain and the blood shed that night became unbearable. Her hands searched for the sword. There would be comfort in its blade, silence from its touch. She could sleep forever, join her husband. The man she had killed.

Megan's fingers shook as she unwrapped the bundle. When she had threatened to kill herself before, it had merely been an excuse to anger Hweol, to irritate the monster. A petty revenge. This time was different. She could do it. She knew she could. Beyond the cave was the grey sky of dawn. In the Weald were family who, whilst mourning her passing, would be relieved at the removal of the constant reminder of their own failure. It didn't matter there would be pain. She had suffered that before in so many ways. At least this time, it would be quick and with a definite end. She could do this.

The sword lay across her lap. Ragged bits of wood at each end of the blade; the remnants of its handles. How it had not all been destroyed was beyond her. But Betty had moved quickly when he'd come to the rescue of the swords. Betty. Though it was Tommy who manipulated situations, wrote the script, there was something worse about the giant. She had been promised to him in some manner and despite events, she felt as if there was a strange tie between them. It left her feeling unclean.

Her fingers, blue with cold, drifted over the surface. How long had it been since she had last touched the metal, touched John? And still, she wasn't quite touching the blade. Movement beneath the steel became evident, clouds of grey, tracking her hand. A storm in the making. She reached for the blanket and then stopped as she berated herself for her cowardice.

"John," she whispered, allowing a tear to drop on the exposed blade.

There was no answer, only a slight deepening in colour.

"John," she tried again.

He had spoken to her in those early days. Reassured her he was alright, that he was in no pain. They had talked of happy days, of plans for their future. Cheerful discussions of things which would happen once she freed him from his prison. But then time went on and his voice became angrier, colder. And he was thirsty, oh so thirsty. He needed a drink.

The shock of his demand the first time had led to an accidental cut, her blood spilling out onto the sword. The few drops had vanished swiftly beneath its surface, lapped up. After that, the demands had become more insistent.

"Don't you think you owe me?" he'd asked.

"I need to be strong when I come back."

"If you loved me, you'd do it."

Megan rolled up her sleeve, studied the hatchwork of scratches. Offerings she'd made when her mind had closed down and she had lost herself to months of madness. Even Hweol had remained silent during that time.

As she recovered, she would try to talk to her husband with the sword safely at arm's length. But even then, she would hear his wheedling demands, his poisoned darts of guilt replaced by more loving words, words which were still a lie. It was then she had begun to doubt John's true presence in the sword. Smoke and mirrors, hallucination. That was all it had been. A desire to hold on to some small comfort, some belief John existed, that she hadn't lost everything. A belief not dismissed by Hweol, Tommy or the Mother, leading her to distrust herself further.

"You're not there, John. Are you?" she whispered, holding the metal closer to her than she had in a long time. "Even if there is a tiny bit, it's not all you, is it?"

The clouds swirled and pulsed across the blade's surface. There was no other reply.

The sword had become a mere remnant of a past horror. Time to discard it.

"I'll give you peace," she said. "This time. I promise."

And how will you do that?

Hweol had come back.

"If you're in my head, you should know," she said, speaking aloud as she always did when she was on her own.

Only fire is strong enough. And not all fires have the same strength.

The memory of the Forge and its inferno roared up before her. She threw the sword from her, unable to bear touching it. She felt the heat, smelt the roasting of her husband's flesh anew, an unbearable flashback. With a cry, she ran out of her cave, into the forest, ignoring everything around her. Imps jumped out of her way, Wyves looked curiously on, Lords followed her flight impassively. She barely noticed, hoping that by running, she would leave her pain and her guilt behind.

Out of the forest, she ran, stopping only when pain stabbed at her side and her lungs could take no more. She found herself in the middle of a field, sloping at its edges so that the ground beyond was visible and anyone on the other side had a clear view of its centre. With horror she realised she was in the Fallow Field. The site for the Fifth Turn of the Wheel. Though left untended, barely anything grew here. Only the barest of green covered the soil, allowing patches of dirt to peer through as if waiting for its offering.

In response, her stomach cramped and a warm trickle ran down her leg. Blood. This land always cried out for it, demanded it from anyone who could give, not caring who it was. This field had taken her mother's unborn and so many others, she would not allow it to take even a drop of hers.

Megan moved swiftly until she was on the other side of the hedge, the cramps deepening as she did so. Her monthly cycle had been irregular ever since her miscarriage. That her period should start now, and so violently, at this site jarred her. To be reminded of her pain in this way and at this place, was beyond comprehension. The Mother was cruel.

She threw herself down onto the grass, gasping for breath, crying out as she cramped again.

As she lay there, she heard a snuffling in the hedgerow; an Imp appeared, sniffing the air. Then it crawled towards her, another following hard on its heels.

"Thirsty," said one.

"Thirsty," repeated the other.

They could smell her, her blood, but she couldn't move. They were at her feet, sniffing their way up, tongues flicking out. She kicked at them in disgust and sent them yelping back into the hedge. A Wyve appeared behind them and scooped them up, throwing Megan a disapproving look.

She didn't care. The Wyves regarded the Imps as children, and she had too—once. When her father had taken her to Umbra, he had encouraged her to play with these creatures, and she had enjoyed their company then. As an adult, the scales had fallen from her eyes and she had seen them as they really were. Slightly recovered, she pulled herself to her feet and turned herself reluctantly back in the direction of her shelter. Her jeans stuck to her skin, clammy, uncomfortable. The smell of blood, the dull ache, not just in her womb but her back, her legs, a painful throb refusing to go away. Her stomach roiled. More than once she had to pause and wait for the waves of nausea to subside, but she eventually found herself back at the cave. She quickly changed, wiping herself down, found a sanitary towel to at least make her feel clean, human, for a moment. The Wyves had shown her how to make old-fashioned clouts with rags and moss, the few occasions she had needed anything, but they hadn't been comfortable.

It was a reminder she could still become a mother. No. She would never allow such a thought to cross her mind again. The dull gleam of the sword caught her eye. She quickly hid it in its blanket and curled up on her bed. Hoped she could sleep without dreams or nightmares, until the aches, the betrayal of her body, had passed.

CHAPTER FIVE

TOMMY

Clumps of trees turned into a forest. The trio moved along paths which Tommy knew would take them to the cliffs at the Seat of the Wheel. They had to move carefully as they followed the rocky base. A pit lived in this place. Normally it would be at the foot of Hweol's throne but it sometimes had a tendency to shift when it felt particularly hungry. Megan had starved this area too, being, as it was, the site where her mother had been turned on the wheel and sent down into the depths of the pit to feed the demons inhabiting the darkness.

"Do you miss her?" asked Fiddler, nodding his head in the direction of hole.

"She warmed my bed, cooked a good meal, was obedient—"

"Except at the end," interrupted Fiddler.

"Yes, except at the end. Didn't really see that coming, did I? Women, eh, they'll always surprise you."

Tommy felt no regret, despite her suffering. They had all been forced to witness Liza Wheelborn's last moments. She was the example held up to those who crossed Hweol. Was it that little ritual which the Mother had decided was beyond the pale?

Nor did he feel any guilt. Liza had chosen her own path and in doing so, had fed the creatures of the dark. They would sleep a while longer. Should those demons stir and not be fed, then Umbra itself would be in danger. He would leave that knotty little problem to Megan to deal with. She had been lucky so far. The pit had been sated. He chuckled as he thought of how little his daughter knew of her Umbran 'subjects', especially those like himself who were not necessarily all they appeared to be. She thought she knew him. Soon she would realise she didn't know him at all.

They left the gaping mouth of the pit behind them and continued along a rocky track which led away from behind Hweol's seat. Nobody trod that path without permission when their father was free. But all had walked it once—when they had followed Hweol on their exodus from the Layerings and into the Weald. Now he was returning, but it had been a long time. He needed to focus and already Betty was starting to wander about.

"We have to tread carefully," he called out to his brother. "Until we know how things are, you can't go running ahead or dancing or …"

Betty's face fell. He'd been on a tight leash and Tommy could sense he needed to run. He would let him—when there was no danger. Even Fiddler needed to stay his hand from the music.

Their feet crunched over large pieces of slate, the track meandering along the bottom of a hill before it tapered to the entrance of a gorge. How the land transformed itself so suddenly and so spectacularly never concerned him. They could easily be walking from one world into another, this particular threshold was a gateway. Like the path which took the Folk of the Weald quickly from one village to another via the Weald, this was an old Ley Road. Full of energy, it was part of the ancient network of tracks which guided them across the country as a whole. Nobody, apart from their Folk, had ever walked them. No one, from the ancient Celts and Viking invaders to modern day man, had been allowed to know exactly where these paths were, nor were they allowed to follow them. Any strays were always dealt with.

It had been interesting listening to Tobias tell him of the preoccupations of modern man. A conflicted people, he considered, with their continual pushing at the boundaries of technology whilst developing a yearning for the assumed 'spiritual' nature of early pagan times. Possibly an audience of his for the future? The idea amused him as he considered his own 'spiritual' nature.

There was also this modern pre-occupation with Ley Lines, a misguided idea of hobbyists feeding the myths of Olde England. If the Leys were ever exposed then the world as they knew it would come to an end. To let the creatures out which guarded its borders would be to unleash Hell on earth. If those creatures still existed. Tommy considered this. What would Megan say should a Wyrm burrow up beneath the Fallow Field. How would she cope with the DeadEyes? What would she make of the Skin Walkers when she understood the truth? Skin Walkers like himself and Fiddler. They had held this form for so long it had taken hold. He had become fond of his appearance, had no thought to change himself.

"Will you Walk?" asked Fiddler.

"I don't know," said Tommy. "I don't want to, but I feel it might serve our purpose when we come back if we present a different face to my daughter."

"I've been thinking on it, before you suggested we return to the Layerings. A temporary transition only. Enough to escape her beady eye and then change back again."

"Remember when we could alter in the blink of an eye?" laughed Tommy. "Several shifts in a minute?"

"We were young," said Fiddler. "Had no sense of self. My present skin serves me well and this is, I think, how I wish to remain."

"I think you're right," said Tommy, thinking of how long he had worn his current shape. "At least it's something to fall back on should we need it."

Betty had remained quiet as he walked alongside Tommy. "You change?"

"You saw me once. Remember?"

Betty frowned and Tommy could almost hear him thinking, he was trying to remember so hard and then suddenly the man's face cleared.

"You were wearing furs!" he said. "You were fat!" And he started to laugh.

Tommy grinned. That had been an entertaining Tudor experiment. He had enjoyed the wives. A diversion Hweol had condemned as foolish, though he was laughing when Tommy had told him the details of his escapade. Changing was something they kept away from Betty. Confusion could have unintentional—and horrific—consequences.

"Lost a bit of weight since then," said Tommy patting his growling stomach, feeling hungry. The thought of taking action had fuelled his appetite. Perhaps they could afford a little hunt, let Betty off his leash.

"Betty," he said. "I think we need a snack. Do you think you can rustle us up a small something?

Taking in their surroundings, he wasn't too sure what his brother would be able to find for them. They were walking through a gorge from whose sides strange and contorted trees projected. The grotesque trunks, laden with heavy branches, looked as though they might slide down the outcrop at any minute, but Tommy knew the roots were buried deep, anchoring them firmly. The trees swayed and moved as they passed beneath them, not from the breeze, for there was none, but from creatures which danced and leapt amongst the boughs. A glimpse of grey fur revealed a squirrel. Then another and another joined the first one. A grey cloud peering down, unafraid. Their numbers indicated a lack of predators in the area, explained why they seemed so unconcerned. A cull was probably long overdue.

All Betty had to do was reach up into the foliage and pull down a handful of the squealing creatures as if he were plucking apples from a tree. Their high-pitched shrieks were brief, then followed a quick snap as he twisted their necks. He handed one each to Tommy and Fiddler, kept three for himself.

Squirrel was often their food when they were on the road. Tommy hoped they would find other things to hunt, get a more varied diet. He salivated at the thought of trying new delicacies.

They ate as they walked. This was only the start of their journey and Tommy didn't want them to take a break. Heads were ripped off and tossed aside, hands were bloodied as they expertly slipped the body from its skin, Betty demanding the pelts from Tommy and Fiddler, adding them to his pack. He had already declared he would be making a dress from animal fur for the year's Yule celebrations. Betty would need a lot of skins for that, considered Tommy.

They carried on in relative silence, broken only by the crunch of bone. The animals that had watched them so incautiously had disappeared. They had learned quickly.

He felt as if they were walking in a deep trench; the further they went on, the higher the banks on either side. The walls also grew smoother, so they looked as though they had been carved out by someone or something and were not a natural occurrence.

The stones had changed colour beneath his feet. They bore rusty marks, murky browns. This was where the blood had flown so freely in the past. Betty was sniffing the air, he recognised the scent, faint though it was. He looked questioningly at Tommy.

"Blood drains," he said. "There are four carved by the Layering folk. They leave the land north, south, east, and west. They are filled only during Blodmanoth."

"Blodmanoth?"

"The Festival of Blood," said Tommy. "It was the purest form of the Turns. If our timing is right, we will get to see it again. I wonder if that is what the Mother wants? For us to return to those old, early ways. They were her ways after all."

The thought of it sent a shiver of delight through his body, added to his certainty they were on the road to forgiveness and return. He would even tolerate Sister, for such an event. During those early years of family when they were being instructed in the way of things, she had invariably been a nuisance, always playing tricks. Moving things to places they shouldn't be. Put herself where she shouldn't be, causing upset to Betty. When they had left the Layerings, they had left her too.

The Folk had left en masse; he, Betty, and Fiddler, had followed behind Hweol. Their father had not commented on her absence, and when Tommy glanced back, he saw her defiantly standing firm in that first home of theirs and had said nothing. It had been her choice. Mothers and sons, fathers and daughters. Was that the reason behind her staying? That look on her face had been calculating, assessing. Had she been given some foreknowledge then of how things were to be? Was this all part of the Mother's plan? Something cooked up because of Betty and that little misunderstanding?

They had arrived at the edge of her territory. As they walked the lanes of the Layerings, he felt the scene around him ripple and he wondered how fixed it was, what really existed beneath. Then he dismissed the thought. Sons of Hweol saw things as they really were, nothing could be hidden from them, even in a land he hadn't visited for centuries.

Sister. Was this vision the normal cloak she cast on her land or had she created something new especially for him? He would have to be on his guard. He sighed. Little sisters could be so irritating.

Tommy thought of the children in Cropsoe, how sometimes they would shrink from their parents when they had overstepped the mark and caused trouble and annoyance. He felt a little like that now, despite having grown to his intended span. Their family reunion had been spoken of in the past, something which would happen when the three returned to the place of their birth and received their renewal. A fable, a myth. In the telling at least, that was how it had long been regarded.

Tommy knew the truth of it and understood that before the granting of their next span, they would be weighed. The Mother had not destroyed them after the Five Turns so he had no fear of her, the vanishing fires had confirmed their favour that much, but Cernunnos? Whilst they had worshipped in the name of the Mother and lived according to her laws, they had not performed the same homage to the Father or taken the steps to bring about his return—unlike Sister and Tobias.

What view would the resurrected Cernunnos take of his faithless sons? For the first time, a cold feeling crept over Tommy and he shivered. This was a doom he had never felt before, an unwelcome uncertainty. Then he cast it aside as mere nonsense. The Mother had gained the upper hand in those ancient struggles, and Cernunnos had been banished to the Corpse Marshes to stand as a reminder to those who dared to cross her. He could only be freed with the libations of centuries. Tobias had performed this duty, but after all this time, Cernunnos would be hungry, hungrier than ever Hweol had been. Yes, he would challenge the Mother, but she was strong, stronger than any of them—he hoped.

CHAPTER SIX

BETTY

The squirrel had silenced his stomach, made Betty feel slightly more himself. The pelts in his pack cheered him up as he planned the robe he would make for Yule. It didn't cross his mind those celebrations might not take place, that he might not be there for them. As he had slipped the fur from flesh, he had heard a distant whisper, a soft voice deep in the dark of his mind, telling him of the time to come and what he could look forward to. *She would remain with him*, she said, but he couldn't say anything to his brothers. This was to be their secret.

Betty smiled happily, started to thread the bones through his hair, a mane which reached below his shoulders. To dress himself as nature was more than the fur or skin you wore. The adornments were also important.

Thoughts of Megan returned. She had been promised, not in the way the Wheelborns had thought—as some sort of incestuous offering—but as another cloak. The Mother had said he could wear her and he had coveted her skin, her bone, her heart. Betty was not a creature for marriage, for any impulse regarding sex, he left the rutting to others. Let them breed, bleed. Offspring were troublesome, required nurturing, and he had no time for that. His driving force was to take, to feed, to exist in the manner in which the Mother had created him, to show the joy of life in the Dance and the Wheel. He was also the destroyer, the one to bring back the balance. He was the volcano, the earthquake, the plague, and the famine. The balance was even more important than the Wheel. Without him, there would be no turning.

A lot of his brothers' conversation had gone over his head as they walked. His attention was continually being grabbed by the scuttling of a creature, the cry of some animal, the sway of a branch. One word managed to filter through to him. Sister.

"Sister? I remember no sister," he said.

"No?" said Tommy. "Perhaps it's for the best."

"But shouldn't we—" said Fiddler.

Betty noticed the look his brothers gave one another.

Tommy was frowning, and for the first time in a long time looked uncomfortable.

"It's something I hoped we could forget," said Tommy. "An unfortunate incident."

"Unfortunate incident doesn't quite cover it," said Fiddler. "She's not going to be happy."

Another look between the two. Betty felt something tug inside, it was a pain that crept up when things were happening and he didn't understand. It made him want to lash out.

Tommy must've seen something in his expression. "Sit down, Betty. Before I start, I want you to know no one blames you. It was an accident. The Mother understood."

An accident. Had he done something? His anxiety built.

"Mother," he said, sending his voice into the dark. "What did I do?"

Don't worry, it's all in the past. A childhood mistake.

Her silent answer reassured him. It didn't matter how bad it was, she had forgiven him.

He calmed and sat next to Tommy, who regarded his change of mood with some surprise.

"When you were young, although not that much smaller than you are now," said Tommy, "you were being taught how to create the cloth of ritual, how to wear the skins of animals, create your dresses."

Betty pushed his mind back, struggled to remember. He saw meadows and animals, he was running, creatures were fleeing from him. The warmth of those days remained with him.

"You were also being taught how to control yourself."

Tommy stopped and the three looked at each other and burst out laughing.

"Well, that pretty much failed until we discovered your affinity with Fiddler's music. Anyway, there were one or two mishaps, as I said, and Sister was one of them."

Sister. Again.

"I still don't remember."

"She was a little girl, tended to get in the way, forever playing tricks on all of us. She, um, got caught up in one of your hunts."

"What did I do to her?" asked Betty, curious rather than sad. He carried the Mother's forgiveness inside him.

"You took her cloak," said Tommy.

"You mean I killed her?"

"No," said Tommy. "You know we said earlier some of us could change appearances? Sister was one of those too, so she was able to survive, take another form. But—well, you were both young, we all were—things got a bit messy. It was all smoothed over."

"So I only hurt her a little bit?" That didn't sound too bad, considered Betty.

"Just a little bit," agreed Tommy. "She didn't cry for very long."

"She forgave me?"

"Yes," said Tommy. "The Mother explained it all to her, dried her tears. If she's annoyed with anyone, it'll be me."

"Why? Did you do something?" asked Betty.

"It's more what I didn't do," said Tommy, sighing. "You'll find out when we get there. Hopefully she will let bygones be bygones."

Betty felt the knot in his stomach dissolve, the inner pressure recede. The Mother had been right, there was nothing for him to worry about. His eye tracked a beetle scurrying around his foot. He let it go. Betty didn't always kill or hurt things.

Noise caught his ear, a low hum of traffic. The human world was close by. A city. An underbelly to explore. It frightened him, but it offered so many possibilities. He could almost hear its voice.

CHAPTER SEVEN

AIDAN

"What the bloody hell do you think you're doing?"

The scream pierced his brain, set the hammers clanging at full blast. He held his head in his hands, afraid to move in case she upped the tempo and triggered a migraine. Bad enough he had a hangover and his daughter was there to witness his disgrace.

"You couldn't keep sober for one weekend? After all this time, promising the court on your daughter's *life* you were a responsible adult. What sort of shitty father are you?"

Kate was right. He couldn't raise his eyes to hers, was afraid to see the hate, the contempt, the disgust he knew was there. Nor did he want to look at Chloe. What did she think when she looked at her father?

A hand touched his shoulder and he reached up to pat it, but it vanished before he could reassure her. Her mother had pulled Chloe back as if he might contaminate her.

"Dad?"

"Not now, Chlo," said Kate. "We'll leave your father to consider the error of his ways. I think it would be a good idea if you didn't see him next weekend."

"No!" Chloe's voice pierced the rock inside his skull and he buried his head further in his hands.

He hated himself. She probably thought he was hiding from her. And she'd be right.

"Dad!"

Still, he didn't look at her, kept himself curled up in his tight ball, hiding from reality, pressed in on himself until he heard the door close and the sound of Kate's car drive away. Then came the silence.

Full and as heavy as a boulder weighing down on him, he could hardly bear it. Slowly he raised his eyes and looked about him at the dismal flat, the gloomy light. This was no place to raise a child, to ask her to spend an hour in its damp, mouldering walls.

He had failed. Like so much of his life, he had allowed those things most important to him to escape. He was on his own. Being allowed to become a parent had become a fluke, or a cruel joke on both himself and his daughter. *Unless she's not yours.*

The thought which had wormed its way deeper and deeper into his brain rose up. It was one of the reasons he drank; to drown out its voice, deny the possibility. He had heard the whispers and confronted Kate. She had denied it and he had believed her, but something—*something*—kept eating at him, asking him if he was sure. Could he really trust her? Wasn't she exactly the same as those other leeches who had sucked him dry?

That was being unfair, the reasonable part of his brain insisted. He couldn't help himself. He scratched away at the idea until it became a festering sore. There was nothing to lance the poison and now it had contaminated him utterly.

Yet when he looked at Chloe, he could see so much of himself in her. In the colour of her eyes, the tilt of her chin, the line of her jaw. Physically, there was no doubt. So why did he allow himself to be deluded? Because he had always destroyed anything which had been good in his life.

He pulled himself to his feet and dragged himself over to the window. His second floor flat overlooked a grim park with rusted swings and broken fencing. A gang of teens were gathered there, smoking and drinking. It was a school day but nobody ever checked round here. The social services and the police were too frightened to come onto his estate. Sometimes he wondered how Kate felt bringing Chloe here. Was she terrified every time she passed that welcome sign?

Everything stank of neglect and decay. The physical embodiment of his own miserable state. His letterbox clattered, and he heard the thud of letters landing on the carpet. More brown envelopes to add to the pile on his desk. Final demands and threats from the bailiffs. They were asking more and more of him and he had nothing else to give. He could bear it no longer. Without giving it any further thought, he grabbed a backpack and threw a few clothes in, a torch, his phone—which would soon be useless—a knife, and then he left, pausing only to drop the keys on the doormat. He would not be coming back.

Aidan's stomach growled. He had not eaten and his cupboards had been empty. He made his way to the city centre and took up a position near the ATM. It was a coveted pitch and he was surprised no one already sat there. Hopefully, someone would toss a few coins his way soon. Like the others in the precinct, he kept his eyes on the ground. An attitude equally important when gangs of predatory teens roamed the area. He prayed the youths he had spotted on arrival would keep their distance, that the truancy officers would sweep them up before they came any closer. It was not to be.

"'Ere, isn't that Chloe's dad?"

He recognised the voice, a girl. He couldn't remember the name but he could picture her, blonde and freckled, a pretty little thing who had taken charge at the sleepovers Kate had organised for their daughter when they were still together. Now there was a harsh, spiteful edge to her voice. He cringed. Even here, he had brought shame on Chloe. The tone in this voice was one which would echo through school corridors for years to come and remain with their target for a lifetime. He tucked his chin in closer to his chest, tried to hide in an invisible shell.

"It's him," said the same voice. "She said he'd left home. Didn't realise he was on the street, a tosser."

"Probably a druggie," said another, "or a drunk."

"And we used to go to her sleepovers," squealed a third. "Shit, anything could've happened to us."

"Just cos someone's fallen on hard times," said a male voice, "it doesn't mean they've become a monster."

"Ooh, but I bet he has," said the first. "Chloe barely mentions him. Now why d'you think that is?"

"Probably because she's too upset," said the lad, "doesn't want the whole world knowing her business. Thinks people might take a pop, jump to the wrong conclusion. Can't say I blame her."

"You're too soft-hearted, Matt," said the girl, her tone becoming light and flirtatious, "like father, like daughter. Bet she'll be sitting here soon enough."

Aidan felt sick. Already Chloe was being painted as someone who would never amount to anything.

"And you're a bitch, Moira," said the one she called Matt. "Let's leave him alone. He doesn't deserve this."

There was silence for a moment and Aidan thought for one blissful minute they had gone.

"Thinks I'm a bitch, does he?" muttered Moira. "I'll show him."

Aidan could see a hand reach down, the arm come close, stretching out for the cup nearby in which people tossed the few precious coins which would see him through the day. Chipped varnished nails disappeared into the cup. His own hand shot out and grasped her wrist. She let out a squeal.

"Leave it," he hissed.

"Help!" she shrieked.

"Hey, let go of her!"

"Filthy pervert."

The pink nails disappeared, were replaced by fists and boots which connected with ribs and jaws.

Matt's voice filtered through from somewhere. "Hey! Leave him! He wasn't doing anything to her. She was trying to pinch his money—"

It faded out as the blows continued to pound into him. Nobody paid any attention to the rights or wrongs. It was his own fault, he decided. He deserved this. Darkness descended.

He didn't know how long he'd been out. Only that night had fallen. The moon of the same day or sometime later, he couldn't say. Nor was he in the precinct. He woke to find himself buried amongst a pile of filthy blankets and sleeping bags, a tattered piece of canvas draped above as if the awning of a tent. Squinting round, he recognised the layout of a multi-storey carpark. This one however, held no cars.

As he looked up and down, he saw small groups of people, scattered around a variety of fires, others more solitary sitting a little further away. Voices were muted and more than a few glances were cast in his direction.

"Why'd you bring him here?" said one man.

"He needed somewhere safe and Oldingham is pretty far from the precinct," said another. That lad again, Matt. "I needed to get him away before the police arrived. They'd side with Moira. He'd have no chance."

"So you thought of me."

"Yeah. Well, you're still my brother. Said if I ever needed help to come to you or Tobias. So, here I am."

"Thought it would be you who needed help, not some geezer old enough to be our dad."

"He's Chloe's dad," said Matt.

"Ah, that's the way of it is it? Got a soft spot for the girl?"

"She's a friend," snapped Matt, his defensive tone belying his words. "It didn't seem right, what they were doing to him."

"No, you're right," said his brother. "It wasn't. But it happens all the time. You live on the street, you're regarded as less than nothing."

"You could come home," said Matt, going back to something which was obviously an ongoing conversation. "Mum wants you back."

"But Dad doesn't, does he? You know what he's like. Doesn't like to be shown to be wrong, to be weak. He's a bully."

"I wish you'd come home, Vic," Matt's voice was softer now, pleading.

"I can't, Matt. We'll end up fighting and Dad'll push me too hard."

"Well, if you stopped—"

"I don't want to," said Vic. "Can't you see that? I'm sorry. But this is my escape. I haven't got anything else."

"You've got me." Matt's voice was a whisper.

"I know," said Vic, "but that's not enough."

The way they spoke, the clear anguish between the brothers, brought tears to Aidan's eyes. He swallowed and moved slightly. Matt and Vic noticed and came over to him.

"You alright, mate?" asked Vic. "My brother says you took a pretty good beating out there."

"Yeah," said Aidan, struggling to sit up, only to be pushed back down by Vic.

"You need to rest, mate. Even if no bones are broken—though I still say we need to get you to a hospital—you're going to have some killer bruising. You won't want to move for a while."

"Sounds like the voice of experience," said Aidan.

"Yeah, well, I've been in a similar position meself a few times. Picked on for no reason other than I'm on the street."

Aidan didn't know the man but he felt safe, allowed his eyes to close and let sleep claim him.

CHAPTER EIGHT

BETTY

The world around him continued to shift and slide across his vision. Tommy kept them on a path which held them to the edges of the illusory landscape. They would not be travelling deeper into the Layerings until they had been to the city along its border. Betty understood the diversion was necessary but he disliked the thought intensely.

As he walked, images of the world beyond theirs slipped in and out of view. It was a world he normally loathed. The speeding cars flashed by; metal containers keeping the tread of a person from the soil, their breath from the air, their bodies from the hunt. They moved too fast for him and he resented their advantage. It wasn't natural. It wasn't fair.

It also unanchored him. When a stream of cars rippled past, the sound of their engines, the vibrations they transmitted through the ground broke the throb of the pulse which grounded him, silenced the heartbeat waiting.

He hated the towns and cities as much as the cars. These too, were an unnatural separation. The spread of concrete and stone stained the land he had known and loved. He wanted to destroy it. Perhaps when he had his strength back, the Mother would let him loose to bring back the balance.

Betty's stomach rumbled. He needed more than rabbits and squirrels. He sniffed the air, started to look at his surroundings, trying to assess the possibilities. Their path had become similar to the one he'd often walked in the Weald, thankfully moving away from roads and mechanisation; a tree-shrouded route invisible to human eyes unless they were given leave to walk it. The rippling became more noticeable, unbalanced him so he found himself swaying.

"Betty? You alright?"

His brothers' voices pierced the fog of his mind. He ignored them and sank to the ground, burying his hands into the earth, searching for the beat which guided him. He focused on his breathing, shut everything out, let the rhythm of Nature ease itself back into his body.

The soil was cool and damp. He felt the tickle of a woodlouse, the slithering of a worm, the business of ants. These were creatures he knew. They brought with them their own rank in the cycle of life, fixed him once more in place. Their animal urges filtered through him, reset his own and with a sigh he opened his eyes. Reconnected to the heart of all, he felt strengthened, but still he needed more.

He looked at Tommy. His brother would know what was wanted—what was always wanted. He watched as Tommy moved to a fork in the path, opened up the Ley track to the world beyond. He could see a woman riding a horse. The beast tossed its head and twitched its ears, looked directly at them. Tommy was crooning something, softly clicking his tongue. Horse and rider turned towards them. Smiling. Trusting.

"Enough for now?" asked Tommy.

Betty barely heard him, his hunger roared so loud. Everything faded from his vision except for the animals approaching. He had never regarded humans as anything else, for all their conceit of superiority. They were just part of the food chain like all creatures on the planet. Beneath, the heart of his mother drummed its encouragement, a rhythm matched by the beat of the two hearts in front of him. Hearts he would soon hold in his hand.

CHAPTER NINE

TOBIAS

Tobias surveyed the Oldingham estate. Small groups were dotted around fires in front of the empty warehouses and factories. It was one of his favourite places. It was also the most sacred of spaces. Protected by Sister, it was where Cernunnos awaited his summoning.

"Time for the harvesting. The last harvesting for the Father," said Tobias to the shadowy group behind. They drifted in and out of view. Hungry.

Sister had drawn her layers over the edge of the city. She had found it the perfect place to cast her net for what was needed in her world of the Layerings. Like the veil drawn between Umbra and the villages of the Weald, this land was camouflaged but differed in that it was hiding in plain sight.

Nobody wanted those who lived there. Those who gathered in this place found others like themselves, formed bonds of friendship and often dependency. Tobias' work in the hostels and the soup kitchens had brought him trust from many who wouldn't give another the time of day. When beds were full and there was nowhere else to go, he would persuade them to this estate, saying it was safer than the precinct in town. There would be no kickings from the gangs of youths lurking in dark corners, no being spat at or mocked from those who left clubs, there would be no one trying to set fire to them like poor old Fred the previous night.

There was always one sacrifice, a little window dressing to add to the sense the precinct and its parks were places to be avoided. Fred was a harmless old man, slept rough after his marriage broke up, could be seen ambling around the precinct with a carrier bag full of cans during the day. When sober, he was a perfect gentleman and most of the shop owners had a soft spot for him, sending out sandwiches and coffee, alerting him to news of a bed whenever one became available.

It was a pity it had to be Fred, but persuading the rough sleepers to come his way had proved hard of late. They had grown an extra veneer of cynicism, disbelieving anyone who tried to help them. Insisted they could look after themselves. It had made Tobias—or Toby as he was to them—consider himself, wonder if he had given himself away somehow. Had they seen him? Seen through him? He could be compassionate as well. Fred's death had been quick, painless.

Tobias knew he would have to reinvent himself soon. Pamela in the kitchen had commented how he never seemed to get old, and they had been working together for twenty-odd years. She bemoaned the fact he aged so much better than her.

"Hey, Bert," he called across the lot as he made his way to a brazier around which a number of huddled shapes had gathered.

The man grinned, raising his can to him in a toast. "All right, Toby."

He stood aside and allowed Toby to join their circle. Toby rubbed his hands over the flames, pretending to keep warm even though the temperature had no effect on him.

"Kelvin, Gary." He nodded to the other men. Familiar faces from the drop-in. "Col, Vic. Bitter out tonight, isn't it?"

"Yeah, chilly for this time of year. Can't say I'm looking forward to the winter."

"This place is pretty sheltered," said Toby. "There's one or two units round here we can make nice and cosy. I've been speaking to the local vicar and the press. We're gonna do a bit of a fundraiser and make them habitable. Council have agreed at least a temporary shelter. No one's come forward to buy this land yet."

"Always wonder why that is," said Gary. "This is good land round here and must be worth a bob or two. Reckon somebody could buy it at a knock down price and make a killing."

Toby smiled in agreement. How right Gary was. He didn't know that the purchase had already been made and the second part of his statement was also true and would come true again soon enough.

"You're like an old nursemaid," said Col, "coming out to check on us."

"Delivery boy on occasion, eh?" laughed Bert.

"Sorry," said Toby, holding his hands out to reinforce he had come emptyhanded. "Nothing for you tonight."

At those words, Bert's expression changed, became angry, menacing. "You said you'd bring some stuff. Told me I didn't need to worry and you'd get it. You know I need it."

He didn't need it, not really. Toby knew that. Some of those on the lot had real addictions. Bert's was very much in the mind, a convinced dependency on drink. A show for those he mixed with in order to demonstrate how much alike they were.

"Look, I might not have it on me but I've got a stash over the far side. Didn't want to bring it over to you in case we'd been inundated tonight."

"Inundated? It's like the bloody Marie Celeste round here."

"Seems busy enough." Toby made a point of looking from fire to doorway and across the unit.

"Nah," said Bert. "Space like this and no one here? Makes you think something's up somewhere."

"They might have got beds for the night," said Toby.

"There's not that many spaces in the hostels," said Vic.

He was right. The available beds were all full and the others had found their rest elsewhere. A place this small group would soon join.

"Look!" said Col, as another fire sparked up over on the far side.

"Didn't see them arrive," said Gary, ever suspicious. "How'd they get in? Nothing but solid boulders over that way. Break your neck if you try it."

Some old blocks of flats had been demolished years back. The developers who owned that bit of land had gone bust and the brick and rubble had remained. Like their estate, the council merely advertised 'exciting new development' plans every now and then, they always came to nothing, blaming lack of money and imagination. After a while, locals stopped seeing the area, almost appeared to forget its existence.

"Oh, they passed by a moment ago," said Toby, "I saw them." He wasn't lying.

"Well, we didn't see them," said Col.

They hadn't. Those who passed would not be seen until they were good and ready. For the moment they were setting the scene, creating the backdrop for Toby's evening event.

"I promised you a little entertainment, didn't I?" he said. He grinned at them, turned on the friendly smile they always responded to. His mask was accepted as genuine even when they saw beneath the mask of so many others.

"Does it involve food and drink?" asked Vic.

"Doesn't it always?" said Toby. He had held one or two events already, simply to soften them up. Marinading, he liked to term it. "Come on, lads. Let's go and have a bit of fun."

"Wha hay," cheered Gary, making to take the lead.

Toby restrained him lightly. "Let me lead the way. Don't want you having an accident, do we?"

"Accident? Here?" queried Vic. "What could possibly cause us a problem here. There's nowt on the ground between here and there."

"Perhaps," said Toby. "But the dark hides many things."

"Yeah," laughed Bert. "Like us."

They all laughed at that but followed obediently in Toby's footsteps. The other two small groups also joined them, led by friends he'd brought along for the evening. There were calls of greeting as they merged, most had come across each other on their travels.

A chargrilled aroma of something cooking drifted across.

"A barbie!" cheered someone from the back.

"Remember your pulled pork from last time?" said Bert. "Hope we're getting that again."

"Oh, yes," said Toby. "There'll certainly be pulled pork aplenty."

CHAPTER TEN

TOBIAS

They had neared the edge of the dark circle, could only see the flames dancing up ahead. The fire seemed further away, deeper into the pitch. Toby cast a glance back over the heads of his herd. The few streetlights which flickered over the lot had gone out, as had the fires the homeless themselves had built. Behind them, it was becoming as dark as ahead. He continued to watch the outlines of the buildings fade, pulse slightly, and then vanish. It was as if someone had rubbed everything out. His group did not notice, they were paying too much attention to whatever freebies lay ahead.

"Got a candle?" Vic asked.

"Here comes a candle to light you to bed," said Toby, obliging and striking a match, putting it to a candle an arm held out from the darkness.

"'Ere, who's there?" asked Gary, as the candle seemed to hover in the air.

"Here comes a chopper to chop off your head," said Toby, and a flash of silver flickered near the flame.

"Chop, chop, chop, chop, the last man's dead." Another voice finished the rhyme, deep and dark and cold.

It changed the mood of the group who became a bit more wary. Instinctively, they shuffled closer together, responding to the ancient herd mentality of safety in numbers whenever a predator was near. Their problem was, they didn't actually know how close the predators were to them, or how fully the trap had been sprung.

Toby felt the air change. The Layers were shifting and he relaxed. The men moved closer to the fire. It was a monstrous inferno.

"How'd you build this without us seeing?" asked Col. "Gotta hand it to you. You don't do things by halves."

"I'm known for it," laughed Toby.

He surveyed the bonfire with satisfaction. Its size hid the pit it encircled, the Layer on which they stood rippled, the men didn't notice.

The darkness made everything look solid, closed in behind them, building another Layer. Layer upon Layer was now forming, interweaving between those gathered, *within* those gathered. They were sharper than any blade. Toby thought of Tommy's knives and their place in ritual. Oh, they looked good no doubt when everyone was dancing and drinking, but it was all for show. The knives could gather one or two at a time, but they could not harvest a crop. Tommy plucked blades. Toby reaped a field.

Already the Layers were honing their movement, thinning themselves into a dimension too narrow for the human eye to see.

Toby watched. He had promised an entertainment, although this was for himself and those assisting him that evening. It was always fascinating to watch this stage, as the layers thinned and thinned, multiplying and building, so that in the end, nothing looked different at all. Unless you were from the Layerings and could recognise what was happening. There would be a moment soon when the Layers would have taken all they needed and split apart. Toby's assistants moved to his side, watching the Layers work on Bert, slice through Vic, split apart Col. And the men never realised. They didn't feel anything apart from the brush of a breeze on their skin, a tingle inside they put down to hunger, a sudden pulse in their heart which they regarded as little more than a beat of goodwill.

Toby felt as if he was holding his breath, if he had any breath to hold.

"I still don't know if they feel anything," said the man to his left.

"If they do it's for the mere blink of an eye," said Toby.

"That long? The Layering is faster than that," said his companion.

Bert turned and looked at the three. He was smiling. Then his expression changed as he looked beyond the trio.

"Hey, I can't see the lot anymore. Those bloody lights have gone out again."

"Don't you worry about those lights," said Toby. "Dodgy electrics didn't you say? I'll check the hook-ups in the morning, see if I can short-circuit something for you."

"Cheers," said Bert. "You know," he leaned forward, as if sharing a confidence, "you know I'm not that keen on the dark. Hated it since I was a kid."

"Well, the fire's giving us all the light we need at the minute," said Toby. "And by the time that dies down, it'll be dawn and you won't have to worry."

A man sleeping rough afraid of the dark. It was surprising Bert had lasted as long as he had.

Bert cast another anxious look into the pitch and then faced the fire once more, allowed the flames to hypnotise him. The gathering was in a trance-like state, the flames dancing and holding them. These too weren't real, were merely coloured Layers pressing in from in front of them.

Toby would have to give the signal soon. It had taken him years to refine the Layering Reaping to this point. He knew if he went too far he would destroy the harvest, and that had happened on occasion. In those days he had plenty of others in reserve, but now, when the movement of the modern population was monitored so closely, it was harder. The fixation with cameras filming every movement was an annoyance. Toby and his friends would never show on the video, their bodies too fluid for the cameras to pick up, but they would catch those he gathered, and it was those gatherings he needed to keep on a low key.

His signal was simple. One he borrowed from film directors galore. He was, after all, directing the action.

"Cut"

On cue, the Layers vanished and as they slipped back into the Regions belonging to Sister, the bodies they had been holding together disintegrated, falling to the ground, carved into slivers nanometres thick. Blood gushed, was directed into gullies which gathered the liquid in buckets, flesh and blood sank onto mesh which acted as a sieve. From each, the three watchers reached in and pulled out the heart. These had not been affected. Were still beating, under the impression they remained part of a human whole. As soon as they were tossed into the basket Toby had brought, they stopped.

Then he turned his attention to the grey matter. Tiny sparks flickered amongst the remnants of Bert and his friends. These were the final impulses of the brain. Like the heart, its separation from the body had not yet registered, a feature of the Layering, which seemed to cauterise all sense of separation. The sparks, like the heartbeat, would also die out, although their death was accompanied by one final burst of energy. The death spike. This was what they had come for and what they harvested. With the spike came the soul and this was the food of the Layerings. Sister would be pleased. He would visit her, make sure she understood *now* was the time. There had been too many false rumours of late. Then he would call to Cernunnos, Father of All. With his power would the Wheel, stilled in the Weald and in trouble in so many little pockets of Britain, start to turn again.

CHAPTER ELEVEN

BETTY

When Betty returned to his surroundings, carcasses of horse and human lay intermingled at his feet. Steam rose from the deflated stomach of the beast, the entrails lay nearby and Fiddler had already started to gather them up. Food for later. Betty reached out a bloodied hand and stroked the mane, the soft coat, and yawned. A big meal always tired him and he had not had one like this for a long time, it overwhelmed him.

Sightless eyes gazed at him from a head which had rolled towards the fire Tommy was building. Her chestnut hair was tangled in the wood. Tommy picked it up and placed it in the fire pit.

"Anything you want?" asked Tommy, indicating the head.

Betty regarded the eyes again. Brown eyes. Their taste was sharper than blue, carried a more bitter flavour. He wasn't in the mood for such fare.

"No."

"All the more for me and Fiddler then," he laughed. "Now, sleep. We have time for you to rest. And while you do that, I think Fiddler and myself might be able to rescue this fur for you."

The thought of the horse's chestnut pelt cheered him as much as the food he'd eaten. He would add it to the squirrel and rabbit fur he'd already gathered.

"Maybe we can find you another such," said Fiddler. "You'll get that new coat of yours that much quicker."

Betty lay himself on the ground and curled up into a ball, resting his head on crimson hands.

Fiddler began to sing the old Umbran lullaby and Betty drifted into the past.

Sleep, nature's child,
born in blood and with love.
Let your eyes close against night.

The words soothed him, took him back to his early days when he remembered being held close by Nature, wrapped in its soil. Songs were always sung to him then. Stories filtering down to him in the darkness, sending their words, their pictures, preparing him for the world he would be born into. It was as if the past year was being erased.

There was movement around him, his brothers' careful tread, the rustle of leaves and branches. All was peaceful.

In his semi-conscious state, he could smell the reassuring scent of burning wood, hear branches crackle as a fire took hold. Its warmth reached his skin, lulled him deeper into sleep. His earthen mattress relaxed him further, the Mother's heartbeat pulsing next to him, the cord between them stronger than it had been for some time. His strength was slowly building. It would take more than a feast such as this, a sleep such as this, but it was another step back to the beginning. Only when he arrived at the point where he had started from would he be at full strength and vitality.

His face settled into a smile as his dream sent him running across meadows, hunting everything, creatures great and small. Somewhere in the distance, he could see fires leaping over the horizon as day turned into night. A fire blazed and his mother was calling him, the tie between them shortening the nearer he got. It tugged at him insistently so that after a while, he forgot about the rabbits and squirrels, cast aside the lamb in his hand, and dutifully headed towards the blaze. By now, the beat of the heart was loud in his ears, drowning out all voices, his brothers, Hweol, everyone. She was calling him, and she would be his.

CHAPTER TWELVE

SISTER

Sister studied the Layerings. The weaving was getting harder. The quality of the material provided had dropped in recent years. Sister blamed Tommy for that. He had created a captive audience—so to speak—in their part of the world. It meant she had to be more discrete in her actions, working at the edge of society, nibbling away in comparison to the great chunks Tommy and his brothers took. It left her with the underbelly, poorer quality but better than nothing, and at least they fed the Layerings, helped her weave the landscapes she loved. Usually delivered by Tobias, her stock was getting low—where was he? She was roused from her musings by approaching footsteps.

"Sister."

Tobias approached, a broad smile on his face, an excited glint in his eye. He could barely contain himself. She felt her spirits rise in response.

"Your brothers have finally taken the plunge and left the Weald."

She had sensed their movement, but received no confirmation. This was good news indeed. Within his world, Tommy regarded himself as lord of all he surveyed, indulged by Hweol and the folk of Umbra, all sucked into those cruel rituals of his which he claimed honoured the Mother. He rarely went beyond its bounds, knew his reception by those near Winchester, in the grey edges of the Layerings, not to mention within the Layerings themselves, would be cool. Tommy, Betty, and Fiddler had claimed much and abandoned and neglected many, including her. If he had left, then he was coming to her. She wondered whether he considered the little sister he had left behind, what form she now took.

"So, Tommy was unable to tame his daughter? That girl, Megan, actually kept him in check?"

Tobias had fed her the news from the Weald and Umbra, told her of the disruption to the rituals of the Five Turns of the Wheel. Those bloody rites carried out over five nights took much from the nearby villages in terms of flesh and blood. She had heard the Fifth Turn itself, when the sacrifice of the unborn had been sabotaged by Liza Wheelborn in order to save Megan's child. A wasted gesture it seemed, but one which drove Megan back to Cropsoe, the village at the heart of everything. Oh, how Sister wished she had been there for that Sixth Night, when Megan had destroyed Tommy's fun—where she had destroyed his swords. A pity she hadn't been able to wipe out Hweol completely. You couldn't have everything, could you?

It was enough for Sister, however, to imagine her brothers having to obey someone else, especially a *daughter*. Hweol and the Mother had insisted she forgive them for what had happened to her as a child, and she had, at least she'd told them she had. Now they were returning to *her* land, at a time when they were weak, needed the rites of rebirth. And where was the Mother in all this?

She regarded her visitor. There was no fear to be seen in Tobias. He was family of sorts, a cousin, another cast-off like she had been, left behind to make her own way as Hweol had taken her more favoured siblings to the Weald. Despite the Mother telling her of the role she would play in the return of Cernunnos, the Father of All—once he had been officially punished, that was—she had still felt some resentment at her treatment.

Tobias looked content, a satisfied expression on his face. He wore the clothes which allowed him to blend in with those he hunted, filthy jeans, worn boots, a tattered army jacket—though he had never served. A dispiriting uniform which nevertheless failed to disguise his robust health. With a face as pale as ever, and teeth sharper than any razor, he exuded the strength of his kind.

"The city air agrees with you, Tobias."

This time he laughed outright. "More a matter of blood. I dine well and the Master often allows me to drink from his table. And speaking of matters of blood—"

Sister leaned in, aware this was an important moment, the one she had been waiting for all her life.

"The daughter, Megan, stopped their hunts, weakened them. Tommy, Betty, and Fiddler are near their time. And there were no longer any fires around Umbra to stop them leaving."

His words confirmed the rumours and gossip. It also told her the Mother had forgiven her sons. She would have to be careful with her tricks.

"So they have risked everything on the promise of a legend."

"Is it a risk?" asked Tobias. "Would you deny them?"

Sister threw back her head and laughed until the tears rolled down her wraith's cheeks. "Oh yes, I would deny them. For a short while at least— I doubt I would be allowed to destroy them completely. Such an action belongs to the Father, and even he bows to the Mother. But I would like to give them a taste of what it feels like to be abandoned by family."

Tobias nodded. "If it's a comfort, I've read the signs. It is time for the Father, for Cernunnos, to return. I've fed him well."

It had been even longer since she had seen the Horned One. Not the pale imitation of his son, Hweol, but the Father of All. She considered her preparations, all those years she had spent weaving her offerings so everything would be in place when He returned.

"He will reward you," said Tobias. "You have been faithful, not neglectful like some."

"As have you," said Sister, "although he can be capricious. Our devotion does not guarantee our safety."

"True," said Tobias, "but it puts us in better standing than some. What is left to do?"

"Raise Him," said Sister. "You have attended Him for so long, it should be a matter of a heartbeat. But remember to save one. Another heart will be needed if the Father demands it, and better an outcast than one of mine. My people deserve better than that slaughter."

He raised his eyebrows at her in query.

"We've both been playing a long game," she said. "We've served the Father, and the village contains those I've gathered for the Mother. I've grown quite fond of them and would like them to have at least an illusion of peace at the end."

"You've grown soft," said Tobias, laughing.

"Who, me? No. Let's just say I prefer to save my venom for others."

"Good to hear," said Tobias. "We'll need to keep sharp when our brethren arrive. Do you realise," he added as he turned to leave, "we will be a complete family for the first time in centuries."

Sister nodded. "But who knows how long that reunion will last. You'd better go. We both have work to do."

She watched Tobias walk the snaking trail out of her phantasmic village and disappear onto the shrouded Ley track. The path would have him back at the Oldingham estate in no time. Another Layering, hiding so much more than any of the humans who slept there bargained for. She had woven that particular canopy long ago, a shroud to protect Cernunnos against modern encroachment.

She had mentioned her folk, the people inhabiting her village of Kinlet. The community had been created with His return in mind. She had built up the village, given her people a good life, although appearances could be deceptive. There, her Layerings were thick and textured, appeared real to all intents and purposes. Sister thought of her little pocket of apparent humanity, her congregation. It was a false idyll, a fiction of her own making. Whereas Tommy's folk lived beneath blue skies, her own existed in a barren world beneath eternal grey cloud. They didn't know it however, as she had painted their Layers with an illusion to match the reality of their known world. They thought it a paradise. Trees and grass remained lush shades of green, clouds were white and fluffy, animals and humans alike appeared well-fed and healthy.

Would she remain and recast her Layers after His return or would she follow Him—or the Mother—wherever that may be? It didn't matter. Life had become too humdrum, every day the same. Tommy had assumed the upper-hand and claimed Hweol's ear. She would ensure the balance shifted in her favour this time. A world to rival the Weald, one which had its share of sweet meadows and clear waters, which would also include a few towns, a city. There were so many dissatisfied souls to manipulate, so many who had no resilience to the hardships of life, who would do anything if they were simply looked after. She had visited nearby Southampton, watched the planes take off and fly across the world. The humans they had for so long regarded as insignificant had created technologies she was determined to enjoy. The Wheel, the cycle of nature, *their* nature, would turn again and this time, she would be at its hub. This time, when the rites were complete, she would not be left behind. She was no longer that little girl.

With Tobias' departure, Sister allowed herself to drift to Kinlet. As ethereal as her Layerings, she became more fixed in time and space as she neared. For them to see her as she truly was would be a shock. The drift became a walk and she felt her shoes crunch satisfyingly on gravel. Adding the aural to the visual had been a great challenge and taken many years to perfect. She had created a complete world, and yet it could vanish in a blink with no sign of ever having existed in the first place. Her world carried none of the carbon footprint she had heard many speak of, their desire to reduce such a thing so that the planet flourished. She allowed herself a chuckle. How could they disapprove of her manner of living?

Sister continued to take in her surroundings. Chocolate box thatch, overflowing hanging baskets and cottage gardens in full bloom—despite it turning to autumn. This was the layer presented to the traveller whenever an engine passed by. Should someone be on foot, the road would weigh the age of the walker and their time, then it would show the appropriate layer. Decide if they should be permitted to leave.

Sister was proud of her handiwork. The layers coating the village protected her and those who had not followed Hweol to the Weald. This land had been scarred by the Wheelborn when the Wheel had turned for the first time. He had not read the land correctly and too many had died, taking the land with it. All that remained was a husk of countryside, discarded by Hweol as a disappointment, but not one to be worried over, and ignored by the human world, so few in number at that time they scarcely noticed it. Those who did remark on the place would often accompany their words with a prayer to whichever god they believed in.

With the destruction of the land's fertility, animal life died and the Layerings had become deserted, unhallowed. Dead soil, poisoned air. None could walk here. None of flesh and blood anyway. The spectres bound to this tormented place did need feeding however, and they could only flourish in the presence of flesh, taking at the end of each life, the death spike, manna supplied by Tobias. The numbers were maintained as well against the day of Cernunnos' return. He and the Mother would demand offerings, and she wanted to make sure she had a feast for them. Something else to raise her up in their eyes.

So Sister and her kind used their talents to paint the layers of the land and bring in the humans needed to sustain it. Their eyes could never pierce the veil. They were unaware of the true nature of their surroundings, or themselves. Life in Kinlet was never anything less than perfect.

Tommy had never returned to these parts. He had seen the destruction and the barren lands and dismissed them—and her—from his thoughts. That would be something else for him to consider. Her evolution into a being which occupied more than one world. Sister was of the same material as the Layers, was a Layer in herself.

She continued along the main road into the village, children were playing ahead of her on the green where she had built a small play park at its side. She passed a mother and her daughter in their front garden. The daughter was digging small holes with a trowel and her mother was handing her seedlings to transfer into the hollows. Then they were watered in. Both stopped as Sister approached, their smiles bright and welcoming. The people loved her.

"Good afternoon, Sister," said Denise Morton, nudging her little girl at the same time.

The girl paused in her work and looked up, offering a shy grin. "Hello, Sister. We're planting lots of flowers. Our garden's going to be the most beautifullest in the world!"

"I think it already is," said Sister, leaning against their gate and breathing in the fragrance of the roses still in bloom.

"I can't believe how everything grows," said Denise. "I couldn't care for a Yucca plant before. Everything died on me."

"I know that feeling," said Sister, laughing, knowing it would not be taken the way she meant it.

CHAPTER THIRTEEN

BETTY

"Time to get moving, brother."

A hand was shaking his shoulder and Betty groaned as he pulled himself into a sitting position. He felt comfortably full and his body was more relaxed than it had been in a long time. He stretched himself and scratched at his chest, dislodging the spider which had started to weave its web there. Under other circumstances it would have found itself tickling the back of Betty's throat, but today the spider was free to weave another web. Betty watched it scuttle away.

"Ready to travel again?" asked Tommy.

Betty noticed the sparkle in his brother's eyes. "You've fed too?" He looked around for evidence and saw a pile of bones, the horse's coat rolled up.

"You left us enough to drink," said Tommy. "Meat is not so necessary for Fiddler and I. The iron within is another matter. We are the blood and you are the heart."

The heart. He could feel it beating again, louder beneath his feet. Neither Fiddler nor Tommy appeared to hear it. It was a voice meant solely for him.

"How far to the city?" he asked.

Tommy gazed along the track which still held the same grey light as it had when he closed his eyes. This land gave no sense of time.

"A day's travel," said Tommy.

This surprised Betty. "These paths are supposed to allow us to travel quickly."

"Yes, but Sister seems to have slowed things down somewhat. It's not just what you see but the passage of time within her realm that she's played with. She knows we're coming, she knows where I'll go first, and she intends to have her bit of fun. She won't stop us, wouldn't dare—we're needed by the Mother, by Cernunnos—but it doesn't mean she won't pull a trick or two."

Betty pondered Sister. She had cried when he had slipped her from her skin, assuming she was merely another of the animals around him which he was free to disrobe and digest. His mother's forgiveness had brought with it the memory. Of blood and screams, of tears and sulks and silence, it didn't disturb him. *Sisters liked gifts*, he thought. Perhaps he could take her a present. He thought of his small pack of fur, the larger horse hide, and dismissed those from his thoughts. Those were for him, his Yule. Nature expected him to wear her clothes. He would find her something else, maybe someone else.

He'd risen to his feet, waited for Fiddler to stamp out the fire, and then followed as Tommy led them in the direction of the city. Part of him felt they could travel quicker than Tommy indicated, that there was some other reason for the delay in their progress, but he didn't question it.

"Sister expects me to rush," said Tommy, reading Betty's thoughts. "I'll not give her the satisfaction. We are known to be abroad; our story was told long ago. We can afford to delay slightly, annoy the brat."

Betty smiled. His brother insisted on calling their sister a brat, as if she was still the child of long ago. What word would she use to describe her brother? He felt a slight ache begin to weigh across his brow. This always happened when he considered his family, their problems, the games they played. He dealt with it the way he always did and dismissed it from his mind, turned his attention to what he could see in front of him, what he could hear around him. He needed to be nowhere else except in the moment, part of the hum of the land.

"Do you want a song, Betty?" asked Fiddler.

Betty nodded and as Fiddler sang the song of his childhood. He gambolled around his family as if a pup.

"Will you play me a tune?" he asked, as he came round to Fiddler's side.

"Not yet," said Fiddler. "Once we've been to the city. Then I will have my music back."

Thoughts of the city troubled Betty, but his brother's need for music was as central to him as Betty's need to be free to run and Dance, to feel the heartbeat of the land. Fiddler continued to sing his song and Betty remained at his side, happy to have at least a song to soothe him.

"Will you play us a Dance when you have your music back?" Betty asked.

"Not in the city," said Fiddler. "When we are returned to the Mother, when we are reunited with the Father, then I will play my music in their honour and we will all Dance."

Betty felt a pulse beneath his feet as if in response to Fiddler's words. The rhythm was changing, becoming more regular, less random. Betty felt as if he had entered a tunnel as the air around him constricted, pushing him on. The rippling in his immediate area had stopped; a shield forming.

Tommy seemed to notice. "The Mother's protecting you. She's with us! Fiddler, another song if you please!"

Their mood had lifted considerably, Tommy's air of grievance which had stuck to him like a storm cloud finally evaporated. It felt as if they were going on a happy family outing.

Betty, always sensitive to his brother's moods, especially those directed towards himself, started to run and jump and act the fool. He knew he needed to conserve his energy. There was still some way to go, but the impulse could not be denied, and he was a creature—a child—of impulse.

A mouse scurried through the undergrowth ahead and caught his eye. Immediately his brothers vanished from his thoughts as the tiny heartbeat sang its own song to Betty. The giant responded to the summoning and ran.

CHAPTER FOURTEEN

AIDAN

The plunge into darkness, the gathering silence, roused Aidan from his sleep. He didn't open his eyes at first, his head still pounded from the earlier headache and he thought a migraine might catch him. Nor did he want to take in his surroundings. Knowing where he was felt as much a kick in the gut as the boots which had attacked him earlier. Whilst his body felt alien, not belonging to him, neither did his life. He had sunk so low. Chloe. What had she seen? He had come here thinking he would be better off as far from her as possible. But right now, he would give anything to be holding her, to remind himself he had something worthwhile in this life to cling on to.

He groaned as he tentatively moved each leg and then his arms. His limbs were heavy and reluctant but they responded to his commands. No serious injury there, then. Still keeping his eyes closed, he eased himself into a sitting position, leaning on his elbows as he did so, tucking his legs in, using the wall behind him to gain support. Only when he sat upright and had taken a few breaths did he open his eyes. Nothing. The sleeping forms which had decorated the floor, the mounds of rags, empty supermarket trolleys, and sheets of cardboard had vanished. As had the car park. But it must be there! How else would he be sitting upright against the cold concrete pillar?

It's still there, he told himself. Those few lights outside had finally gone on the blink and the fires had been allowed to die down, that was all it was.

"Bert!" His cry came out as a whisper, as if he didn't want to disturb anything. There was no answer.

"Bert!" This time he raised his voice and it echoed back at him as if he was in some cavern.

"Col. Vic!" He called out the names of those he'd been introduced to before he passed into unconsciousness. Still nothing.

Feeling behind him, the solidity of the pillar felt reassuring and he walked his hands over its uneven surface, using it to pull himself to his feet. Once fully standing, he leant back, trying to gain as much contact as he could with the column. He felt strangely unanchored and sensed if he let go of his support he would float off into oblivion. It was easy to imagine how those astronauts felt on their space walks. Still with his hands clasping the pillar, he shuffled his feet around its base to see if anything was visible from another angle.

Total darkness. Except in one framed image. A hollowed-out window enclosed an orange blaze. There was something strange about it. It didn't look quite real, as if it was a projection of those images created as screensavers. A digital layer of fire hanging in the night. He could see a crowd gathered around the edges, Bert and his friends. Why hadn't they responded to him when he had called out? They hadn't been that far away. He went to call again and then stopped. Saw the man introduced as Tobias—Toby—and two shadowy figures standing slightly to the side. He couldn't quite put his finger on it, looking at them sent a chill down his spine. Tobias raised a hand and it was as if a switch had been flipped. The fire vanished whilst the silence remained.

No footsteps made their way back to their miserable hotel, no curses or drunken songs, no stumbling feet or half-hearted fights. With the disappearance of the fire, his new friends had blinked out of existence.

Everything rippled, even the ground beneath his feet, and now Aidan felt truly terrified. Had he been drinking so much he'd damaged his grip on reality? The black shifted, seemed to split into infinite layers so he felt he was looking at a book, its pages flipping before and slamming shut.

Lights returned. But not the streetlamps which buzzed blue shades in the cold night. Small golden orbs danced in front of his vision. The edges smudged by tiny halos. The nearest thing he could associate with them were the corpse lights, or will-o-the-wisps, he had seen on some of his late-night rambles across a nearby marsh.

It had been known as Corpse Marsh for centuries by virtue of the number of people who had disappeared into its depths. The present-day marsh was a fragment of its former self, having been drained and dredged, with very few bones turning up to everyone's surprise. Just a small remnant remained, protected by local environmentalists for the habitat it provided. He had walked the area, contemplating those areas fenced-off with dire warnings about the consequences of leaving the marked paths, contemplating doing just that. During the long nights of winter, he had gone out there when no one else was about and would sit and try to summon the courage to jump into the mire. As he sat there, pondering his miserable existence, he had seen dancing orbs like those he saw now. And each time, they had stopped him taking that final step. He had regarded them as guardian angels.

These orbs, however, seemed cold. There was no warmth emanating from them. It dawned on him that the chill came not merely from their appearance but also from his surroundings. The pages—as he regarded the layers—were fanning out again, shifting and transposing themselves on each other, the effect was disorienting. Aidan continued to cling to the column, still feeling exposed as his hands were behind him, effectively leaving him defenceless.

Carefully, without breaking total contact, he turned round so he clasped the column in a tight embrace. Only when he had completed the manoeuvre did he become aware he had closed his eyes. Slowly he opened them, realising that what he held had changed in texture and form.

Smoother, carved and curved, cold, oh so cold. His fingers traced runes which burned beneath his touch, sent a spear of terror into his heart. He swallowed, reluctantly stepped back and raised his eyes. The column he had been embracing so tightly was monstrous. A statue to some beast god he had never seen before.

As he looked up, he saw it wore three faces and the eyes of one of them was looking directly at him. They burned even though they were blacker than the pitch which swamped his sight.

Then he spotted Tobias. A friend! He almost called out until he saw there was something strange about him, saw what he was carrying. He felt sick.

"Cernunnos, we bring meat," said Tobias, walking towards the statue and placing a mound of raw meat and bones at its feet.

Aidan was convinced he could be seen, yet for the moment they chose to ignore him. He wished he could move his feet and run but found he was frozen in place. Whether through terror or some spell he had no idea. If he had been able to run, where could he have gone to?

"Cernunnos, we bring drink," said one of Tobias' shadowy assistants. A basin filled with dark, viscous liquid was placed beside the first offering. Its coppery tang filled Aidan's nostrils. He recognised the scent of blood.

"Cernunnos, we bring the soul," said the other, holding out a long grey scarf. No, not a scarf, matter of some sort, a writhing, looping skein which struggled to escape the hands holding it. It had no human form, but Aidan could almost feel its terror. Other emotions too, coursed through the mass which was now being wrapped around the outstretched arms of the statue they had named.

Then Tobias stepped forward again. Dipped a ladle in the blood, took a sip, and passed it to his companions. He poured the remainder over the hands holding the shifting skein. He dipped the ladle in the bowl again and began to wash the statue's body in blood. Aidan, still to the rear of the carved creature, took a step backwards, only to find Tobias at his side, holding out the ladle.

"Here is the last drop," said Tobias. "It is for you to drink."

There was no surprise in his eyes to find Aidan there, it was almost as if he had expected it.

Aidan shook his head. Tobias stepped closer, held the ladle up to his lips. The smell of raw meat and the blood was turning his stomach. He pressed his lips together, tried to regulate his breathing. Continued to refuse.

"Drink," said Tobias. "It was what you were born to do."

The words hit him. Truth in a different form. But this. No. This was a travesty. He turned his head away like a toddler refusing their food, lips still clamped. The ladle was pressed up against his mouth, its edge forcing its way into the crease of his lips, urging them apart.

He could barely breathe, wanted to swallow, take in air, but knew he would be ingesting more than that if he did so.

"Drink," insisted Tobias, his voice a command.

And Aidan drank, unable to fight the insistent urging. Thick and clotting, the last drop slithered into his mouth and down his throat. His stomach clenched as he fought against what they were making him do. He wanted to turn and vomit out the poison he suspected it to be, but Tobias was holding his jaw closed, preventing him both from regurgitating the blood and from moving. The man was far stronger than he had ever thought. If he was a man.

"Now you are our blood brother. A fit offering for Cernunnos."

It was an unwanted connection. "Who are you? *What* are you?"

"Something long forgotten but never gone," said Tobias. "You'll find out soon enough. I think it's best if I let you enjoy your journey of discovery."

The smile on Tobias' face was cruel and wicked. He thought of him now as Tobias, not the more friendly Toby, the man who had rescued so many.

"Come," he said, taking Aidan's arm and guiding him round to the front of the statue. "Look." He gestured at the statue, which like Tobias and his companions, appeared to be the only solid thing in this rippling world. "This is Cernunnos. This is the night of His return. He will walk with us."

Aidan gazed on in horror as the horned creature began to shift, pulled cloven hooves from the mud at his feet. The stone façade faded and he took in a man, a beast—a devil. The antlered skull turned one of its faces to Aidan, held him with his dead gaze. Aidan almost sank to his knees beneath that look, felt his trousers, warm and wet as he pissed himself. His stomach churned and he fought to hold onto his sanity.

"It is time to return to the Layerings," said Tobias. "Sister has made preparations for Cernunnos' return to the land, and for the three to Dance again and be reborn—if He wishes it. You will be our guest of honour."

Aidan could barely take in his words. Didn't even puzzle over who the three were. He had no idea what was going on. It was as if he had fallen into some terrible nightmare from which there was no escape. He had no energy left to defy them. He had no choice except to follow.

The orbs he had seen danced ahead of the group. Guiding lights leading them across the marsh which was now vast compared to the size he remembered.

"The Corpse Marsh was never destroyed," said Tobias. "We disguised it with our Layerings. It meant we could continue our traditions without any interference from the human world. We noticed you get a touch sensitive these days at any hint of sacrifice. A disappointment, I must admit. Your people had stronger stomachs once."

"How—how can you hide a marsh as big as this?" said Aidan. "It's impossible."

"All is possible in our world," said Tobias. "Open your mind and make the most of your time here."

The words felt like a sentence. "How long do you intend to keep me prisoner?"

"Prisoner? Oh, you're free to go if you want." The group laughed as Aidan gazed around him. If he made a move in any direction, he would be done for. Wasn't that what he wanted though? An end to the misery? Oblivion?

Cernunnos had started to walk ahead of the group, the orbs dancing around His horned crown. Lighting His features so any who saw Him would know Him. The ground shook with every step the monster took.

Perhaps we will come out somewhere more normal, thought Aidan, trying to conjure up hope from somewhere. He would continue to walk with them, seek out his chances. For the moment, it was certainly safer to stay with these devils. To lose himself in this place would most definitely bring him that oblivion he had craved not so long ago. His decision calmed him, strangely comforted him, until he started to pay closer attention to their conversation.

"It's been a long time since we've seen them," said Tobias's companion.

"Yes," said Tobias. "The renewal is due and they need us. And they need a blood offering."

That term again. The one they had gifted him.

"Who are you going to see?" asked Aidan, casting a glance at Cernunnos, who continued to stalk ahead, silent and uncommunicative. Was he going to meet more creatures like that devil?

"Tommy, Betty, and Fiddler," said Tobias, cheerfully, as if Aidan should know who they were. "A bit of a family reunion you could say. We've been expecting them for a while only they couldn't get away until now. Sister's going to be throwing quite a party."

The names sounded vaguely reassuring. Normal, human names. A family reunion. It sounded relatively harmless. Then he thought of the blood he'd been forced to drink, looked upon Cernunnos as he walked, and then at the faces of his companions. They had called him an offering. The terror returned.

CHAPTER FIFTEEN

BETTY

They had walked many miles, allowed themselves a mere few hours' rest. Betty could feel the cold seep up through the ground. Normally he would ignore it, burrow himself deep as far as he could, feeling in it the sense of the womb, of the Mother. Today though, cold fingers poked and prodded at him. Insistent he should wake and rise. Betty grumbled and twitched, turned over, tried to lose himself in those happy dreams of hunting across the meadows of the Weald. He ran with the hounds and the horses, outstripping them and often reaching the prey first. This was his element, his heaven.

The chill creeping into him reminded him that such a place could only live in his mind at present. Megan had forbidden his hunt, forbidden his dresses, his Dance. He growled at the thought of the woman once promised to him. She had become his darkness. Her face swam through his thoughts and he opened his eyes to avoid seeing her. Found himself moving closer to the fire which Tommy was stoking up on the opposite side. Betty's legs had crossed the threshold and the burn ate at him. He welcomed its heat. It was how he had Become after all. Soon he would have to be washed again in flame, but the hunt had to come first.

"Early," he said to Tommy when his brother noticed he was awake.

"Not early enough," said Fiddler, coming over to join them. He had a couple of rabbits tossed over his shoulder and slung one over to Betty.

The three quickly skinned the animals and ate the remainder, spitting the bones out into the fire which sputtered in response. They did not cook the meat. They had time, and their preference was for the rawness of flesh, the tang of a life recently gone.

Once he had finished, he picked up the bloody pelt and rubbed it against his cheek. So soft and warm. A dress made from such fur would be a true prize. He snatched the pelts from Tommy and Fiddler, slipped them into his pack. He would need to capture a fair number of rabbits to achieve his aim of a soft trim around the horse's coat, these three were a start. Three. The number was a portent. It represented the brothers' power. Who they truly were.

"Hunt," he said, knowing what the answer would be but determined to try.

Tommy and Fiddler shook their heads. He sighed.

"You'll have to make do with what you can find on our travels. You must remain close," said Tommy. "Once we've performed the rites, are renewed, you will be able to hunt to your heart's content. We will change a little, but ultimately be the same. You will still be Betty."

"So long ago, I can hardly remember," said Betty. "And now I must take another into me."

"It has always been so," said Tommy. "Each donor gives you their heart and their soul for you to feed on. Predator and prey. You take and you Become."

Betty's spirits rose at the thought of a hunt. Not of rabbits but of man. From his prey would come the heart he needed. The soul itself a discarded wraith. Everything came back to the heart in the end. The steady pulse beneath his feet quickened.

CHAPTER SIXTEEN

MEGAN

"You don't have to stay." Sister Sarah's words broke into her thoughts.

Megan hadn't heard her approach; she was still buried in the misery of the pain from her cramps, the ache in her legs. She'd even considered returning to The Five Turns just to get a hot water bottle and curl up in bed like she used to. Sleeping the period pains away, as well as her father's remedy of a port and brandy, had long been her solution. She doubted the Wyve was going to offer either water bottle or drink.

Megan looked up at the Wyve, into the darkness beneath her hood. She had never got used to these creatures.

"Where would I go?" She could not return to Cropsoe despite her occasional visits, could not bear the looks that came her way. Guilt. Resentment. Worry she would bring the monsters back. Knowing her bloodline would bring the monsters back.

"There is another place. It is where Tommy and his brothers have gone."

Megan had heard the news of their departure. Had actually heard them recite the words of the Turns. Closed her ears to the horror of the memory. Tommy had made sure she would hear, it was a challenge. Two days ago now? More? She should've been angry, should've demanded their return, sent others out to bring them back. Instead, she had felt relief at no longer being the focus of Tommy's mocking gaze. Out of sight, out of mind. Another guilty respite from the knowledge of her failure to change things.

"Where?" She didn't want to know.

"The Layerings. Where we originally came from. It was destroyed by the Umbrans, by us. We drained the land of its nourishment, failed to sustain it. The Mother was furious, sent us—Hweol and the Folk—here. The Father, Cernunnos, was banished to the Corpse Marshes. He is shackled by the weight of the dead. With the right offerings He can be freed, and I have heard Tobias, a long-faithful servant of His, has fed Him well. Cernunnos is returning. He is walking. It is He who can relieve you of your burden.”

Megan stared at the Wyve. To hear of a Father and a Sister, of the same kind, no doubt, as Tommy and Hweol, made her shudder.

“You need to go,” said Sister Sarah. “It is why Hweol was spared. A mother cannot destroy her child, no matter its crime. But the Father can. He can free you of Hweol’s presence and decide his fate.”

“But he’s here,” said Megan, tapping the side of her head. “Always watching, listening, whispering … what makes you think he would let me go, knowing what awaits?”

“Because it’s a risk he’s willing to take. It’s his one chance to regain another form. To remain inside a human——as the parasite he is——”

Megan heard a growl from the depths of her mind. He had been quiet for a precious few days. He always was during her period. This was the time, outside of pregnancy, which linked her more to the Mother and gave protection to her inner thoughts and feelings; much as she had been able to when she had carried her baby. The baby Tommy had killed with his words whispered in darkness. She turned her attention back to the Wyve.

“——means he *will* die. He can only exist as long as you exist, and he cannot escape on his own. No one has that power except the Mother and the Father.”

“And what of John? What of my husband?”

“His spirit can also be released by the Mother and Father, but he cannot be remade. Being held within the sword corrupts those who are trapped.”

Megan recalled her husband’s thirst, the scars on her arm. She began to allow herself to believe the crone, but she needed to be sure. “I was told they could bring him back. Hweol, Tommy——”

“They lied. They feed you hope to lead you on and then take it all away. It is time you let your husband rest, set yourself free.”

It was a view she had come around to on her own. A decision she needed to make. “And after?”

“Go anywhere you want. Join the rest of the world. Leave us behind. Despite what Hweol wanted, we are fading away and it is for the best. We have become cruel folk, forgetting who or what we once were. That much I have come to realise since the Wheel stopped."

Sadness and regret coated the Wyve's words. Megan could barely believe it. To find someone willing to help her, to listen, and even to understand, was difficult to accept. She had been on her own for so long, she suddenly felt the need for company. She couldn't do it on her own anymore.

"Will you come with me? To the … Layerings?"

The Wyve chuckled. "You ask me, one of those who did nothing to stop the women's suffering, who betrayed their own sex?"

"You had no choice," said Megan, thinking of the years of coercion and force, Tommy's tricks of the trade.

"Oh, I had a choice. I was a coward. Preferred to hide in the shadows; in this robe. I betrayed so many. Your mother was one of them."

Her mother, Liza, had died in a vain attempt to prevent the loss of Megan's unborn child. Before that, she had suffered, offered as Wyve to Hweol and Tommy. Yet Megan felt no hatred or disgust at the Wyve's presence. Not any longer. When one understood the history, the violence and fear, the need to protect oneself and their family, she understood a woman would do what she had to. Decisions which meant justifying those actions for the rest of their life. She too had made decisions which ultimately had led to the loss of those closest to her. Despite keeping them at arms' length, she no longer condemned the Wyves.

"I am no better," said Megan. "And I would value your knowledge – and company."

"You would trust her?" whispered an unwelcome voice. She ignored it.

The Wyve remained quiet for a moment, then nodded her head. "I will come with you. It can be my pilgrimage, my repentance, if you like. I will ask Sister for sanctuary."

"Tell me about her." Megan noticed the silence that had crept up around them. The Imps who'd been playing and chattering nearby had moved closer, sat quietly at Sister Sarah's feet. Other Wyves gathered behind them, as did a few red-eyed Lords. The air seemed to ripple. She felt if she blinked they would all vanish, including herself. This unreal reality had become more unreal.

"Tommy, Betty, and Fiddler had a sister. She has never been known by any other name—as far as I could recall. They left her behind, left her to the desolation of the Layerings. She has made it her own, however, as is the way of women. We are all experts at making the best of a bad job."

"Tell me."

Umbra faded from her vision as Sister Sarah told her the stories of that blasted land and Hweol, from his corner of her world, shared his memories and his crimes. She doubted his return would be welcome.

Not exactly, murmured Hweol. *But it is where I can be freed. Where your husband will find peace. And you will be released. We will both be reborn.*

"Tommy, Betty, and Fiddler. What do they hope to achieve by returning to the sister they left?" she asked Sarah.

"The three are near their time, as you know," said Sarah. "They need their own rebirth or they too will vanish. You stopped this in Umbra, so they travel to the Layerings. With the return of Cernunnos, the Father of All, the Mother is rebuilding her family. In the Layerings, they will be able to perform the rituals needed."

"Rituals?" Remembrance of the Five Turns forced themselves back in. The burning, the harrowing, the crushing, the rupture——and always the blood. A year in the Weald was lived in death's shadow.

"Their rebirth resets the Wheel. It will Turn again."

Megan could've cried. Everything she had done, that her mother had done, was to stop the Wheel turning and now it seemed it was all for nothing. Unless she stopped it.

You can't, whispered Hweol. *There's nothing you can do.*

Maybe not, she thought grimly, *but she would die trying.* Laughter echoed inside her head.

The gathered crowd faded away. Wyves shooed the Imps, formed a barrier between her and the Lords, the Ostlers who had crept from the dark, and other shapes shifting in the gathering gloom.

"They know you will go. They will offer you an escort," said Sarah.

"Escort? Make me their prisoner more like. I will accept no help from *them*." The Lords had hunted down Simon Wheelborn, the man she had always called father, they and every other creature she could see gathered—apart from the Wyves—had ripped him to shreds. "I will travel, but only with you," said Megan. "It's bad enough I have *him*, up here." She tapped the side of her head.

"The path we take first will be into your world. Hweol fades in that place. You will barely notice him for a while. It is not the quickest way, but I have a feeling I know where they will have gone. Their energy was low, and to make such a journey, well I know where I would go. They will lead us to the Layerings, albeit unaware."

Megan considered. She had no real idea of where to go, how to get there. She had two choices: to put her trust in Sister Sarah—or Hweol. In the end, an easy decision.

You trust too easily, said Hweol.

No, said Megan. *I trust no one. But I prefer to take the lesser evil.*

Evil. Was that how she thought of the Wyves? No. They had been formed through an act of violence against themselves, then they had built their shell and encased their bodies beneath it, hiding their faces from the world in the process. Hiding from themselves, if they admitted it. She would give Sister Sarah her chance of redemption, even if she didn't fully trust her.

"When do we go?" she asked.

"Now," said Sister Sara. "No time like the present."

Hweol remained silent and she sensed his satisfaction. In the end it didn't matter who guided her. The destination was still the same. He could be patient.

Three Wyves came forward. One held Megan's backpack containing the few belongings she had brought with her to Umbra. Another held a sling in which a sword—*the* sword—was wrapped. The other, a pack for Sarah. The needs of the Wyves were few. She wondered as to its contents.

CHAPTER SEVENTEEN

BETTY

The wind stirred the grass around them, riffled the leaves of the few nearby beeches standing over the remains of an old chapel. The steady drone of motorway traffic irritated Betty. He preferred the buzz of bees and wasps, even hornets. The 'speech' of living creatures meant more than the rumble of the motor car. Beyond travel, there was no other point to them, and they were part of the poison destroying the Mother's world. As his brothers turned their faces to the city, he looked to where the motorway carved its path through the hills. Beneath this soil, he didn't just feel the beat of the land, he heard its ghosts. The murmur of their voices joining the hum.

Hundreds had been buried in that place when the plague had roared through the city. Amongst them had been many of the clergy, although the Master and his kind had been spared. Pits had been dug, into which bodies had been thrown regardless of station. Over time, those bones had settled, but now their remnants shifted unhappily. Betty cocked his head and listened to their whisperings, absorbed their stories. Another wrong to be righted. Death was to be honoured and respected, not dug up because it represented a barrier to some development or other.

As he listened, he silently promised to return and let the ghosts walk. He continued to circuit the hill as his brothers talked, returning to their side and discovering one thing which hadn't vanished in the name of improvement. The Mizmaze, a grass labyrinth traced out by long-ago monks remained. He glanced at Tommy.

"We've got time," said his brother, apparently more relaxed now they were almost at their destination.

Betty set his feet to the winding track and, concentrating hard, followed the labyrinthine path to its centre and then out again. A simple pleasure. He repeated the circuit and then heard Fiddler calling him. Reluctantly, he returned to his brothers' side and they made their way down the steep hill. They paused briefly at the river to have a drink and then followed the footpath across the road and into the meadows.

Unlike other towns, Betty could smell the history of the city. Ancient walls and old colleges, rambling paths, and the ruined bishop's palace intermingled, with the more modern kept at arms' length.

The day was young but there were already walkers out and about, dogs yapping at the swans, children laughing in a playground between the meadow and the city centre. The area was coming back to him. It had been more rustic, carried the smell of the livestock which travelled through, the odour of the unwashed who crowded round the city's outskirts, seeking to enter and beg for alms. He had preferred spending more time with them than behind the sophisticated walls of the Master's building. This time however, he felt it would be safer to stay close to Tommy. He wanted to hear Fiddler's music again and it was this visit that would allow it to happen.

A swan glided by. The graceful neck hypnotised him, the enticing softness of the feathers tugged at him. He barely noticed as water rose up around his legs, soaked through his boots and trousers. The bird's plumage was warm, the white of a cloud, a pillow. Pillows were for your head, to bury yourself into. This was soft against his face, the individual barbs tickled his skin. Something yellow and gold stabbed at him but he clamped a hand over it, snapped it away. Somewhere, someone was screaming.

He ignored the sound, the fluffy mass in his arms was his sole focus. The heart beat fast beneath the feathers, summoning him. Betty pushed his hand deep into the centre of the writhing mass. Warm blood splattered his face and he noticed with no small sadness the disappearance of the snowy plumage beneath a crimson stain.

"Betty!"

Tommy was calling him but the heart had a stronger voice and he continued to rummage within the bird's cavity.

"Betty!"

This time, Tommy's hand was on his shoulder, an iron grip surprising in one who was half his size. He was being steered back to the bank.

"You've drawn attention to us," said Tommy, indicating a couple who were trying to console a distressed child whilst trying to understand what they had witnessed.

"I'll go and speak to them," said Fiddler, as the man pulled out a phone. "Maybe sing them a song. It'll soothe the child."

Betty smiled. "Can I come? I'd like to listen." The dead bird in his hand was semi-forgotten as the thought of a song attracted him.

"No," said Tommy. "You need to come with me. We'll find a quiet corner and you can finish your meal. I'll even help you pluck the thing! When Fiddler's calmed the family, he can come and give you a song."

Betty looked down at the dead swan and then at Fiddler and the family beyond.

"Come on, Betty. If we stay here any longer, others might come and we can't deal with large numbers at present. You know that. It's safer if we go for now."

Blood was continuing to soak into his skin, his clothes.

"You must respect death. Not waste it," said Tommy, tugging at him slightly.

The reminder of the Mother's decree, one he had recently considered when they were up on St. Catherine's Hill, pulled him back to their situation. He followed Tommy to a secluded corner of the meadow, leaving Fiddler to sing to the family. The screaming stopped as Betty found the heart.

CHAPTER EIGHTEEN

TOMMY

"Winchester," said Fiddler, more at ease now the family had been calmed. He gazed around. "Music to my ears!"

Tommy laughed. "Of course. A cathedral city, there'll be a choir for you to choose your strings from. I hear a number of them can be found by its walls at night."

"It's been a long time," said Fiddler, taking in their surroundings as Betty moved over to the river, swishing swan feathers in the water to clean them. "Nice to see the old stomping ground again."

Winchester. The ancient capital of England. Tommy and his brothers had spent many happy hours sat atop St. Catherine's Hill, gazing across to the city, working out who they would claim. Those were the days they travelled freely from the Weald, before the risks to themselves became too great. He wondered how much it had changed. There were still many travellers and performers thronging its streets, and he found their own presence did not attract attention. Their garb fit very much with the outfits worn by the many buskers and artists.

They walked slowly along the road towards the centre. On their left, the river Itchen flowed peaceably, an old friend in which they had often bathed. Some of the almshouses had become sheltered accommodation, but one still followed old traditions. It was that one they would go to first.

"Fancy some bread and ale?"

Betty smiled. "I could murder something to eat." Hungry again. The swan a distant memory.

"Might come to that," said Tommy, thinking of the Master and his black-robed Brothers.

"Do you think he's still alive?" asked Fiddler.

"More than like. He does his own turning."

"Don't think he'll want us here," said Fiddler. "Always got us turfed out of the taverns. Scoundrels, he called us last time!"

Fiddler's indignant tone made Tommy laugh. Scoundrels, rogues, all the names the Master had called had been true to a fault. He would call them worse after this visit. The three took the steps down from the bridge to the riverside; this path would take them to the remainder of the water meadows and the Hospital of St. Cross. Families ambled along the wide path, couples strolled. One or two raised an eyebrow at Betty, his size was notable, but most barely paid any attention to the men. Their mummers' clothing was no different to that worn by many at the summer Hat Fair or by the New Age Travellers on the road. *That was one of the blessings of modern times*, thought Tommy. *Nobody seemed to care what you looked like.*

Ducks and swans approached the banks expecting food. Tommy could see a sudden shift in Betty's focus, his nearing to the water. *Not again!* He moved quickly. It wouldn't do to upset the nearby toddlers and their parents. Not yet. It wouldn't matter once they were returned to full strength—and power. Betty's look as Tommy restrained him mirrored that of the toddlers themselves. All it would need would be for him to throw a tantrum. And Betty throwing a tantrum was not a pretty sight.

"Come on," he said. "Let's go and see the Master. He always had a soft spot for you. Might have a robe for you to wear."

"I liked his but he wouldn't give it me," said Betty, his voice sulky.

"Well then, I think it's time for us to change his mind," said Tommy. "Come on."

He picked up his pace and soon the group had left their fellow walkers behind and were walking across the meadows. The poet Keats had once walked this way. He had recorded it for others to follow. Many asked why he described half his route, leaving out the return journey.

"Seasons of mist and mellow fruitfulness," began Fiddler.

"Close bosom friend of the maturing sun," responded Tommy.

"Thou watchest the last oozings, hours by hours," said Betty, jumping ahead.

"Never did like that poem," said Fiddler. "No life to it, no rhythm. He didn't describe the 'oozings' properly. Cyder! Hah! Said he was going to talk about Nature, bloody and unbowed, and look at the result. An airy-fairy ode to Autumn!" Fiddler spat on the ground. He didn't have much time for poets.

"I liked the oozings," said Betty, his face taking on a dreamy quality.

"They were good," admitted Tommy. "Some of our best, if I say so myself. Keats didn't say no either. Though I think that might've been due to the poppies. Ever the adventurous soul, was our John."

"Do you remember his face?" asked Fiddler. "When he woke up and saw what we'd all eaten and drunk? What *he'd* digested, imbibed? I near pissed myself at that."

The three laughed at the memory; so long ago, but one they looked back on with fondness.

A breeze carried the cries of privileged youth in their direction. The rugby fields were full.

"No, Betty," said Tommy, seeing his brother distracted once more. "We'll find more meat at the Master's, and Fiddler can string his bow."

"The meat will not be as tender," growled Betty.

"But better clothed," said Tommy.

They had neared the walls of the Hospital of St. Cross and were following their familiar path to the gate. Then it was through an ancient archway and it felt as if time had stood still. Ahead of them were neat lawns. To one side was the almshouse—a building housing the Brethren—and on the other side was the chapel.

"I don't hear any singing," said Fiddler.

"Strange," said Tommy. "The evening air was always filled with the sound of the choir." The sun had started to set, begun to cast long shadows across the quad. It brought with it an uneasy silence. Something else was at play here.

"He's here," said Fiddler. "I can smell him, but it's as if he's hiding."

"The Brethren?"

"No," said Fiddler. "There's no one in there. No one alive anyway. Might find something of use though."

Fiddler was thinking of his strings. If they didn't have to work for them, all the better. It depended on how fresh they were.

"Do you want to go and look whilst Betty and I track down the Master?"

Fiddler shook his head. "I think we need to stay together for the moment."

Tommy was surprised. Fiddler was always ready to go off on his own, ready to face any danger. This undertone of doubt was something new.

"I'll be alright once I've got this damned instrument restrung," said Fiddler. "But at the minute, I feel as if there's something else going on and we're not as strong as we once were. Not yet anyway."

"Ah, caution," said Tommy. "You're probably right. The Master was always an untrustworthy old goat."

They headed over to the almshouse and Betty pushed open the heavy oak door. Man's voice in the Hospital might be silent, but the wood and stone sang with the centuries. Tommy touched the wall, felt its weight and density beneath his hands, the energy buried there. Voices floated up at his touch and then shrank away as they sensed who he was.

He looked around the lobby, neat and comfortably furnished in a modern style, it was empty. Fiddler guided them across a hallway and then into the high-ceilinged rooms. Stained glass windows ran along the upper reaches of the wall, and the growing moonlight cast its glow onto those within, illuminating the company sat at the table.

The Black Brothers, so-called because of their robes denoting them as members of the Order of the Hospital of St Cross, sat on one side. The Red Brothers, their claret colour proclaiming them as belonging to the Order of Noble Poverty, sat opposite. All were statues, leaning back against the high-backed chairs. Eyes were closed and mouths open.

"They're asleep," said a voice emerging from the gloom. Another figure clad in black. The Master. "I could feel you coming, thought it wise to take precautions. Wouldn't want any of this lot dropping dead of a heart attack. The press would have a field day."

"So this is for their protection and not your own?" said Tommy.

"I am perfectly safe," said the Master. "My position is one you have no permission to challenge."

Tommy laughed and his voice echoed across the rafters. "Why would I want to challenge you? Living in a city. Constrained by walls and tradition?"

"Then why are you here?"

Tommy regarded the man who had moved closer. Like himself, he had barely changed with the years.

"You have not kept up with our news?" said Tommy. "I find that surprising."

"Oh, I know everything that's been going on," said the Master. "It's about time we had a change. Someone with fresh ideas. Ironic though that she's your daughter and won't give you the time of day."

"And you would know all about daughters, wouldn't you?"

The Master had the grace to look embarrassed. There were vows he had to make when taking on his position, a large number of which were conveniently forgotten in the mists of time or swept under the carpet.

A wave of exhaustion swept over Tommy. They had walked, the thought of rebirth giving them the energy to keep going. Barely two days!

"Enough of this," said Fiddler, stepping in between the two. "We can talk more later, first I need to restring my fiddle. So, Master. Tell me who I can take or would you prefer I hunt in the close, in the cathedral grounds, in the cathedral itself."

"No," whispered the Master. "You cannot bring such attention to us at this time."

"Then one of these," said Fiddler, waving his arm in the direction of the sleeping men. "They are all of an age. Their cords will be mature, perhaps not as vibrant as I would like, but beggars can't be choosers, and I can always get a second set on our travels. Nobody will notice the death of one through natural causes."

"Natural?"

"What could be more natural for the likes of us?" said Fiddler.

Betty had been following the conversation and had moved over to the table. He was waiting for them to direct him to the chosen victim. The Master reluctantly joined him and took in the sleeping diners. Eventually, he pointed to a man sat at the head of the table. He seemed heartier than most, slightly florid looking.

"He's had a heart attack or two in recent years. Another one won't cause any ripples."

Tommy nodded at Betty who picked up the man quite easily, although not as easily as he would've once done.

"Into the chapel," said Tommy.

Betty nodded and headed in the direction Tommy had indicated. The Master following reluctantly and Tommy and Fiddler coming up behind them.

Betty laid him out on the altar, an action some might call blasphemous, unless they knew who the altar had been originally dedicated to. The table was stone, like that with which the building had been constructed. Traceries were carved in the side, illuminations etched and painted by expert masons. In these images were the stories of the land, although to the uninitiated they looked as if they were mere retellings of the Bible.

Tommy took a small package from his bag and unwrapped it on a nearby table. Three sharp knives lay there. Silver glinting in the dark. These knives were not for the Dance but for the Song. And they were not for him to use but Fiddler.

"Hear the voice," said Fiddler, taking the first knife. "Let him sing." He made a cut at the top of the throat and carried on down the length of his abdomen.

"Hear the song," said Fiddler, taking the second knife. "Let him cry." He made incisions at the man's sides and opened the flaps of skin to reveal the glistening interior.

"Hear the man," said Fiddler, taking the third knife. "Let him howl." He used the knife to hook out the guts, trace out veins and vocal cords. Operations beyond the skill of any normal man, even with the aid of a microscope and fine-pointed instrument, were achieved by Fiddler. The bodily ribbons were like silk in his hands. He met no resistance.

Betty had lain himself out on the pew and picked up a hymn book, idly flicking through the pages, occasionally bursting into song as he found one he knew. None of them were complete heathens. The Master had taken a seat in the choir and Tommy joined him there. Nobody helped Fiddler with the stringing, although in times past, Tommy had set the stage in a rather more dramatic manner, especially when they were putting on a show. There was no need for any of this. Today's restring would be perfunctory, and Fiddler needed simply to be business like. A pity. Tommy missed the songs sung at such times. Perhaps when Fiddler set about collecting his second set they could have a bit more fun.

Eventually, Fiddler took the ribboned tissues and sat on the altar steps. He lifted a candle and proceeded to run it along the bloody skein. The light would flare up briefly and then fade down again. He did this for each of them and then took out a small bottle. The liquid inside was taken from the rivers of Umbra. Fiddler poured it into the chalice he'd taken from the altar, raised it not to the cross over the table but to the figure in the stained glass. This was Her church. He took a sip and then proceeded to dip the slivers in the liquid. Once all had been baptised in this manner, he started to peel them further. Splitting them down until they were barely more than a hair's breadth. As each was finished, he hung them over a nearby rail, and then he took out his fiddle and began to wind a string around each peg and down over the bridge, checking the tension carefully as he went. In all this time nobody spoke.

Then Fiddler took out his bow and ran it over the strings. The bow did not need any such repair. A low thrumming vibrated through the chapel. It echoed around the building, entered Tommy's body, his mind, his heart. It gave him a pleasant jolt, and suddenly he felt a slight lift and the years dropped away a little.

Fiddler was smiling. "Not perfect but it'll do the job." He looked happier than he had done in a long time.

Betty too had perked up, was standing and swaying, waiting for a song to which he could dance. Fiddler looked at him for a moment as if in thought, then started to play. It was the lullaby Betty had danced to before. The one usually played on their return to the Weald. It was the song his long-forgotten mother had once sung to him as a babe before he was claimed for Betty.

Because that's how it was. Betty was never born in the normal sense. He was an elemental of the Weald, housed in skin until the heart failed and another heart was gifted. Then he would rise again from the ashes, a phoenix from the flame.

Betty started to swirl around the nave, spinning and twirling. It should've looked comic or monstrous, grotesque even—it was none of these. It was a moment of memory and pure happiness.

CHAPTER NINETEEN

TOMMY

"He still remembers her," said the Master.

"Somewhere, deep down," said Tommy. "We all remember our mothers, the Mother. Although I wonder if you have forgotten yours?"

It was a while before the Master replied. "I haven't forgotten, but I have grown tired. Sometimes, I think I would like to return to the soil and rest awhile. The world is too busy these days for the likes of us."

"Busy, yes. But weak. They believe in things they can't see, yet show them something like us and they refuse to believe the evidence of their own eyes. We have power and we can reassert it if we build steadily, carefully."

"Ah, so that's your game," said the Master. "Create your own base, challenge your daughter even though she has the Mother's backing."

Tommy laughed. "You forget the survival of the fittest. That is the one contest the Mother is interested in."

He did not doubt he would win favour. It would be a shame to have to challenge Megan, but if it meant he could restore Hweol to power or, a small voice whispered, himself, then the Mother would be proud. He stretched his body, looked at his brothers. If nothing else, it was time for a change. The future, although dangerous, had suddenly become exciting. How stale had they become repeating the same rituals year in, year out. Now they could travel the breadth of the country, root out old traditions fallen by the wayside, find land more suited to their requirements. Once they had been reborn.

Eventually, the music stopped and the four men regrouped around the altar, gazing down at the eviscerated body. Stomachs grumbled in the cavernous chapel. Tommy would've been hard put to say whose had rumbled the loudest.

"Seems I can offer you a light supper," said the Master. "And I've a particularly delicious mead to go with this."

Betty wrapped the fleshy remnants up in the altar cloth and slung it over his shoulder as if a knapsack.

"To the kitchens," he said.

An hour later saw the meat bubbling in a broth, the bones cast aside, remnants of clothing tossed into a rubbish bag. As the food cooked, Betty cleaned the kitchen. He had always been houseproud.

The Master put dishes out on the kitchen table and poured them all a drink. For the first time in a long time, Tommy felt content. He was warm, food was on the way, and he had a drink in hand. They also had music after a dearth under Megan's edict. Their life was returning to normal.

"Who'll clean up the chapel?" asked Tommy.

"I'll do it," said the Master, "after we've dined. My Brothers will be out for some time yet so there is no need to hurry. And if they wake, Fiddler will be able to soothe them with a tune. For the moment, we can eat, drink and share our stories. I know a little of what has been happening in the Weald."

Tommy swirled his honeyed drink in his glass. The crystal glinted beneath the lamp, added to the warm tones of the amber liquid. He was not sure how much to tell the Master and was fairly certain Tobias had kept him fully informed. The man would surely use the opportunity to put one over on Tommy; the pair of them had always vied for supremacy in this world of man. Then he considered. Better to know exactly where he stood. Deal with the Master once and for all.

"Our rites have been discontinued," said Tommy. "The Daughter does not honour the Mother—"

"Or the Father," laughed Fiddler.

Tommy shot him a glare. "The rites are what gives life to our people and to those of us who are beyond the Weald." He looked at the Master who nodded. "When the rites stop, it affects us. The land dies, we die. We are all at our time of rebirth. Betty sooner than us. We left to fulfil this ritual. The Daughter refused permission to do this in the Weald. She would have us cold in the ground."

"I could say that might not be such a bad thing," said the Master.

Tommy smiled. "I knew you'd say that. But consider this. You too, are of the Weald. You too, have a prescribed time. If she does not permit the ritual, then the same fate will befall you as well. Do you want that?"

"Maybe, maybe not," said the Master. "I said I would like to rest and part of me still wants to. Much as it pains me to agree with you, you are right, it should be as a matter of choice. The ritual is not for the Daughter to forbid."

"We will strengthen ourselves and then, when we return, we will be able to release Hweol. Allow him to experience his own reincarnation. Then all will be as it was before."

As it was before. Oh, how he enjoyed that time, that calendark. Yet he had learned lessons from this hiccup in the way of the Wheelborn. He would bring in more new blood, expand the land they controlled, be more present in day-to-day lives. There had to be visible worship. That was something modern people liked. Their need, their search for spirituality had been evident on his travels. He and his folk could fill a hole and if they were dismissed as crackpots and cranks by the world at large, all the better. They would be left alone and be able to perform their own celebrations in plain sight.

"Will you travel with us?" asked Fiddler.

Tommy was surprised at the question. His brother had no love for the man.

"We should gather together all the Wheelborn on this side of the veil," explained Fiddler. "When we travel, it may be that we need our numbers."

"You make it sound as though we should have an army," said Tommy.

"Perhaps," said Fiddler.

"I think," said the Master. "I would be better off here, maintain the status quo. But I wish you luck."

They finished their food in silence, and when the last drop of mead had been drunk, the three took their leave of the Master. What he would do with the remains of the dead man, how he would explain it away to his sleeping Brothers, none of that was their concern. If the Master decided to blame it on them, that too could wait. A more pressing matter required their attention.

"It'll be easier to travel now I have my music," said Fiddler.

Tommy nodded. When Fiddler played, the world listened—and nobody argued.

The bells chimed the hour as they left the grounds of the Hospital. Three o'clock. Tommy relaxed as they walked. They'd dined on food denied them by Megan, drunk liquor no longer brewed in the Weald. When they returned, these would return to their menus. The Wheelborn would eat as they had done for centuries, whether Megan liked it or not. After all, other animals fed on their own kind and the Mother did not love them any less.

The three did not talk as they walked. Fiddler was composing new tunes in his head and Betty was lost somewhere in memories which always pulled him back at this time. The hoot of an owl or the occasional twitter of an early-rising bird broke the silence as they made their way back across the meadow to town. A soft rush of wind stirred the branches of sturdy oaks, trees he remembered as saplings. The ground beneath his feet was soft and springy after recent rains. Nobody was around.

It would be different further in. He wanted to see what pickings could be found on the streets these days. Not everybody lived in houses, and the cathedral's grounds and the ancient city walls housed many who had no choice but to lay their heads upon the pavement. These would come to no harm. In Winchester at least. Here, they could prove useful in other ways. They had, after all, discarded their morals—and their pride.

The tramp of their feet grew louder as they turned on to the riverside walk, the rush of the water seemed to push them along. An invisible current guiding their movement toward the bridge and the pub alongside.

"Pity it's closed," said Fiddler, eyeing the building. "I'd like to see what passes for ale in these parts."

"Really?" Tommy was surprised. Fiddler had been very much a puritan in certain tastes, preferring that which came from the Weald or was made according to its recipes.

Fiddler grinned. "I have new music, perhaps I should try other things whilst we're abroad."

"I can see you having one sip and then returning to our more traditional brew," said Tommy. "I can guarantee you'll find it insipid. No body. Literally."

They both chuckled, and Betty stopped and smiled back at them despite not having heard a word they said.

"You know," said Tommy. "I think this break from Umbra will do us all good. Something we should make the most of."

CHAPTER TWENTY

TOMMY

They passed the statue of Alfred. It hadn't only been the beer which had been insipid. Tommy shuddered at the memory of the man's piety. If they had to trace the gradual retraction of their world, the lessening of their power to any point in time, it would be to that man.

There had been that brief moment when the Vikings harried the country, when the Normans took control. But they all succumbed to the new ways. Preached religion and morality in holy robes, spreading the Word—although they didn't always live by it, used it as a means to control the people. A little like Hweol and his folk did with their songs and traditions. All religions were the same in the end. Merely another way to claim authority.

They left Alfred behind and went up into the pedestrianised precinct. Old buildings housed modern shops, shadowy doorways housed the homeless. Through an ancient archway leading to the Cathedral close, a group of men huddled. They were not asleep and could be heard, arguing fiercely. Their ripe curses flowed as freely as the cans of lager they pulled out of a carrier bag in their midst.

As the three approached, one of them pulled the bag protectively towards them. The conversation stopped and hostile looks turned on Tommy and his brothers. One of them, a large, bullish figure, rose as if to challenge them. No doubt they thought there was the possibility of easy pickings. Strangers did not walk these parts at this time of night. The quaint old streets of ancient Winchester could be as dangerous as any city centre.

"I should introduce you to my brother," said Tommy, keeping his tone mild, friendly. In reality he could deal with this group himself, but Betty often added an additional amusement if he became involved. "Betty."

"Betty!" The man laughed. "What sort of name's that for a man?"

"Why don't I let him show you," said Tommy, and beckoned Betty closer.

As Betty turned his attention away from a shop window full of strange mannequins and came to join the group, the challenger fell back. His friends also moved, shuffling backwards along the concrete, although there was no real place to go, backed up as they were against stone. The furthest of them pushed himself to his feet and started to sidle away.

"Stay," said Tommy. "Betty won't harm you. He might ask you to dance!"

"I have music," said Fiddler, taking the cue. "Let me play you a tune. You have drink. We have music. Tonight is a night for new friendships."

The men were looking anxiously at each other, Tommy and Fiddler's apparent friendliness had done little to reassure them. If anything, it appeared to heighten their anxiety.

"I'd like to dance among the trees," said Betty, nodding through the archway towards the grounds surrounding the cathedral, the spotlights illuminating its famous architecture.

"Always a child of Nature," said Tommy. "But why not? Trees and grass provide as good a ballroom as any paved square."

Fiddler had moved to the other side of the group and the three formed a barrier, forcing the men to their feet and through the arch.

In the daytime, these grounds were filled with visitors, many sitting amongst—and on—old graves and monuments. Now it was Betty's turn to dance on their graves. He offered his hand to the man who had challenged them. His chosen partner recoiled. Betty stomped his foot in annoyance and Fiddler immediately plucked at the new strings on his fiddle. This would be a good chance to give them a trial run. A little rehearsal before the main event.

It was a gentle tune but it made the men, drunk as they were, cry out as if they had been stabbed. And stabbed they had been. Fiddler's music created daggers of moonlight, slivers which darted mischievously at them, pricking and pinching their skin so they had no option but to start leaping about. Betty grabbed the hand of his reluctant partner and started to twirl him around. A sedate waltz, quite gentle by his usual standards. There was an occasional crunch of bone and a brief scream of pain, yet the man was still living at the end of his dance.

Betty led the gibbering dancer back to his friends. They cringed, bloodied and broken in a group.

"Don't worry," said Tommy. "Look upon this as friends well met. Our paths will cross again one day, perhaps. Maybe we will share a drink then."

The troupe turned away and left the close, carried on up the hill and past the old castle keep, and then they walked away from Winchester.

"I don't think I can stay inside a city's bounds for long," said Fiddler. "I found it draining."

"I like the trees," said Betty. "I want the open air."

Tommy nodded. "Then let us be on our way."

Betty looked at him, opened his mouth, and then closed it again. It was always Tommy who oversaw his rebirth. He trusted his brother. It was something he could not go through on his own.

"So. Where?"

They stood at a crossroads, considering the signpost, the names and mileage. The name Tommy had in mind was not included.

"Kinlet," said Tommy. "We take the Old Track."

"I'd forgotten that path," said Fiddler. "It'll cut miles off our route. But the Leys …"

Tommy knew what Fiddler was going to say. The folk who lived in the shadow of the Leys had once been family but they had lost contact centuries ago. What form they took now would be hard to say. Nor did he particularly want to meet one or two characters who could still possibly roam those paths.

"It'll get us where we need to," said Tommy.

A public footpath sign was buried in the hedge; it directed their feet onto the track, although it wouldn't be long before they diverged from this. They would be taking another right of way.

Like the path which provided the shortcuts between Cropsoe and the other villages of the Weald, theirs led them into a shadowland. Another little pocket of rural England placed beyond the Veil. Nor was this place under Hweol's influence. Restrictions had meant no one from their corner of the countryside had walked this way for a long time. What state it was in now, nobody knew. Had anyone remained behind? Was it under Sister's control? It was possible.

With another step, Tommy led them into this other world, taking them from morning to another twilight.

"No moon?" asked Betty, gazing up at the sky.

A fine mist obscured their view, a filmy transparency cast across their surroundings. Like their own well-trod path, this was lined by walls of trees. It was not as wide, although it looked as though it had been once, until the foliage had advanced to claim it. The temperature had dropped. The trees looked dead; the air smelled dead.

"It feels as if nothing living has passed this way for a long time," said Fiddler. "Not our kind, not an errant human, or any other creature. Nothing. Nobody has walked here."

Tommy shivered and realised it was not from the cold but from fear. An emotion he had not felt for so long it felt alien, shaming. When he looked at his brothers however, he saw the same expression reflected there.

"Do you have a tune for us, Fiddler?" he asked.

"Not for these parts. I think it best to remain quiet for the moment. I wouldn't like to disturb whatever sleeps here."

"Sleeps?"

Fiddler nodded. "Yes. The place felt dead at first, but I sense something else—a certain rhythm travelling through the soil. A pulse. If you concentrate, you can sense it too."

Tommy nodded. His brother was more tuned in to the pulse of life than he was. Over time he had grown lazy, allowed his brother to relay the information to him. Now, he needed to hear it for himself. He stilled every part of him, emptied all his thoughts, cast aside his fear. All of these would return soon enough, instead he had to create a large enough void in himself to fill with whatever life inhabited these parts. There was nothing at first, a deep, dark emptiness, and then … then there it was, a slow, steady pulse. Like a heartbeat, a drum, it beat its way underground and up into the soles of their feet, up and up into their bodies, their hearts, their minds. Like bindweed, its rhythm wound itself around their thoughts. Chaining them.

As Tommy realised what was happening, he gave himself a sudden shake, cast off the shackles of the intruder. Fiddler had decided to disregard his earlier caution to silence and was now sending his bow across his fiddle. The music danced over to Betty and caught his attention, brought him back from wherever he had been travelling.

"Whatever's here," Fiddler said, "has already heard us. I don't think a touch of music is going to make any difference."

"What is it?" asked Tommy.

"Something that's very hungry," said Fiddler. "If we're to go this way, I suggest we move as quickly as we can."

A scream from behind them caught their attention.

"A stray?" asked Tommy, looking at Fiddler.

His brother focussed on the direction of the sound. "Yes, something came in after us. Two somethings."

As if in direct response to his words, two figures came crashing through the mist and almost cannoned into them. The new arrivals pulled themselves up short, throwing terrified glances over the shoulder at the same time as gazing in horror at the three ahead of them.

"Hey, hey, Clive, it's okay," said one. "They're normal, well, sort of normal."

The one called Clive took a step closer to Fiddler, probably figuring he was the safest of the three to approach.

"Yeah, they look alright. Not like that ... that thing behind us."

"You look as though you're in a spot of bother, lads," said Fiddler, keeping a smile on his face, continuing to try and appear as normal as he could. There would be a point where the mask would slip, for now normal would do.

"Yeah, mate," said Clive. "Hitched a ride and then the bloke dropped us at the path. Said it was a short cut to Oldingham."

"And you believed him," said his friend. "Bloody fool."

"You didn't have to come with me, Ethan," said Clive. "Too scared to go off on your own."

The two men glared at each other, using their anger to hide their fear.

Tommy considered their words. They had been directed here by an outsider. This path, supposedly hidden from modern eyes, was unknown. And yet here these two were.

"Do you know the person who gave you the lift?" asked Tommy.

"Some old boy in a strange frock," said Clive.

"Habit," said Ethan. "Or a robe, black. He was getting on a bit. If I'm honest, he was probably too old to drive. Then again, beggars can't be choosers."

"The Master," said Fiddler. "He must've cleared up quick."

"Know him, do you?" asked Ethan. "A friend?"

"In a way," said Tommy, trying to puzzle out the meaning of their presence. "Did he say anything to you in the car? Anything strange?"

Clive and Ethan looked at each other. "Everything he said was strange, mate."

The 'mate' was beginning to grate.

"Like?" prompted Fiddler.

"Like there would be people to show us the way. Even though he didn't know which way we were going."

"But you said Oldingham."

"That's what he told us," said Ethan. "And we went along with it. It's not far from Fodderbridge, so we kept quiet. You learn not to give too much away, these days. Don't know what sort of lunatics you're going to run into."

"Yeah," said Clive, looking at the three for slightly too long.

"Something wrong?" asked Betty.

"Um, no," said Ethan. "Look, don't take what we're saying seriously. We got a bit spooked back there and if you're heading in the direction of Oldingham, then I reckon we can keep you company. If you don't mind?"

There was the tone of a plea to his voice, an anxious look thrown back behind him. Whatever they had seen had seriously scared them.

"You keep looking behind you," said Tommy. "Is there anything we need to know?"

"Not sure," said Clive, suddenly reluctant to speak.

"Well, you screamed loud enough to wake the dead," said Fiddler.

Clive paled, swallowed hard. He looked at Ethan. The latter was the one with the most backbone out of the pair, Tommy decided.

"Yeah, there was something but we couldn't make it out. Bloody huge thing, stank to high heaven. Seemed to be trampling the trees down. All we could hear was the crashing as wood fell. Whatever it was, it was coming after us. So we legged it—and here we are."

"Still reckon we should've gone back and hitched another lift," said Clive.

"Then why don't you bloody well go on and do it,?" snapped Ethan. "I'm not going back that way with that thing on the loose. I'm not stopping you."

Clive glared at him. Took in Tommy, Betty, and Fiddler. Looked again at Ethan. "You know something, mate? I think I will. Whatever's back there? Well, it's gone quiet now. Reckon it's gone. Think you'll have more trouble with this lot than that thing. And it's a quick ten-minute walk. I'll be out in no time. See ya." He spun round on his heel and headed back the way the two had appeared. Ethan watched him go.

Tommy thought he would run after his friend but he made no such effort.

"He might be right, he might be wrong," said Ethan. "But I think I'm probably safer with you lot and I've got this for you." He pulled out a small package and handed it to Tommy. "The old boy in the car said to give it to you if we came across you. If we didn't, he said we could look at it and decide whether we wanted to keep it or not. He said it was the toll price. Although he also reckoned we might pay the toll in another way. Wouldn't say how though."

Toll price. Tommy searched his memory. Something stirred in the darkness. He took the package from Ethan. For its size, it carried weight. It gave beneath the press of his hand but did not spread out. It felt like, it felt ... he unwrapped the cloth and gazed down at the dead brown heart. Without saying anything, he knew it was from another of the Brothers at the Hospital. It could not have come from the one chosen to string Fiddler's fiddle as they had already dined on that one.

A human heart. Another scream pierced the forest. Clive's voice, shrill and terrified, reached out to them. Ethan blanched and almost burrowed himself into Betty. The toll.

"Seems he's paid," said Fiddler, understanding. "But ..."

"But?"

"But I think whatever it is, it's still hungry. It's been so long since it's eaten."

"Well, it'll find plenty to dine on here, if we don't get a move on," said Tommy. He regarded Ethan. "Reckon you'd best come along with us."

His tone was an order, not an offer, and for the first time an element of reluctance appeared in Ethan. As the silence behind them grew, he considered his position and moved forward. The four continued along the path and headed further into the dead, misty forest.

As the group approached a bend, Tommy looked back. The mist had thickened, but he could still see something moving, the shape splitting the fog like a curtain before allowing it to fall again. It was enough to make him shiver. He remembered that particular monster and had no desire to meet it face-to-face.

"We'll need more than your music if we come across that fellow," said Tommy, as Fiddler followed his gaze.

His brother raised a questioning eyebrow.

"Lyndwyrm," explained Tommy.

"Oh."

It was the answer Tommy expected. Many years had passed since they had crossed the path of such a creature. The music had not worked then and would not work now.

"I thought that monster was long gone," said Tommy. "When Hweol guided us this way on that last journey, she wasn't here. He said our path was clear, that no such dangers existed to challenge us any longer."

"Seems he was wrong," said Fiddler, gazing back at the shifting shadows. "Do you ever consider he might not have told us the truth?"

Tommy burst out laughing. "Of course he lied to us! We all lie to each other, but it doesn't work, does it? We can read each other like a book. We cannot close our minds to each other. We knew he was lying, but we chose to believe him.”

“We wanted to believe him,” said Fiddler. “You know, I can barely remember those early years. There were many more of us then. Numbers spread across the countryside, clans travelling freely. It seems it changed without us really noticing.”

Tommy had noticed, he just hadn’t given it much importance. Too caught up in carving out his position in the Weald, his enjoyment of the human world had closed his mind to the antics of those of his kin left behind. And when he looked, his old companions were no longer there. When he considered that, he’d merely shrugged his shoulders. Everything had its time.

“What are you all on about?” asked Ethan.

The man’s interruption made them pause. It wouldn’t do to scare him too much at the moment. If they were unable to find what was necessary in the next few days, then Ethan could serve their purpose. Tommy took in the man’s build, his general attitude. Not perfect, but he would do.

“Family stuff. You know what it’s like.”

Ethan laughed. “Yeah, I know. High expectations and eternal disappointments. That’s what my dad always says.” He shivered and peered ahead into the gloom. “You sure we won’t get lost in here?”

“No,” said Fiddler. “It’s been a while since we walked this way, but the path is the same. It’s a right of way that cannot be changed. A little further, maybe a mile, and we’ll get to where we want to go.”

“Good,” said Ethan. “This place gives me the creeps.”

“It’s why we’ve avoided it,” said Tommy. “Betty doesn’t like it either.”

“Betty? Strange name for a bloke.”

“It’s the part he plays in our little mummers troupe. When we perform, he puts on a dress and makes people laugh. We got used to calling him that.”

“Fair enough.” And with that, Ethan fell silent, apparently happy with the explanations.

A man of little imagination, thought Tommy. The path narrowed further and they were forced to walk two abreast. Tommy and Fiddler led the way,

Betty and Ethan followed. Low scrub bordered the edges of the track, and a little further back he could make out splintered and grasping boughs. Some bore foliage, yew and holly, their main guards of honour. He breathed it all in, inhaled the damp, mouldering decomposition beneath their feet, the rotting wood close by. It had not always been like this, had been on a par with his home in the Weald with its living forest, the wildlife and inhabitants. This mist wasn't white and silvery with the magical glitter that lifted the spirits. This one was heavy, dirty, dead. What else lived here apart from the Lyndwyrm? Something that didn't breathe.

Tommy quickened his pace. At full strength, he never feared anything. In his current state, they were too weak to deal with much at all.

CHAPTER TWENTY-ONE

MEGAN

Megan tried not to think of the last time she had gone beyond the Weald. Hopeful of a future of sorts, it had turned into another layer of the nightmare she had been living. One of the darkest. She was leaving again, this time without any sense of that earlier hope. Whatever events were at play—and she had no doubt she was no more than a pawn in a bigger game—it was time for it to end.

"You think you have no future," commented Sister Sarah, as they stood at the threshold, "but fate—and luck—can turn on a whim."

Unconsciously, Megan's hand floated down to her empty womb. Another dark and empty place.

"You are still young. You could meet someone else, start a new family.

"But, John—"

"Your husband is dead. Forget Hweol's lies. Only John's spirit remains and he needs to be free."

Death. There had been so much in her life. She was not sure she could put this all behind her. It would haunt her for the rest of her days.

"You can forget," said Sarah. "There is a potion I can make you—"

"No," said Megan. "That would be another betrayal. It would be as if my parents, John, my friends, had never existed."

"And would that be such a bad thing?"

Megan didn't answer as together they stepped out from Umbra and walked the lanes of the Weald once more.

"We were more than Wyves once," said Sarah. "More than a womb. We were seers, healers, Wyse Women." Her voice, wistful, faded.

Megan had given the Wyves little thought. Repulsed by their appearance, their submission to Hweol, she had dismissed them. No more than subjugated women become a monstrous perversion of the female. She had regarded them as not of her kind, did not trust them.

They continued along the lanes taking them to the extent of what she had known for most of her life. The few trips beyond regulated and rationed. Enough to enable them to function appropriately in the presence of random strangers, obtain an education of sorts.

School was hazy. From the village schools, they had gone on to the nearby secondary of Oldingham, yet it was as if their day was wiped away on their return. Their learning would be retained, but so little of friendships and awareness as to the nature of society beyond. How would the families of the Weald be coping now?

"The borders are still intact," said Sarah as they approached the boundary. The Weald will only release those who have permission."

"The Mother hasn't spoken to me since I walked through her fires into Umbra," said Megan.

"She has a plan," said Sarah. "I cannot admit to knowing what it is. Our next step will show us if we are part of it."

"What will happen if we cannot go beyond?" asked Megan, feeling the heat of the memoried flames.

"We think again."

There was nothing ahead of them, an unchanging landscape of fields glowing beneath the sun, now at its highest point. The sky was a brilliant blue, dotted occasionally with a cotton wool cloud. Megan felt the breeze, sniffed the air. Despite appearances, the seasons were changing.

"Here," said Sarah, and stepped off the road and through a gap in the hedge.

Megan cast a look at the path she had assumed they would take and followed. "I thought we were following the roads. You said ..."

"I know," said Sarah, "but our first stop is Winchester and that is a journey of many miles to humans. We follow the Leys and will get there soon enough."

Megan's heart sank. She waited for Hweol to start his whispering, ask her how she could trust Sarah, start her doubts again.

"Don't worry," said Sarah. "In those parts he will remain quiet. He is not regarded kindly for his past troubles."

"I thought he was all powerful."

"In Umbra, and there only to a certain extent. He was dependent on the Mother's favour."

The track put her in mind of the one joining the villages. The difference here was the silence. A muffling of everything—sound, vision. A shifting grey revealing terrifying sculptures which, on closer inspection, turned out to be the distorted limbs of aging yews. One trunk, huge and ancient, stood guard right against the track. Into its bark had been carved a face, its mouth open wide in a scream. The Wyve did not explain, merely beckoned her on.

Their way was carpeted with fallen needles and mossy earth, making underfoot springy and easy going. This did little to allay her growing sense of unease. The occasional snap of a twig somewhere in the undergrowth provided jumpy punctuation marks as they continued forward. She saw nothing but felt a presence, something watching from all sides. The grey veil moved and rippled, revealing other forms. *Trees*, she told herself. But after seeing another agonised face etched onto a nearby trunk, she no longer felt sure. She could almost hear their silent cries.

A beat in the air drew her eyes upward. She was able to make out the shape of a wing before it disappeared. It was nothing feathered. Megan moved instinctively closer to Sarah, fought against the impulse to grab the woman's hand. She had felt her touch before and it had been cold, oh so cold.

They had barely covered half-a-mile before Sister Sarah stopped and looked around.

"What?" whispered Megan. She could hardly see anything. Felt the murk getting thicker, heavier, smothering. A panicked sensation fluttered in her chest and it was if every breath had to be fought for. She felt herself sinking.

"Megan!" Those cold hands held her upright. Those terrible eyes gazed into hers. "Megan! It's nothing. This place plays tricks on you, turns your mind against yourself. Breathe!" The words were accompanied by a hard shake rousing her from her stupor.

Megan gasped, gulping in the damp air, forcing herself to take steady, deep breaths.

"I'm sorry. This place is smothering. It felt as though it's wrapping itself around me, choking." Megan put her hand to her throat as if to remove an invisible tendril.

"The nature of the Leys, I'm afraid," said Sarah. "It plays on people's fears. Although they are the only paths resistant to the spells cast by the Umbran folk. These tracks were born with them, but not of them. They have proved a useful escape route on more than one occasion"

Megan gazed about her. She would prefer any other escape route to this. Still, it was a useful snippet of information to file away. Rarely did you hear of anything which was beyond the control Hweol and his kind. "How much further?"

"Another mile—" Sarah's expression changed as they both heard a scream. One of sheer undiluted agony. It went on and on, and when it finally stopped, Megan continued to hear it echoing around her head.

Then she heard a steady thud, regular cracks and snaps of undergrowth. Something was approaching. Megan started to back away but Sarah's hand shot out and stayed her. They remained frozen in that position for one, two, three seconds as it came closer and closer and then stopped. Something flew out at them, landing with a sickening splat at their feet. Again, Megan moved back, hand over her mouth to prevent a scream. This time Sarah did not stop her.

"Turn away," she ordered.

Unquestioningly, Megan did as she was bid. The body, and it was a body, although barely recognisable, was not something she wanted to look upon.

"Wha … what is it?" she asked.

There was no answer. Instead, she heard a sickening slurp and crunch, chewing. She started to turn, could see the Wyve crouched over the body, enveloping it. The movement reminded her of her cat when it was devouring one of its kills. She swallowed. Tried to speak but no sound came. Megan started to move away but distance did not smother the sound.

"Stop." Sarah's voice halted her retreat. "It's not safe for you on your own. I won't be long."

As she spoke, some of the grey shadows edging the track solidified into black. Six of them. They reminded her of the Wyves in their black robes. Similar but not the same. Their darkness seemed deeper, colder. She didn't want to look at them any longer, or for them to look at her. She felt like an insect under the microscope. Sensed a hunger in the air. She retreated nearer to Sarah.

"Thought you might be thirsty." The voice was dry, brittle—dead.

Sarah had risen, come to her side. She laughed. "Generous as ever, Hilda. There was barely a quart."

Megan didn't want to look, but felt her body betray her and turn to the shredded mass on the ground. Human. Probably. Bone and tissue remained, the flesh dry and shrivelled, like a deflated balloon, the essence squeezed out.

She had never given a thought to the Wyves, how they lived, what they ate. It dawned on her she had never seen them eat or drink in her presence, had assumed they dined elsewhere.

"Well, you've a live one with you. Portable supplies you could say."

The words brought Megan's attention back to the group. Understanding seeping horribly in.

"No," said Sarah. "She carries Hweol's spirit within her."

"All the more reason to kill her now, enjoy the feast."

CHAPTER TWENTY-TWO

MEGAN

"No!" Sarah's voice became sharp, commanding. "I know how you feel about that monster. I do too. But I would rather revenge myself directly upon him. Face-to-face. It will be so much more satisfying."

The six had come closer, formed a dark ring around the two. Their robes covered them utterly, as did Sarah's, with the same deep hoods hiding everything but their eyes. Orbs of a black so dark it defied every depth of every shadow. She could smell blood.

"That we would like to see," agreed Hilda. "I think we should accompany you. It is a long time since we had such entertainment."

"And the Wyrm?"

"Our little pet? Oh, he's dined well the past few days. He won't trouble us."

"There have been others."

"Oh yes. The three have walked this path. Running after Mother as always. And …"

"And?"

"Others move too. All go to Kinlet."

"So do we," said Sarah. "But I have a call to make in Winchester first."

"From what I understand, Tommy has already been there. There is no need—" Hilda turned her gaze once more upon Megan, "—aah, I see."

The way in which she said this sent a chill down her spine. Megan could feel her weakness, her vulnerability in the centre of that circle. Understood she could not question or challenge the statement or tone. She bit her tongue. Hweol's silence was also ominous.

"We'll accompany you to the Edge," said Hilda.

"Will you wait for our return?" asked Sarah.

"I think not. We'll meet again at Church. It's about time we paid our respects and this is going to be so much fun."

"You do not fear for yourselves—after everything?" asked Sarah.

"How can you fear something when you are already dead?" said Hilda.

Not all Wyves were the same. Megan understood that Hweol chose them from every community, every race. This, though. To have taken something already dead, without possibility.

Megan looked at Sarah with new eyes. "What kind of creature are you?"

Sarah laughed. "You almost said monster, didn't you? Don't worry, we've been called many things. No offense taken. You've never asked before."

"I thought you were an unfortunate. Women like my mother. Except you chose the path Hweol offered in Umbra."

A cackle burst out from the group, as sharp as the crack of a whip sending dark-winged creatures above into flight.

"Shall we tell you our story as we walk?" said Hilda. "It will fill in a few gaps in your knowledge. Prepare you for what is to come."

Hilda didn't wait for an answer and Sarah remained silent.

"We may look like Wyves, but that is a state achieved after you have mated with Hweol. Though from what I understand, it is more akin to rape. It is certainly not a loving act, is more a declaration of ownership—"

"He does not own me," interrupted Sarah.

"No? He chained you to the Weald, didn't he? Stopped you travelling beyond, returning to us. You wouldn't have been able to leave at all except this little human stopped the Wheel."

Prisoners. The Wyves had never given that impression. Asserting their choice gave them freedom from any further attention from Hweol.

"We have been called many things over the centuries. The most common term these days is vampire. That is not who we are. We are the Blodgitan. We were created by the Mother to verify the purity of a soul. When a human child reached thirteen in those early days, we would drink of them. Only a sip mind. That taste would allow us to detect whether the child would go to the good or bad. We were living then. Not the undead monsters you think us."

"You were human and you would drink another's blood?" Megan couldn't fathom it.

"It was a position of honour within each clan. If someone was measured and found tainted, they would be banished. Sent into this place."

"They were children! How could you condemn them?"

"You measure everything by today's understanding. You grew up quickly back then. You had to, to survive. Those who passed our test were prized. They would make the best marriages, achieve the highest status. As time went on, we realised we too were changing. the small amount we took was soon not enough for us to judge and we would drink more. And we aged but did not die. Each of us realising our hearts were no longer beating and yet still we walked.

As this became common knowledge, people's attitudes changed. Hweol was to blame. He poisoned minds. Asked how grotesques like us could possibly be considered a judge of good or bad. It came to a head when I tasted his son and proclaimed banishment. The people turned against us, and instead drove me and my sisters out, and here we've roosted ever since, evolving, changing."

Initially revolted by the women, Megan found herself sympathising, the bloodied corpse left behind.

"You see six of us—and Sarah. There are others, although our numbers are few."

Megan glanced up as a shadow passed overhead. Another chuckle.

"Oh, dear. Those stories have a lot to answer for. Unlike some races, the Blodgitan do not transform. Bats have a certain kinship with us but no more than that. They are our eyes and ears. Pets, if you like. The Mother left us here. Like bastard children you don't want to recognise. We had done her bidding and were abandoned by her, betrayed by Hweol. But the Father, He will honour us. I know it."

How like human children, that need for recognition. Would they receive what they desired?

"Sarah was taken by Hweol to the Weald. He thought unwillingly, a hostage. He likes to feel such power. And we played along. She went for us so that we would have a spy in his camp. He could never read her mind for the home of the undead is a place forbidden to him."

"I would pretend," said Sarah. "I would allow him to access me. It fed his vanity, protected my true family. It meant he assumed a greater power than he had."

"He knows now," said Megan.

"It no longer matters. Everything has changed."

Megan could see little as they walked. The Blodgitan continued to surround her, preventing her from studying the path. All she could do was occasionally look up, see the forms hanging from the branches.

"We do not waste the meat when we have drunk from it. It is food after all, and there are animals who need feeding."

Like strange birdfeeders, the bodies swung occasionally as something would fly in and peck at it before taking off again. Others looked as though they had remained attached for longer spells and the bodies moved violently as they were ripped and torn.

"Do not judge," said Hilda as they passed the last one and Megan sensed from the shift in the air they were near the end of their path.

"We are all children of Nature, whatever form we take. We were made for a never-ending battle of survival. There is nothing that is romantic or honourable about any of us—even humans. It is the way of things. We are all animals, obeying the instincts and appetites we were born with—or gifted. How we act on these impulses is our own choice. If it is moral to survive, then how can we be judged?"

"At any cost?" asked Megan.

"Cost? What cost is there when there is only one goal and you have two outcomes? To live or to die. We were created in both worlds. We were made like this. Do not condemn us for that."

They had reached the edge of the track, another border crossing in this strange world, so much of which had been kept hidden from her. She thought of the Weald, and despite her memories, she longed for the blue sky and open fields. Innocent normality, at least in appearance. Ahead of her she could see no green pastures; abandoned industrial units and a weed-infested lot greeted her. She sniffed at the traces of something burning.

"We leave you here, Sister. Do what you have to. We hope it brings you peace."

As one, the Blodgitan stepped back, their darkness receding, soon covered by the mist.

"Come," said Sarah and marched out onto the concrete.

Megan followed, immediately picking up on the vibrations of modern life, the hum of cars, a plane's engine—noise. Voices. Shouts from somewhere. It crowded in. An overwhelming assault after the muffled silence, the weighty suspense of the Ley track.

"Where are we?" Megan took in the industrial estate, felt its sense of being on the edge of things.

"You'll see." Sarah said nothing else but marched forward. Determination obvious. An alley here, a turn there, and then suddenly she found herself in another world. Crowds every which way. Gaggles of tourists playing follow-my-leader. Oblivious individuals plugged in to another wavelength. Eyes transfixed on small screens rather than ancient walls. She thought her companion might attract strange looks due to her garb, but nobody paid much attention. In fact, nobody seemed to see them at all.

They were in Winchester, the ancient capital of Wessex. She had visited the city a couple of times, her father had brought her when she was a child. Her mum had stayed at home—somebody had to run the pub after all. Where had they gone when they came here? She pushed back into the past as their direction took them away from the bustle of the city and across the water meadow to the Hospital of St. Cross.

Old gables and leaded windows peered over its high-walled border. She remembered a church. An argument, the last time they had come here. A priest of sorts who kept looking at her, her father shaking his head furiously. Unconsciously, she raised her hand to her neck.

"You remember," said Sarah, noticing the gesture. "My father was, is, Master here. You were too young to be measured in that way. Simon Wheelborn was so angry. He had come to take a census of the Brothers at

Tommy's request. Took you to give you a day out, a treat. You were protected, or supposed to be."

It all came back. One more horrific memory buried under so many others, hidden by scenes of an idyllic childhood.

"Whilst Hweol can't destroy your memories, he can bury them. He did it at your parents' request, to give you back your childhood."

Their feet crunched on gravel paths running between trim squares of grass and late-flowering borders. The few remaining bees buzzed amongst lavender bushes. *Another false idyll*, considered Megan. She could see the Chapel's heavy oak doors in the distance, a mouth waiting to eating her up. The thought brought the last visit roaring back. Candles had flickered along the wall as the sun set, casting a bloody beam the length of the aisle. She had been sat on the steps of the altar, feeling the chill of the stone seep into her legs and wishing her dad would hurry up.

The Master had returned first, sat beside her on the steps, talked about—talked about what? She could not recall, her attention had been on his teeth. Unnoticed before, they now seemed longer somehow. Twin daggers so sharp and then—nothing. Her hand was still at her neck, rubbing at that place. Tiny scars. An insect had bitten her, according to her parents, and she had never questioned how something so small could leave such a mark.

"Come," said Sarah, seeing her reluctance. "I have business, I need to attend to, and you are perfectly safe."

She didn't move.

"You are serving as a vessel—albeit unwillingly—for Hweol. He would do nothing to harm him. He wouldn't dare."

Bizarrely, Megan had almost forgotten the monster lurking inside her. He had gone so quiet. Did he still exist? Her grip on reality felt as if it was slipping. Could it all have been hallucination, her mind playing tricks to convince her John still existed? That spirits could exist beyond the flesh? The strangest offering of hope. Sarah's words did little to reassure her.

"I thought you were the only Blodgitan," said Megan.

Sarah shook her head. "We were at first, then my father saw how long our span was becoming, even against his allotted time. He played on my affections. I was young, you understand. Said he couldn't bear the thought of me being on my own with no real family, blood family. He made me look into a future where I saw myself alone. He explained to me how it worked, the one bite, the amount to be taken. So I did as he bid. I've been a dutiful daughter and dutiful wife. And I've paid for it, lifetimes over." The bitterness in her voice was evident. "When the other Blodgitan found out, they were furious. My role as Hweol's Wyve was my penance."

A thought struck her as she considered her bite. "Does that mean I will become like you?"

"No," said Sarah. "You were lucky. He bit you but was unable to drink, your father's swift action prevented that. Others weren't so lucky. He built his own Chapter here. But it was an impure bloodline. He has never been able to build the army he wished, and after each census, if it was felt the numbers were too many, there would be a cull."

"Why was he allowed to exist here? Outside Umbra?" asked Megan.

"A useful army," said Sarah. "Something to have on standby should Hweol need them."

CHAPTER TWENTY-THREE

BETTY

Betty couldn't understand his brothers' unease. Already they were stronger, had had music and food sufficient to carry them as far as they needed. The soil pulsed beneath him, as it had done since they had left the Weald. He had tried to tell Tommy and Fiddler there was no danger, but they saw things differently to him. That was one thing he knew. They both liked to exert control over those around them, even himself. The Lyndwyrm was something beyond Tommy's capability.

Betty had no such qualms. All he sought was to exist alongside his fellow creatures. That the strong would prey on the weak, that one would eat another, were tenets to which Betty paid tribute. Regardless, he was protected by the Mother, he was the same as the beasts of the land.

Ahead of him, Tommy and Fiddler walked with Ethan, paying no attention to Betty, who fell back. He sensed a presence in the mist, the miasma thinning to his left so he could see the burning eyes of a dragon-like face. He turned away from his family and made for the giant serpent. It slithered towards him, coiling around his feet to Betty's delight. This Wyrm remembered him! He had known it as a wyrmling, wanted to keep it as a pet but Tommy wouldn't let him. There had been the usual arguments, who would feed him, who would clean him, who would exercise him. The Lyndwyrm was too obvious an animal to travel with them once it had outgrown Betty's pockets.

Those who had seen the Lyndwyrm and survived had described it as a monstrous serpent, but to Betty it was beautiful. All life was beautiful.

The Lyndwyrm raised itself up and pulled Betty into its arms, they swayed together for a while, heartbeats in sync as they had been when both were much younger.

"This place is too dark for you," he said to the animal. "When we make our return, you will come with me to Umbra and the Weald. None of us will hide away again."

The Lyndwyrm coiled around him, almost purring. The sound made Betty happy.

"I'll be back," he murmured as he eased himself from the creature's grip. "Just be careful what—and who—you eat until then!" It was a phrase Tommy had often used on him when they had parted, it suited them both equally.

As he walked away, he felt the ground vibrate. The Lyndwyrm was following him. He stopped and waited for it to catch up. "A little way," he said, "and then you *will* have to wait here for me."

Tommy and Fiddler had stopped and were watching him. The man, Ethan, had paled, was looking wildly around for a proper escape route.

"It's fine," called Betty. "He just wanted company. I said he could come with us to the Edge."

Tommy looked as though he was about to say something and then shrugged. "I said we'd return with the Old Folk. I think that includes some of your pets as well." Tommy grinned and Betty smiled back.

Pets! Betty tried to remember the others he had left in similar dark places, worlds shrouded from human minds.

Humans had got away from them, and the Folk had hidden themselves for their own protection. Now it seemed that had been the wrong decision. If they had made a stand, shown their strength, then none of them should've had to hide away. All could share the land of the Mother equally. No one species had superiority over another. All had equal value, an equal right to feed from the land.

"You'll enjoy yourself once you're out there," he whispered. "More food than you can imagine!"

The land needed to rebalance, and Betty and his pets would be part of that. Betty looked again at the Lyndwyrm's skin. It had developed a beautiful pattern on its shining scales. He could see himself wearing it, spinning beneath the sun, light flashing from him. A better diet, freedom under the skies. It was always good for the skin. Some things were worth waiting for.

CHAPTER TWENTY-FOUR

TOMMY AND ELIAS

The streets of Oldingham were almost empty. Only a few were abroad. The last leaving the pubs, clubs, and restaurants, weaving their way home. The smell of alcohol and sated moods drifted towards them. Business owners and security guards pulled down shutters and locked doors. They gazed suspiciously at the four as they passed. Tommy gave them a grin and they looked away.

He knew where he was going. An abandoned industrial park full of empty and disused warehouses, factories, and retail outlets. It was an occasional haunt of his, a place to talk and drink. Shoot the breeze with people who had no idea who he was, who had no idea who they themselves truly were. These were the lost, and Tommy enjoyed them the most. They were the most honest of all people.

Flickers of light could be seen coming from one particular building, an old furniture store. He could see a group gathered outside. Several men, filthy and ragged, were gathered in a circle around a brazier from which insipid flames rose. It was not the sort of fire to normally draw Tommy or to make Betty dance. But it was enough to draw them in. They were as much moths as those involuntary insects.

"Gentlemen," cried Tommy. "Is there room around the fire for four weary travellers?" He didn't wait for an answer, and Betty, who'd gone on ahead, simply nudged the nearest man out of the way so he could claim his spot. The man looked as though he was about to challenge Betty and then thought better of it as he took in the man's bulk. He shuffled nearer to his friends who'd also moved closer together to allow the new arrivals room and not stand too close to them.

"Don't I know you?" asked one, an old man, shrunken and too frail to exist in this world of the abandoned.

Tommy looked at him. Yes, their paths had crossed some years ago. He'd thought then this one didn't have long left and yet here he was. His heart must be truly stone.

"Perhaps, old man," said Tommy. "I've travelled a lot of roads as I think have you. We probably met then." He held out his hand. Not to shake the other's in greeting but an unspoken command for the unidentifiable drink in the man's bottle. Without quibbling, it was passed over.

"Carry on with your chatter," said Tommy as he drank from the bottle. "Don't mind us. We've been looking for a good fire, good drink and good company. I think tonight we have struck lucky."

The men looked at each other, expressions of incredulity mingled with fear. The group emitted an air of menace without trying.

Tommy passed the bottle to his brothers and then Betty offered the last drop to Ethan. Their new companion shook his head.

"No offense," he said, "but with all the bugs and viruses going round these days, I don't want to catch anything."

The old man by the fire cackled. "None taken. But that stuff is 100% proof. Doubt any of our germs would survive long enough to be transmitted."

Betty still held the bottle and raised it again to his lips. He drained the last drops and then hurled the bottle into the distance. They could hear the glass smash as it crashed back to earth. The old man shrugged and pulled another bottle out from a deep pocket.

"Are you all sleeping here?" said Fiddler, looking at the cardboard sheets and piles of rags. "I thought you would prefer indoors. There's enough empty buildings round here for you to shelter."

"Nah, security guards come and kick us out. They leave us alone if we stay outside."

"Then perhaps you might prefer to move to another part of this park. Maybe right over the other side?"

"Why? This is our pitch," said their spokesperson. "You think you can waltz in and take—"

"That's exactly what I think," said Fiddler. "Now why don't you gather up your belongings and go."

"Except for you," said Tommy pointing at the one he had met before. "I think you should join us. Tell us the news of these parts."

The group looked annoyed at this invasion of their turf, their stance becoming aggressive as they moved towards Fiddler, someone whose size indicated an easy victory. Then Betty coughed, deliberately drawing their attention to him. They looked up and their bravado crumbled. They couldn't get away quickly enough.

When the others had gone, Tommy spoke to the man again. "I thought you would be dead by now. Your span is done."

"Who says? I've lived like this for a long time. It suits me. No one causes me any bother, not even Tobias, and he's finally headed off. At least no one until now."

Fiddler was staring hard at the man. Tommy wondered how long it would take for him to remember. It wasn't too long a wait.

"Elias! Elias! Is it you? After all this time? Thought you'd fallen by the wayside."

"Nah," said Elias. "Simply faded into the background. Decided it was easier than being under Hweol's eye all the time. Safer."

"Bloody idle from what I remember," said Fiddler, looking at him. "See you don't exert yourself still."

"No need," said Elias. "People feel sorry for me. They give me money, food, drink. And as for sleeping out. That's always been our way, hasn't it? A life under the stars. That was one thing I couldn't give up. But while it's good to see you again, I must say it's strange after all this time. What brings you out of the Weald? Tobias and his shenanigans?"

Betty came closer to the fire, allowing Elias to study him before taking in Tommy and Fiddler again. "Ah," he said. "Thought Tobias was all hot air. You look as though you're in need of a little pick-me-up." He cackled. It was not a pleasant sound.

"Then you'll understand why we're travelling," said Tommy. "Stay!"

The latter command was directed at Ethan who had started to back away from his travelling companions, his confusion and unease evident. Betty moved to Ethan's side and guided him back.

Elias laughed even more. "You hoped to catch Tobias here when he woke Cernunnos, be there to gain the Father's favour rather than let Tobias steal the limelight! Oh, my, you are losing your touch."

Tommy glared at him. Elias was perfectly correct but that didn't mean he liked to hear him say it. Then he shrugged and joined in the laughter. "Missed the bus, didn't I? You weren't tempted to go with them?"

Elias swept his arm around him, encompassing the almost deserted car park. "I know where I am here, I'm comfortable. Follow you lot, go back to that way of life and I'll probably end up on a bonfire or being chased by the Lords or thrown in a pit—like before. Can't say I fancy that again. Nor do I want to get caught up in any family quarrels."

"And who will you follow when we return?"

Elias regarded his bottle. "Whoever keeps this filled for me!" He looked at Ethan. "Are you sure you don't want a drink?"

This time, Ethan almost snatched the bottle from him, coughing and spluttering as he downed the fiery liquid.

"Easy, lad," said Elias, taking it back. "Too much of that stuff'll kill you, you know."

Tommy looked at his old companion. The man had no ambition, no illusions about himself, and as such, he was useful to keep on side. One always knew where one stood with them. And they were disposable.

"Will you stay a while?" asked Elias.

"How far ahead are they?"

Elias shrugged. "Depends on how far Cernunnos wants to make them walk, bring understanding to that poor sod they've taken with them."

"They have an offering?"

"Yeah." Elias regarded Ethan. "Looks like they beat you to it. Still, he's not a bad specimen." He leaned forward and sniffed at the man who shrank back. "Can you spare him? Save me a trip to that old snob at the Hospital."

Elias hadn't changed. Was still as lazy and idle as he'd ever been.

"Afraid he's already been spoken for," said Tommy.

"And does he agree to that, know what's in store for him?"

"What—"

"Not for you to worry about," said Tommy, as Ethan began to rise to his feet. "Why don't you go and lie down, close your eyes. It's been a long walk."

Ethan shook his head. "I don't live far from here. I'd best be off home." He began to walk away from the group.

Tommy nodded at Fiddler, who pulled out his instrument and started to play. Soft amber notes danced around Ethan like glittering moths. His eyes followed their movement, hypnotised. His body followed as they danced towards a pile of filthy blankets. Entranced, Ethan lay down on the mass and fell asleep.

Elias continued to laugh. "Haven't had this much entertainment in ages, given me an appetite. Sure you want to keep him?"

"I've a feeling he'll come in useful," said Tommy. "One way or another."

"You shouldn't linger much longer, you know," said Elias, finally accepting defeat. "Cernunnos will be able to tell where you are. Know you're hanging back. Don't want him to think you're afraid, do you?"

Tommy wanted to wipe the smirk from the creature's face. But there were other, more important things to tend to first. He would come back and deal with Elias in his own way and in his own time—if they had any left. He thrust the doubt away. Their time was coming. There was nothing to worry about.

CHAPTER TWENTY-FIVE

BETTY

At last. The group were moving deeper into the Layerings, leaving the concrete of Oldingham behind them. Ahead lay miles of darkness. An area of cold, of old things, hung over all. Betty hung back. He didn't want to walk that way. He was a creature of fire and flame.

Tommy waited for him to catch up. "It's a short way, though it looks further. We're walking in Cernunnos' footsteps. Can't you smell him? Can't you hear him?"

Betty had not heard such excitement in Tommy's voice for a long time. Eagerness was written all over him.

"The Father?"

"Yes," said Tommy. "Like us, he is going back to the beginning, to the Mother. She is waiting for us all."

He's right, whispered the voice. *You're all coming back to me, and I shall be there, waiting for you. Follow my path and all will be well.*

Betty looked down, bubbling pools ran along the track. Stagnant water filled with rotting foliage and flitting shadows. Movement beneath the surface sent the water up and onto the banks, turning the soil to mud. Occasionally, tussocks of wiry looking grass dotted the area, their colour a dying yellow.

A slight haze shifted over the landscape, gases rising, sparking into small flames. The sight of such insignificant fire however, raised his spirits. Anything could burn. Then the lights turned into globes, floating ahead to guide them. Betty moved quicker, reaching out a hand to catch the globes, delighted at their appearance. Tommy's hand stayed him. Why did his brother always have to spoil his fun?

"Don't," said Tommy. "These are creatures from beyond even our time. They have aligned themselves with both Mother and Father but sometimes destroy on a whim."

Betty stared at the spiralling gold within gold of the bubble. "What are they?"

"Wyrd Walkers," said Tommy. "You'll see their shape later. This is how they chose to travel."

Betty was half-listening to Tommy, was already imagining hanging a chain of these globes around his neck. A necklace to shine in the darkness of Yule. He reached out again. This time it was the voice that stopped him

No, she said. *I will give you all the jewellery you need from this world. There is enough here for even such a magpie as you. The Wyrd Walkers have their role to play, and we must let them be.*

He looked at the nearest sphere sadly, felt his hand twitch, wanting to reach out but already another image had taken root in his head. The black and white of the magpie was another trim he could use for his coat. A sorrowing necklace of feathers. The design of his Yule coat pushed his surroundings away and he followed Tommy and Fiddler in an almost dreamlike state. A small part of his brain acknowledged the darkness, the descent into pitch behind him, the opening up of a void, but the dark was not for him and he travelled happily away from it.

Some of the spheres had moved further from them.

"Where are they going?" he asked.

"Cernunnos isn't far," said Tommy. "I can smell him and our brother Tobias. I think it best we keep our distance for the time being. I would prefer our reunion to be in the light, with the Mother nearby."

He does not feel you? asked Betty, of the voice.

No, there are lessons to be learned and this is part of it, came the reply.

CHAPTER TWENTY-SIX

SISTER

Something moved through the Layers. Sister sensed Cernunnos' presence immediately. At last, Tobias had harvested well and would be bringing matter she could digest and spread amongst the land. Cernunnos was more ancient than Hweol, was the one creature who could defy the Mother and bring back the Lord of Umbra. If he wished it. Hweol would have to be weighed, his rule measured. It would be an interesting trial. Family together again.

Trial. The word had popped unexpected into her mind. Mother versus Cernunnos and by extension, Hweol. Who would be chosen as judge and jury?

She sensed more than a trial however. Something, someone, else was walking with them. A human. One who had drunk of the blood offering. Sister could see through the Layers, read them as the pages of a book. A blood brother. Her heart rose at the idea. This was cause for celebration, a Dance was on the horizon. One of the oldest and the first to turn the Wheel.

"Oh, Megan. Do you know what you triggered when you restrained the three?" She felt sympathy for Tommy's daughter, understood the need to lash out and punish those who had hurt her, but this emotional response had caused the restart of the one thing Megan had hoped to stop—the Wheel. The woman had turned myth into reality, had shown courage, but she was ignorant of their true history. She did not understand what ruled the land. The true order of things. Tommy had been part of Megan's life. Sister wondered why those old stories had never been told to the Wheelborn of the Weald. A deliberate mistake? Or Tommy playing games.

Sister rose from her chair and pulled a cloak about her shoulders. She would not miss watching this return for anything. She pondered the route they would take and merely blinked an eye and she was there, at the top of Gaast Hill. Below her, the land shimmered and rippled, blurred in and out of view as each settled into the form she had given it. This was her creation and she would never let her brothers take that away from her.

From here, her eye could see into every aspect of her world, and now it was drawn to the edge of the Corpse Marsh. Through the mists rising up from the bubbling mud, she could see the walkers, Tobias and his two companions, Cernunnos, and another. A human.

"Father," she murmured. "And sacrifice." She felt a tingle of excitement, her shape shifting and resettling.

Small orbs of golden light danced around the group. They had not taken on their real form yet. Would only appear as such when they reached their Altar. These were the Wyrd Walkers who travelled all of their lands, whether Weald or Layerings or those other parts of the country almost forgotten. The borders of those places were almost vanished, subsumed into modern Britain. Here though, they clung on.

As her gaze returned to Cernunnos, he raised his antlered head and appeared to look in her direction. He could see her. There was no hiding from him in any of the Layers. He was a terrible sight. Carved from bone, skeletal, with no flesh to clothe him, he was death made manifest. From his antlered stag's head atop the body of man, he claimed the earth on which he walked. Hweol had been carved in his image. A weak imitation.

"Tell me, what is the First Turn?" she asked aloud. Then she answered, not with the words of the Weald but with those of Cernunnos.

"The First Turn is the Turn of Beginning and Rebirth,

when blood runs freely and the moon turns red,

when the soil drowns in a river of death

and we rise again."

Her brother's turning of the Wheel in the Weald was mere child's play compared to the rites of Cernunnos. These were to be feared by all. He could choose any of them to sacrifice. Herself, Tommy, Betty, Fiddler. It was said, he could even claim Hweol, if the whim took him. She considered the village filled with those brought to live within its limits, glad she had read the runes right and prepared a feast on which both the Mother and Father could dine. There would be more arriving soon. The return of

Hweol would require more blood-letting than even Tommy could imagine. The Midwyves were ready, the land was ready.

A dancing globe approached her hill, drifted on the air, to settle at her side. She did not look at it. An Umbran was allowed to see the face of the Wyrd Walker only once, at their naming, when they were shown the truth of the world. Then they learned never to look at the Wyrd Walkers again. Not in the manner of the Wyves, whose age and suffering were etched on their faces in a mask of horror. These were creatures made of horror itself.

The globe grew in size, took its proper form. It cast no shadow in either moon or sunlight. It shimmered as her Layers did, but its matter was black and deep. The shape, although similar to human, was no more than a sac. Occasionally, a limb would appear or an eye or a mouth, their whereabouts in the whole depending on the mood of the Wyrd. Further deep inside was a void as cold and empty as the cosmos which made it; here was the black hole of the beginning, the burial of all things. When it spoke, its voice was sibilant, hissed its way into her ears.

"Sister, the Service will begin soon. It is time to prepare the Church for Cernunnos."

"Tell me what you wish," she said, keeping her eyes fixed on the Father's progress.

"A Choir," hissed the Wyrd. "A Celebrant. A Congregation. Communicants."

"We have them ready. They just need to be placed."

"Then set it in motion. When the moon is at its deepest shade, we must all be ready."

Then the Wyrd shrank in on itself and vanished.

Sister turned her gaze into the Layers, sifted through them until she was in the village. In a second, she was walking down the lane into the village of Kinlet. The church bell was tolling, pulling the worshippers in. It was a Sunday. Appropriate.

"Morning, miss," shouted a little girl, skipping across the green, her mother following close behind. Both looked so happy and healthy, but if one looked beneath, as she could, they would see a scrawny child, thin through neglect with lice crawling in her hair and scabs forming on her scalp. Look at her mother and beneath her veneer, and see eyes bruised through lack of sleep, needle marks on her arms and hunger stamping its claim. Look at the teen who idled along behind them with her peers and see the scars on her arms and on her legs where she took out her torment on herself.

This was her Congregation. The addicts, the hungry, the lost and the lonely. She had cast her net wide. It was a good catch for her Church. Tommy always called her Sister, as did everyone. They had forgotten her other name. It was one she would wear for the First Turn and they would remember who she truly was. The Father would give her her name back.

CHAPTER TWENTY-SEVEN

MEGAN

The knowledge of creatures such as the Blodgitan had disturbed Megan.

"Are there others I should know of?" she asked the Wyve as they walked away from the water meadows, heading towards the cloisters. Regardless of what lurked inside in the Hospital, she felt she could be happy living in a city such as this. So much of the old mingling with the new, but in such a way the modern played a subservient role, allowed history to remain the dominating factor.

The autumnal air carried with it that hint of change; the flowerbeds, though in bloom, were dying. Families walked past them, dogs bounded by. The world could be a happy place. It made her suddenly angry. These people were so unaware of what she and her family had been through, their suffering.

"Possibly," said Sarah, but gave no further answer.

Megan continued to feel the cramps in her belly. Nature's horrible replay of her loss. Her period had not been as painful as this since that night.

"A good sign," said Sarah, noticing Megan placing her hands on her stomach, almost doubling over. "The Festival of Blood is to be celebrated in many ways. A woman's blood is valued."

"You're kidding, right?" asked Megan. "You said we would be ridding me of Hweol, bringing peace to … John." She could barely think of that shifting shadow as her husband, was slowly coming to terms with the idea she had truly been widowed on that night of the Sixth Turn. Mind games, that was all it ever was with the Umbrans. And blood. "You said Cernunnos was returning. You made no mention of a festival."

A tune started to play in her head, Hweol humming a song Fiddler used to play as he led the villagers from the pub to whichever village had been chosen by Tommy for the ritual Turn.

"A birth—and a rebirth—brings blood," said Sarah. "That is all."

"And the rituals you mentioned?"

"You will not be harmed by any of them."

She doesn't know everything, said the voice. *Women bleed and their blood is prized. You should know that by now.*

Megan sat down on a bench. Nausea prevented her from moving on.

Sarah rooted through her pack and pulled out a small flask. She opened it and offered it to Megan. "It will give you strength and stop the cramps," she said.

"What's in it?" Megan sniffed the liquid suspiciously.

"It's a tincture of motherwort and nettle, a little honey to sweeten the taste. It's not poison. It's a remedy that's been used for centuries."

Megan eyed it. Hweol had remained quiet, refrained from any attempts at control. That meant it was safe to drink. She wanted the cramps to stop, the memory to stop. She wanted any reminder of lost motherhood to go away. Megan drank. The honey barely masked the bitter taste and she almost spat it out, but as the tension eased from her body, she continued to force it down.

Sarah took the flask from her before she could empty it. "You might need more later. Ready to move?"

"I'd rather sleep," said Megan.

"We have business here first. But after that our journey is short. Not long now and you'll be able to rest as much as you want."

Think of John, said the voice. *Let his spirit free, let him rest.*

The women resumed their path, Megan's thoughts filled with John, of their plans to flee Cropsoe, of his promise to stay with her no matter what as they headed back to the village to stop the Wheel turning. Hweol's words had turned her into a widow all over again and the pain tore at her, raw and burning. Lost child, lost husband, lost family. She wanted the monster in her head out so she could destroy him all over again. And she would. She would take on both the Mother and the Father if she had to.

You won't win you know. You're too small. Too puny.

I beat you, she answered back. *I did it before and I'll do it again.*

This is going to be so much fun, murmured Hweol.

Megan let out a low scream. The Wyve stayed silent, merely gave her a look.

Regaining control of herself, Megan focused on the Hospital looming ahead. Something told her this family reunion was not going to be a happy one. The shadows lengthened around them as the sun shifted position. Tourists drifted in and out of the cloistered walls. None came over to the doors however, eyes always distracted by something else. They were blind.

The two women had reached the chapel door. Megan gave those families one final lingering look and followed Sarah through the door.

CHAPTER TWENTY-EIGHT

BETTY

Tommy had said they would not have far to walk, but Betty was getting bored. He had designed his robes in his head, had told himself stories, had returned to the hunts of memory. It stirred his cold blood, warmed him, reminded him of who and what he was. He raised his head and sniffed the air, seeking out something which could distract him.

"There are creatures here," said Tommy. "But I don't think they will offer you much by way of adornment. They are already dead. They have no heart."

Betty stopped, cocked his head, and listened. The only beat he could feel was the one beneath his feet, the cord provided by the Mother which bound him to her gift.

There was a familiarity in its pulse. Not because it had accompanied them on their journey, growing stronger the nearer they got to the Layerings, but because of its origin. There was a connection there. A woman, yes. Wheelborn, yes. He longed for the cloth of skin he'd been promised. Megan. Something else taken away from him by the Mother. Would she at last be given to him? Another pulse joined the original. This one, male. A stranger. Two hearts. One which he would take and feed on. Peel away the layers as he had done in the beginning and reconnect with all that made up a life.

Betty began to salivate, his stomach grumbled. Everything else so far had been a mere appetiser, a filler. Something to help him travel the distance they were covering. He held his hand out in front of him, noticed a slight tremor which had not previously been there. Even in the dim light, his pale flesh glowed through the hairs which coated the back of his hands. These were becoming sparse, brittle. He ran his fingers through his beard, strands of hair came away in his palm. Amongst the strands was something small and blackened. Teasing it out, he recognised the tiny heart-shaped charm which had hung from a young woman's bracelet. He rubbed at the tarnish and silver shone through.

"Not seen that for centuries," said Fiddler.

His brother had been quiet as they walked. This was not a place for music, although Betty would've loved to have heard a song, one which told a story, something to relieve the feeling of pressure from the weight of the gloom.

"I can't remember," said Betty, holding it up to his eye and turning it round.

"There were others," said Fiddler. "A deer, a fox, a raven. She loved animals."

"Who?"

Fiddler shrugged. "I forget her name. Does it matter?"

"We are supposed to honour those we take and remember. The Mother said."

Fiddler laughed. "I know the Mother said. But I am old and tired and I feel the weight of my bones. My mind is as muddy as this damned land. If you ask me again when I have my music back—properly that is, without these … these mutton strings—and I am stood beneath a clear sky, then I would be able to tell you all. I could paint her with my music and you could dance with her memory. Until then." He shrugged his shoulders.

"You will be able to do that again?"

"Yes," said Fiddler. "I will be well, once we get this done and over with."

Betty moved closer to his brother, concerned at the admissions of vulnerability and age.

"Don't worry," said Fiddler. "I'm not going to keel over. We took enough from the Master to get us to where we want to go. It's a trial, I know. But it's the Mother's plan."

The small globes which had accompanied them vanished at this point, and as Betty sought them out, he saw a thin white line running across the horizon. Day was coming to this world of night, unless they had reached the edge of the world. All three stopped and looked as the band grew wider. Against this border, shapes appeared in silhouette. One which stood above all others, a horned creature exuding an awfulness unmatched even by Hweol. Others walked alongside or behind him. Some carried the human shape, others were amorphous, barely registering, as if seeking to fool an observer.

"Let them go first," said Tommy. "Allow Sister to greet him."

"Doesn't that worry you she should be first in his favour?" asked Fiddler.

"No," said Tommy.

Betty detected the lie in his words.

"We will enter quietly," continued Tommy, "and I will find Tobias. Judge the way of things."

"Ah, makes sense," said Fiddler. "Just in case Cernunnos has a bone to pick with us."

Betty started to laugh.

A look from Tommy shut him up. It hadn't been a joke.

CHAPTER TWENTY-NINE

AIDAN

Aidan continued to stumble though the reeking marsh. Its extent was vast. He could see no end to the miles of mud and mire, interspersed with rough tussocks of barbed grass and slimy moss. The sludge pulled at his feet, refused to let each step pass easily. It sucked at his strength, his mood. Somehow, he moved onwards, managing to keep pace with his captors. For this was how he viewed them. The smell was foul, sulphurous. Some pits contained a bubbling mass which he shrank from, barely avoided falling into on more than one occasion. One of Tobias' companions had reappeared at that point and guided him back to the invisible path they were following. It was a walking nightmare.

Absolute darkness above, no stars or moon to guide them, only those few strange orbs flitting around the creature, Cernunnos. Part of his mind had already accepted he was dead and was in Hell; the creatures ahead of him, the Devil and his minions. The other part, though alive, had not yet accepted what he was seeing and decided this was simply a dream to be got through. One ooze-filled step after another.

Then the lights stopped moving. A pause in the journey for which he was welcome, although it meant he caught up with the group and had to stand close to the horned Cernunnos.

"What do you think, blood brother?" asked Cernunnos, casting a skeletal hand across the landscape. "A beautiful world is it not?"

Aidan couldn't answer, looking upon this monster's face took away his ability to speak, to think. Eyes swirled with an energy which sapped him as surely as the mud at his feet. When he looked into those sockets, he knew he was an open book. No thought, no feeling, could be hidden.

"What, no words? Never mind. This blighted place has been my prison as well as my kingdom for eons, and now I'm free thanks to my faithful Tobias." The skull's mouth did not move, although the words came out as clearly as any normal speech.

Imprisoned. This implied there was a power stronger than this monstrosity. Would they meet up with it again, and would whoever—whatever—it was, free him? Or would they think him a supporter and destroy him too?

"The Mother has weakened," said Tobias. "When the Wheel stopped turning it drained her, even if those rituals she hated had come to a stop. It means you have the chance to claim back everything."

"The Mother was weak before the Wheel stopped. She worried about the 'innocents'. She forgot there are no innocents. Not even the babe newly born is free of that."

"Something in common with human religion then," said Tobias with a laugh. "So many are hung up on the idea of sin as being something wrong, when in fact, it is something purely natural and which we all grow into."

"And so, God gave his only begotten son," laughed Cernunnos. "We all sacrifice our children in the end."

"It is the way of things," said Tobias.

As they spoke, Aidan thought of his daughter. He had sacrificed Chloe as he pursued his addictions. He hoped she was safe now, cared for. At least they had found him on his own and had no trail back to his daughter. He did not know what he would do should they get hold of her. Or her mother. He owed her too. This would be his atonement. Whatever lay in front of him, it would be a small price to pay if they remained safe.

More globes approached Cernunnos. Five of them taking up point around him, allowing their light to diffuse down to the ground as they took shape. Gradually their illumination faded, and Aidan could begin to make out an outline which refused to hold no matter how often he tried to grasp it.

"Shouldn't try," said Tobias. "You won't be able to see them."

"What are they?"

"Wyrd Walkers. They guide us, they …" Tobias stopped, as if giving up. "Don't worry, you'll find out soon enough."

"How much further?" asked Aidan, still scanning the expanse beyond them. Occasionally, a small flame sparked out of a bubbling pit, adding to his idea of Hell.

"As far as Cernunnos decides you should walk," said Tobias. "We could be out of here in a minute, step through the veil, but he needs you to see and absorb the matter of life. This is not the Corpse Marsh of your own little world. This is the stuff from which you were made. This is not Hell. This is the beginning of time, before the sun and the moon, the stars and the galaxies. Here is everything you were and are."

It was too much to take in. The depth of the growing darkness, the continual pull at his feet, it wrapped itself around him in a black cloak, snuffing out every hope and good feeling inside him. His despair became unbearable.

At that point, the Wyrd Walkers drifted over to him, surrounding him. He felt their energy press at him as clearly as if hands were taking hold and pushing him on. Chains of night coiled around his heart. Cernunnos had stopped again and was looking at him. Aidan understood. He belonged to this devil, and for him there would be no escape. He did not consider the name blood brother any longer. It did not matter what it meant or represented. His fate had been written in this place of the dead.

"Good," said Cernunnos. "You understand at last. And now that you know, we will walk to the light together."

It was as if a day was dawning. Aidan could see a glimmer on the horizon as if the sun was coming up. Hope did not swell however. Nothing had changed. Whether it lived in light or in the dark.

The sun rose and Aidan saw they were in a place he recognised, a small village he had walked through some months back when his troubles had become too much and he had run away from everything. What was its name again? They passed a sign. Kinlet. *A strange name* he had thought at the time, *and it felt stranger now.* If this was their destination, had that earlier visit marked him in some way, brought about this downfall?

Leaving the group behind, Tobias led him down the lane and the pub he remembered came into view. Like all small villages in England, the pub was the centre of things, the place of news and friendship. It was where the community bonded. The Skratte's Arms. The sign displayed a bat flying across a full moon. He had not studied it closely before. Did not want to do so now. The shapes crouching on the ground beneath that solitary creature were disconcerting. His skin crawled. He turned away, smacked his dry lips.

"Thirsty?" asked Tobias. He was grinning. "We'll soon take the edge off that."

"If it's on the house," said Aidan. "I'm not exactly flush."

Tobias put an arm round Aidan. He felt this was more a sign of ownership than anything friendly.

"Oh, you are our honoured guest," said Tobias. That one statement implied ownership of the village and everything in it. Aidan accepted it completely. Numb to everything, he had no reaction to give.

Aidan looked for their companions. All were heading to the church. Cernunnos at their head. A royal procession.

Tobias pulled him back to the pub's door as if he didn't want Aidan to observe what was happening behind him.

Above the door was a sign. Proprietor and Landlord: Nicholas Threape. He sounded like something out of a Dickens' novel. Reassuring in a strange way.

They went inside. The smell of ale, of wood, of the scent of an open fire, and food cooking, warmed him immediately. If it was simply an illusion of safety, he could accept that. Comfort had been in short supply.

"A pint for our friend here," said Tobias to the man behind the bar.

Nicholas Threape. Mine host. Aidan's assumption of the Dickensian felt right at first glance. A rosy-cheeked, hearty fellow. Micawber type— almost. Worn like an ill-fitting cloak, this appearance seemed to hover over something else, a ripple effect Aidan had observed in the landscape. He shuddered, focussed his mind on what he saw, not what he thought he saw.

He could fool himself a little while longer. Until he was ready to face whatever reality he had stumbled into. Had he been so out of it before he hadn't noticed this?

"Wondered when you'd turn up," said the landlord.

"Had a few things to do, Nick," said Tobias. "In fact, I need to go and tend to them now. You'll take care of this one. Give him a room, food. It won't be a long stay."

"Does Sister know?"

"Bound to. She knows everything here, doesn't she? Her place, after all. When you've set him up, come over to the Church. There's someone wants to renew old acquaintances." As Tobias spoke, he raised his hand to an old set of antlers hanging on the wall and stroked the bone. The gesture had an immediate effect on the man.

"He's back? At last?"

"Yes," said Tobias. "And the Wheel will start turning again. I think the Layerings will be the chosen land. The folk in the Weald have a thing or two to learn about the proper ways."

Nick looked at Aidan. "We've met before, haven't we?"

Aidan nodded. "A few months back. Ended up here somehow." The answer was more for himself, than Nick.

"You were in a bit of a bad way then, I recall."

Aidan's memories struggled through the murk of time. "Yeah, but you helped me out, gave me food and drink and a bed."

"And I'm doing it again!" laughed Nick.

"You don't mind?"

"Mind? Why should I mind when it's Tobias who's asked it?"

As he spoke, he poured a pint for Aidan and filled up a jug he placed at the side of the glass. He disappeared briefly, returning with a huge portion of cottage pie. "If you get through this lot, help yourself to anything behind the bar. You can have the same room as before. First on the left."

Nick was half-way across the empty bar by now, heading for the door. He seemed to be keen to go and meet the being Tobias had brought with him. Or rather, who had led them there. The thought of the three-headed monster chilled him.

In response, the familiar copper tang of the blood he'd been forced to drink wrapped itself around his mouth again. He picked up his pint and drank quickly. He wanted to drown the foul taste, remove it forever. As soon as the glass was emptied, he poured again. It was an ale, earthy, initially pleasant until its reassuring tang swiftly faded and the old disgusting taste came back. He attacked his food, hoping for a better result.

The silence soothed him. Free from his strange company, he felt his body relax, his mind ease. He did not dwell on the darkness through which he had travelled. Understood it was still out there and would come back to claim him. There were no expectations anymore, and that reassurance meant he could rest easily. He made his way through the bar and up the stairs to the rooms.

The first one on the left brought back no memory. He really must've been out of it. As he sat on the edge of the bed, pulling off trainers which had all but disintegrated, he saw an old photo on the bedside table. It was the one of himself and Chloe he thought he had lost.

He picked it up and held it against him as he laid his head upon the pillow and slept.

CHAPTER THIRTY

BETTY

One heartbeat pulsed strong beneath him. Its strength told Betty he was near its source. They were still some distance away from the group which had Cernunnos at its head.

"They must know we're here," whispered Betty.

"Oh, they know, brother," said Tommy, "they know. But now is not the time for our reunion."

Betty slowed his pace. Frustrated at having to hang back when the thing which had been promised was so close.

"You can't just take it," said Tommy, reading his mind. "You need the fire as well."

He was right, but it didn't ease Betty's impatience. By now the buried pulse had become a drum, a beat to be marched to. It had become a torment. On they walked, horribly slow. At least they were emerging from the darkness. The Layerings shifted ahead, an almost duplicate of their home of the Weald. Meadows and blue skies, winding lanes, and distant hills and woods. Betty breathed it in, felt himself relax as he shed the claustrophobia and anxiety which had built up in the last stages of their journey.

"Go," said Tommy.

Betty was puzzled and looked around. "Go where?"

Tommy nodded in the direction of a nearby field, a stream ran along its far side. "Not too long, mind."

Betty smiled, scanned the ground. Things were lurking in the soil, crawling through the grass, running across its surface. Above were birds, in the stream, fish. He wanted to know what life was here. Then he could take it. Aware he needed to conserve his strength, he ran slowly but it was still a joy to be off the leash, to have the freedom to move and to take. He reached up into a tree and pulled down a nest. Eggs! He cracked them open into his mouth, swallowed, the white, the yolk, the embryo. Oh, the taste!

There is more in this land, said the voice. *Sister has laid on a banquet for us.*

The mention of Sister caused him to pause. She might still be upset with him despite what Tommy and the Mother said.

A fox sniffed around a hedge, apparently unperturbed by the presence of the giant. Still worrying over Sister, Betty absently picked it up and snapped its neck. The brush would be a beautiful adornment. As soon as the creature died however, it fell apart in his hands. The coat was no longer rich and glossy, was sparse, and spots of mange could be seen on the exposed flesh. There was barely any meat to the carcass, and the plump sensation had vanished to leave a bony structure. The fox's mouth was almost devoid of teeth, the few there yellow and loose, the gums bloody and swollen. Enough to put anybody off it. *A pity*, thought Betty, as he scavenged what he could, never one to waste anything.

He moved on to the stream, swirled his hands in the sparkling clear water, felt the sludge and silt build up, tendrils of algae wrap around his fingers. Fish floated past him, blank eyes gazing up. Betty let them go. When he ate it was as life passed, as the heart slowed and stopped. Death was best eaten fresh. He made his way back to Tommy and Fiddler.

"Thought you'd be longer," said Fiddler. "You've been chomping at the bit for some time."

"Not much there," said Betty. "It's not … right."

"Sister," said Tommy. "As I said, she plays tricks. Come on, we're almost there."

Betty felt as though he was being pulled in two directions. The beat which had grown so strong was overwhelming him, whilst another lay behind and carried an old promise. Its connection to him was as strong as the one in front. It was becoming unbearable, confusing. He couldn't think clearly. Hunger pulled him one way, a long-held desire another.

"It is the Father who gives us leave to Turn again," said Tommy, sensing Betty's mood. "We must pay our homage to him first."

Betty could smell the beast they had followed, understood now how much of himself was created in the image of Cernunnos. He was Nature's form and he was its destructive force; these were his two faces. He wondered at the three faces he had seen of the Horned God's. Where did the third look? There was a darker place and it was one where he suspected Tommy's affinities lay. The void which had followed them through the Corpse Marshes was for Tommy, he was the abyss. Fiddler with his music was of the air. Betty was the land. Three sons, three faces. Of Hweol he gave no thought.

Being so close, any fear of this long-forgotten parent had vanished. The voice had faded.

There is no more need for me to whisper in your ear, it had said. *We will meet in person, soon enough. Family again. A mother and her sons.*

"Come," said Tommy, as the village appeared ahead. "Let's renew a few old acquaintances first."

Again, Betty felt Tommy was putting things off. He could feel his brother's mind whirring, plotting, and scheming. To what purpose, he had no idea. For once, he wanted things to be simple. His head was already beginning to ache as he tried to imagine what Tommy could be up to.

"And Fiddler can sing for us," said Tommy.

Like a warm bath, Fiddler's voice washed over him and his irritation faded. The village was ahead of them. Winding lanes and thatched cottages. Rose-filled gardens and jasmine and honeysuckle clambering over walls. It reminded him of Cropsoe. The imagery jarred, the perfumes from the flowers were cloying and sickly. The colours were garish. It was as if he'd suddenly developed an acute sensitivity to what was displayed before him.

It jarred because it wasn't real. He was a child of nature and this was unnatural.

"Sister," said Tommy. "She has taste, I suppose. Made us a home from home."

"You think she's done this for us?" asked Betty.

"Who else?"

"Why not the Father or the Mother?"

That was another thing about Tommy, he made everything about himself. Why couldn't he just kill what he saw, take what he needed without any scheming? It was so much easier.

CHAPTER THIRTY-ONE

TOMMY

The four walked the final lane into Kinlet. The air seemed to be in a flurry, unsettled, dancing as if unable to decide on its final form. Tommy felt an energy he had not experienced in a long time. Cernunnos was here. He could tell in the way the land coloured itself, how the few people about moved. All drifting over to the church, although they would not find him inside there. Their god was to be worshipped outside in the forests and the groves of Nature. What they found inside the church would be half the story.

The door to The Skratte's Arms stood open. He sighed. What would be, would be. It didn't harm to have a drink of the local brew first. They would be summoned soon enough. Sister would know where to find them.

The three turned their footsteps to the pub, Ethan trailing behind. Tommy looked around at its faux Olde Worlde trappings, polished, shining, new. This was not the honesty of the Five Turns. This was pretence for another reason. His surroundings shimmered briefly and he glimpsed the cobwebs and the rotting floorboards, the rats hiding in the corner. Everything broken and corrupt. Then it glimmered and the shiny new version overlayed it again.

"I must say, the Layerings are looking in good shape," said Fiddler, going behind the bar and pouring their drinks. The cider in the barrels was one of the few things which was genuine and uncorrupted.

"Glad you like it," said a woman's voice.

Tommy turned, elbow leaning on the bar, a casual look to show he had expected this and was not disconcerted. He found it a struggle, however, as her form was rippling as much as the Layers she'd created.

"Hello, little sister," he said. "Thought you'd be over there, praying."

"I'm not needed for the moment. Wanted to see my long-lost family." Sister stood in the doorway, looking over the three of them, assessing their state, ignoring their human companion. She became more solid as he regarded her, no longer a shadow, giving the impression of iron. He began to think she might prove difficult. Especially given the fluidity of the form she had taken. She had become the Trickster. The knowledge rankled. That was his role.

"Been a while," said Tommy, betraying none of his feelings.

She walked over to them, showed her power by pulling the Layers with her, leaching light and colour, leaving the bone. This was the truth of her kingdom, the foundation of the rotten and corrupt was the dead and decaying. The bone of the matter. Her land of Layers was in truth no more than an Ossuary. A Charnel House. But it was *her* land, that much she made clear.

"Cernunnos will summon you soon," she said. "It would serve you to attend Him before he does so."

Her face showed all ages and no age. One moment a crone, the next the little sister of memory, the girl left behind. A deliberate presentation, he considered. One to make him feel guilty. A mistake on her part. Tommy had never felt a moment's guilt. The games had begun.

"Show willing you mean?" laughed Tommy. "Put our heads on the block first. Hope we'll distract him from you? Do you hold his favour then?"

"More than you. I have been preparing his feast for a long time. He knows what I have done for him and the Mother."

He ignored her smirk, sniffed. Another human was nearby, one unknown. "We have a visitor here."

"The Heart," said Sister. "Tobias brought him here."

They had what was needed and his mood rose. The Heart was Betty's.

We are to turn the Wheel again," said Tommy, clapping his hands together. "That is cause for celebration."

"Is it? Who says you will be the one to turn it?"

Tommy paused in his drinking. His little sister challenging him! It didn't matter they were in *her* lands. She was still just the Sister. Like Megan was *just* the Daughter, a little voice nagged at him. He couldn't, shouldn't, let her get to him. When they were with Cernunnos, all would be restored to their health and their rightful place. He bit his tongue. Let her have her bit of fun.

"Ah, lovely to see you all together." Nick had returned. "Think you're wanted over the way," he said.

Who knew so casual a summons could be so threatening?

"Time to face the music," grinned Fiddler.

Tommy smiled. He could rely on his brothers. "Come on, then. Let's go to church."

The four crossed the green behind Nick, who guided them through the cemetery and into the wood. Along the springy track, carpeted with needles and fallen acorns and pods, decomposed leaves, they made their way. Betty seemed happy.

Beneath the boughs of old and twisted trees, they walked, ancient arms reaching out to them. Here were the ancestors of the yews he had planted in the Weald. He allowed his hand to reach out and touch those closest to him, felt their whisperings beneath his fingers, sought to understand their words. Some things had remained. The scaffold on which Sister hung her tapestries of illusion.

Their voices were drowned out by the chants he heard up ahead. It was a chorus whose language crawled through him with venom. These were the words of the Summoning, when blood called to blood.

He paused, letting Betty dance on ahead until he was out of sight. Fiddler remained with him.

"Stage fright, Brother?" asked Sister. "Shouldn't worry. We'll wait for you." She headed off after Betty, leaving Tommy and Fiddler alone.

Tommy looked at the structure, an opening into a hillside, some remnant of an old burial mound. When the air moved, he was looking at redbrick church, solid and modern. This was what its congregation would be seeing. Sister had created a Victorian masterpiece. She'd gone High Church. He sat on an old log and pulled out his pipe. Fiddler copied him, the two remaining in companionable silence for some time.

"Last smoke of the condemned man," said Fiddler, laughing.

"Maybe," said Tommy, thoughtfully. "But I think all will be well. What are our rituals rooted in after all?"

"Blood," said Fiddler, without hesitation.

"And we have never let down whoever we have served. We have delivered blood and meat, bone and spirit. We have always fed the Wheel."

"Nor were we the ones who condemned Cernunnos," said Fiddler. "That was between the Mother, Hweol, and Him."

"Families," said Tommy. "Even gods have their quarrels."

"And we, as the children, can merely obey," said Fiddler. "It sounds as though you are already constructing our defence."

"If we should need it," said Tommy, "but I have the strongest suspicion all will be well." It was a feeling that had grown on him the deeper they had come into the wood. Whilst he had not made out the words of the trees, he had understood their feelings, detected no animosity, no danger.

"Might be in trouble if we're late though," said Fiddler, tapping his pipe against the trunk and emptying out the ash, pressing his foot over it as it fell so he smothered any heat.

Tommy followed suit. "You're right," he said. "We have been Summoned. Let's go and join the Dance. I wish Megan was here as well." He would've been able to put his daughter in her place. "Although the way everything's gone lately, I wouldn't be surprised if she hadn't beaten us to it!"

"She'll be here soon enough," said Fiddler. "Sarah will have seen to that."

"She's been a good Wyve," said Tommy.

As they approached, the chant grew louder, and in the gloom, he could see the outline of villagers kneeling with hands clasped. Their heads weren't bowed but raised, looking up at something he could not yet see.

The chant became an insect hum, a worm eating inside him. He could feel it take over the pulse of his heart, its beat and rhythm. It had already claimed the attention of Ethan, who had remained at Tommy's side since their arrival, taken his mind to the same place as the other villagers.

"A dangerous song," said Fiddler, catching his arm and making him pause. "Do we want to go in when we have to yield so much of ourselves?"

"I think we are safe for the moment," said Tommy. "We haven't done anything to annoy them yet. It might be an idea if you wait outside. Then if I appear any different when I come out you can take me back, bring me back to my senses."

Fiddler nodded and made his way over to a bench a little further back. He took out his fiddle and began to oil it. The bow lay ready alongside. *What notes would rise up in this village?* wondered Tommy.

He turned towards the darkness of the church and crossed its threshold. The chant was continuing, and now that he was closer, he could see mouths did not move. The villagers were not the ones proclaiming the words. His gaze travelled over them, up the aisle to the Choir and the altar.

The pulpit was empty.

There were ten shrouded figures in the Choir. Cowled and hooded like the Wyves. Tommy walked up the aisle, pausing to take his hat off. If nothing else, this was a service demanding respect.

The words of the chant continued.

"Modor, modor hrif, bletsian, bewarian, fedan."

As the congregation repeated the phrase, a figure stepped out of the shadows and took their place at the altar.

Robed in a wolf's cloak, wearing the beast's mask, and crowned with a bone wreath, he recognised her immediately. It was the form the Mother took when she needed her presence to be noticed, not dismissed as a mere imagined voice. She smiled at him.

"Wilcuma, dóc."

He bristled inside. An insult from his mother. He was no bastard, he was the true child of Nature.

"Mother." He fought to control his tongue. Until he knew her mind, he was in uncharted territory.

"Still so quick to anger. I couldn't resist," she said, her tone softer now, a hint of amusement. "You must leave the church for the time being. The service is not over, but you are not part of the congregation—yet. Your human can stay, we will talk after." She held out her hand to him, bone, like Hweol. He kissed her, bowed, and left.

None of the congregation seemed to pay any attention to him. As he walked past them, he took them in. Their eyes were vacant, fixed on the Mother and the Choir. Every body was rigid, all under perfect control. He felt no blood bond with them. Hweol exerted influence through shared blood in the Weald, Umbra and Wheelborn united. Here, things were different. These people were human through and through. They were Sister's gatherings. Folk swept up from concrete streets and despairing homes. These were her tribute to Cernunnos.

He stepped back out into the sunlight and blinked, shook himself to free his mind from the fuzziness produced by the chanting. Fiddler looked up as he approached.

"Play me a song," said Tommy. "A song from the Weald. Remind me who I am."

Fiddler raised his bow and was about to play when Nick sprinted out from the pub and jerked the bow away from the instrument.

"You cannot play your songs here. At least not now. Not during a service." He looked worried. Cast a glance at the church. "Your notes could disrupt the—" He seemed to be struggling to find the right word.

"The conditioning?" offered Tommy.

Nick nodded. "Come. Come back to the Arms and I'll pour you a drink. We can talk a little more."

"How's Betty?" asked Fiddler as they returned indoors.

"Haven't seen him," said Nick. "Thought he was with you. My brothers can keep an eye on things while we catch up."

Tommy looked at the two men sitting at the bar and noticed the family resemblance. They were not going to be hard-pressed for work though. The rest of the bar remained empty.

"It'll fill up after the service," said Nick. "I've got the drinks ready."

Tommy raised his glass to the light. Its gentle amber colour warmed him. A reminder of home. The taste too was of old. Who was added to this mix to further bind the community?

"You saw the Mother?" asked Nick.

"Yes, in all her glory," said Tommy.

"She has not long returned," said Nick. "Sister's been working hard on appearances. She's painted it in her colours for the moment until the people are ready."

"Ready?"

"Ready to Dance. Ready to Turn."

CHAPTER THIRTY-TWO

BETTY

"Brother."

The voice made him jump. Betty turned and found Sister. Unlike the earlier meeting, she refrained from shifting between faces, showed him the one he had last seen. He felt uncomfortable.

"Shouldn't you be in church with the Mother?"

"They won't miss me for a minute or two. I wanted us to have a little chat, clear the air."

"I don't—"

"I want to know what Tommy told you," she said.

"That I … got carried away, I was a child." He looked her defiantly in the eye. "The Mother said it was an accident and I was forgiven."

Sister smiled. It wasn't a pleasant expression. Reminded him of Tommy before he struck. A serpent's smile.

"Maybe," she said, "but she doesn't hold all the power, does she? And you are in my world."

Betty could feel his anxiety build up. He waited.

"Do you know what it feels like to be ripped apart?" she asked.

It was something he had seen many times, and on most occasions he would be the one responsible for it. He heard their pain, saw the shock, felt their terror as he took them. He revelled in it. It was a stupid question. If he'd been torn to pieces, he wouldn't be there. He shrugged.

She moved closer to him, put a childlike hand on his chest. It felt strange. As he looked at her hand, the skin rippled and became old and shrivelled, yellowed talons to claw into him.

"You think I couldn't tear you apart?" she whispered. "Take from you what you took from me?"

"I only took the shape of you—"

"You took more," she said, "I can feel it inside you. All I want is for you to remember."

Her hand remained on his chest, there was a pulse but it came from inside him. He felt as if they had fused together.

"You feel it, don't you? The tie that binds us."

The sensation was akin to one felt so long ago. Something he had claimed, touched. A ruby apple, dissected, held on the tongue.

"Do you remember now? The heart?"

"The Mother gave it to me," he said, more confused than ever. "I didn't take it."

"True," she said. "You didn't, but Tommy did. After you'd—skinned me, before I could recover, he took my heart. If he hadn't, I could've come with you. What he did meant I had to stay here."

He continued to start at her hand, watched almost hypnotically as it became transparent, seemed to dissolve into his chest.

"That tickles," he said, unable to stop himself laughing. He wriggled beneath her searching.

"All I want," she said, "is what is mine."

She plunged in harder and Betty felt pain for the first time, a ripping, burning sensation.

"Daughter!"

Another voice interrupted them and Sister pulled back suddenly.

"You forget yourself."

A shadow fell over them and Betty raised his eyes to the horned creature. He felt small, a child again. His world was shifting around him and he no longer felt sure of his place. He had thought himself protected.

Sister too, was staring up at the new arrival. "I was preparing for your coming."

"Not this way," said Cernunnos. "This is not how it will be."

Betty could feel her anger.

"They took what was mine, left me behind."

"You forget your privilege."

"But—"

A look silenced her and she moved further away from Betty, head hanging down like a recalcitrant child.

"Your brother is protected here," said Cernunnos.

"But—"

"Betty is the impulse, the agent. Everything happens for a purpose."

"But—"

Another look. "You will do as you are bid. We are returning, and we will all take our place in the world, including you. Be patient."

The shape of the sulky child changed, became the woman who'd assailed Tommy and Fiddler. She was smiling.

"Thought it was worth a try," she said to Betty, giving him the same shrug of the shoulders and smirk he recognised as a mannerism of Tommy's. The two weren't that dissimilar. "Better get back to church, I suppose."

The horned creature watched her go and then turned to Betty.

"Don't let your brothers and sisters confuse you. You have only ever done what we created you for."

Cernunnos turned away and stalked out of the village, leaving Betty alone. He tried to empty his mind, but his thoughts buzzed like angry wasps.

Beneath him the ground thrummed, the waves raging into him, land and body alike claimed by fury. He felt claustrophobic, his breath short. Betty felt himself being pushed along a path without any freedom to challenge it. The cord which tied him was pulling tighter.

His hands twitched, itched to destroy. He heard murmurs across the green as the congregation was expelled from the Mother's presence. Not Sister's humans, he noted, but his family, those of their kind who lived in the Layerings. Tommy and Fiddler headed in his direction, the man, Ethan, pulled along between them. Betty's hand twitched again. If he could get him away from his brothers …

"Come, brother," said Tommy. "The Father has summoned us. Time to greet Cernunnos properly."

"I've spoken to him already," said Betty. "Can't I stay here, look after him?" He nodded in Ethan's direction.

"You saw the Father?" said Fiddler. "What did he say?"

"Not much," said Betty, who'd already forgotten most of the words of their conversation, although he retained the feelings from it. "He stopped Sister."

"Stopped Sister from what?"

"She said I had something of hers, something *you'd* taken from her and given to me."

"Told you she'd hold a grudge," said Fiddler.

"And Cernunnos? What did he say?"

Betty noticed the small tell-tale frown of worry on Tommy's face, something very few ever noticed unless you knew him well. "Said it was all in the past. She wasn't very happy."

"But she accepted it?" Tommy's eyes gleamed keenly.

"Yes."

Tommy relaxed. His old smile broad.

"Then I think we can go and join the festivities with a clear mind," he said. "Betty, I'll need you to look after this young man here. Do you think you can do that?"

Betty nodded, his mouth salivating.

"No," said Tommy, as if sensing his brother's appetite. "Not yet. This one is to be shared."

Ethan was pushed towards him and Betty took his arm, inhaling the man's scent. So tempting, those notes of terror buried deep beneath shock.

Tommy remained at Betty's side, Fiddler moved to Ethan's. Betty could hear him singing a low quiet song, something to soothe the man, keep him calm. It annoyed Betty. He wanted to hear Fiddler's music. His songs were for *him* and not for a stranger.

"It will all be for you soon enough," said Tommy. "No need to be jealous."

Others were rambling alongside them, a throng swirling around so it became a tide on which he was carried. They were creatures he knew, and from them he felt their excitement, began to feed on it. The twitching of his hands had lessened and instead it was his feet which moved to a different beat. He wanted to dance. No, not just dance, but Dance.

The beat beneath quickened and Betty was pushed onwards.

"The Blooding," said Tommy. "It's started. We're coming back."

Betty laughed and clapped his hands, allowed himself a little skip before remembering Ethan, who had stopped as if a statue, and pulling him on.

CHAPTER THIRTY-THREE

TOBIAS

The Horned One had camped on the outskirts of the village with his entourage whilst Tobias settled Aidan in at The Skratte's Arms. Free from his human companion, Tobias returned to Cernunnos' side. The next stage would decide the way of their world for the years to come. He looked up at the Father. The beast had turned one face to the east and the monolithic circle which stood outside the bounds of Kinlet. This was His church. He was the stone to the Mother's wood. It was the one part of the Layerings Sister had never been able to disguise or alter. It was their beginning.

Tobias took his place amongst the followers. Others would lead this part of proceedings and already, the Wyrd Walkers were moving ahead, a dancing string of gold, lighting their path. By his side were his companions from Oldingham. More were still to come. He looked at the little village, and the rippling which continued to shimmer in the eyes of those of his folk—but appeared solid to the human—stopped.

From the village and the forest beyond, from the earth and the hidden places, came the familiar and the unfamiliar. Sister drifted towards him. She wore her natural form, the beautiful and the hideous combined. The pub landlord, Threape, emerged ahead of his family. Black-feathered and orange-eyed, a face barely recognisable. He was of the Crow People, and his flock gathered behind him, darkening the sky as they flew down and took their place. They lived in the Roost beyond the forest, nested in the hillside in carved-out caves.

Despite their friendliness, Tobias had learned to keep a healthy distance. A hungry Crow would sometimes make no differentiation between their usual diet of the blind worms beneath the surface and an unfortunate passer-by. Their taloned fingers were as sharp as any blade Tommy could conjure. As he thought of the most recent arrivals, the three appeared and made their way to his side.

Skin Walkers, they formed their own clan. Since the dawn of time, they had never really held a particular shape, were each an unbodied intelligence. As organisms evolved, the Skin Walkers developed the ability to inhabit these creatures, learn their ways, their needs, and drives. Some would continue to flit between shapes, whilst others took the one they enjoyed the most. For folk like Tommy and Tobias, they had taken particular delight in adopting the human. So flawed, so full of senses to be indulged, they were the most satisfying. Hweol himself was the First of all Skin Walkers.

Humans loved their Creation stories. What would they make of the truth?

Others appeared, the Wyves, the Lord and Imps. Cousins to the folk from Umbra, although shaded slightly darker in cruelty, if that were possible. The gathering was growing bigger. Excitement was rising. With the return of Cernunnos came an increasing strength and vitality amongst their kind.

Then came the Whipping Boy. Tommy had promised to return him to Umbra. It would be an extra punishment with which to torment the Weald. The creature was more terrible than Betty and best left alone. Yet he too had a place in the way of things. The cat hung over his shoulder, the nine flails adorned with the agonies of its victims: teeth and bone, shrivelled tongues, and broken skulls. A true demon from the pit, this had become a congregation of the monstrous.

Around the henge they crowded, leaving the way clear for Cernunnos to walk into the circle. The stones, which at a distance seemed shorter than many of their number, had increased in size at his entrance, towering above everyone—even the Whipping Boy. The Temple of the Horned One had risen. After Cernunnos came the Wyrd Walkers, each moving to one of the Sarsen stones of the outer ring, their glow illuminating the shadows cast by the height of the megaliths. Cernunnos took his place at the altar stone and turned to survey them all. Stretching his arms wide, he gestured them inside.

The crowd, usually so vocal, were deathly silent. With the return came change. Tobias shared their anxieties. Only the Father could decide who was to be part of that. The Folk were holding their breath.

"For centuries I have remained in darkness," said Cernunnos, a whispered voice, slithering into the mind of everyone present. "During that time, I have eaten the meat of man. Meals provided by the faithful. Each mouthful gave me insight, taught me all I needed to know when I could not see the world for myself. I have watched the humans take from the Mother. I have watched them cover the soil with concrete and steel. I have watched them take what is not theirs to take. The Mother created and they have destroyed. Balance must return, and that will be by the reassertion of belief in our kind and obedience to our ways. I am the Father, the Destroyer, and I will bring our world back to us."

Tobias found himself nodding along, imagining their future.

"We will no longer inhabit the remote and the rural," continued Cernunnos. "We will go into the towns and the cities. We will bite at the edges and devour the centres. The Mother thought my sons too cruel. I think they have not been cruel enough. We will leave Her to tend to the hills and the meadows whilst we take apart that which has been built and return it to Her as it should be."

Each of his faces wore the same expression—cold, hard, and unforgiving.

Yet the mood of the gathering had changed. No longer sombre, the atmosphere was charged with excitement and expectation. They had held their appetites in check for so long, they sensed a feast coming.

"Our strength is returning. This is more than my return, it is also the time of rebirth for those of you who remained true to the Mother. We are now one family, each with a role to play. All that has gone before is in the past. Those who have erred are forgiven. This is a time of celebration."

Tobias glanced at Tommy. They grinned at each other. Any worries they had about forgiveness had vanished. The shadowy gloom deepened further, the glow of the Wyrd Walkers almost blazing against the pitch, and Tobias realised night had fallen. The moon was crimson, casting a bloody cloak over Cernunnos. He sensed movement beneath his feet, as if the soil was pushing up. The earth was thirsty and needed to drink. As did they all.

"Today is the first day of Blodmanoth, the Festival of Blood," said Cernunnos. "Where is the offering?"

This was the one moment of danger for all of them. Anyone could be chosen despite the blanket pardon. It wasn't personal, just necessary. Tobias looked at Sister. She had not brought any of her villagers with her. A spiteful action, one which kept Tobias and Tommy on edge—as she intended.

"Don't worry, Tobias," muttered Tommy. "Remember we brought a little something along with us, just in case?"

Tobias looked at him and followed his eyes to the back of the crowd where Betty towered over those near to him. He had assumed the giant had remained there because of his tendency to fidget. As Betty pushed through the throng, he saw he was accompanied by a man, and behind Betty came a group of Imps herding several cattle, nipping at their heels to force them onwards.

"Always does to be prepared," said Tommy, rubbing his hands together.

His words rankled Tobias. Did Tommy think he would receive greater favour than Tobias through this one offering when Tobias had been faithful to the Father for longer than any? Then he looked up at the Father again and found Cernunnos regarding him. There was a slight nod of the head and any resentment Tobias felt vanished. Cernunnos recognised his worth.

"Tonight," said Cernunnos, "on this First Night, we will take the sacrament in which we are baptised. This is our Blooding."

The Father moved to the side of the altar stone, and Betty lifted the man high above his head as if offering to the moon herself. Two of the Lords stepped forward, knives unsheathed and glinting. A Wyve also entered this inner circle.

"Beloved family," said the Wyve, "this is the sacrament of our baptism when we are first born. It is the holy rite of the Mother and the Father. It is our gospel. Hear the words of blood."

The crowd knelt before the Crone and the Father, the Lords with their swords bowed their heads. Tobias felt a cool breeze on his cheek, smelt the must of the nearby animals, sensed their fear, the human's terror. Betty still held the man high above the stone, never wavering, never swaying, despite his strength being less than it once was.

"Cernunnos," said the Wyve. "Father of all that is born of blood,
you have given us life and strength.
In your image have we been created.
Through your gift of the vital fluid have we been sustained.
This liquid, when drunk on this night,
realigns us in our faith and belief,
in our obedience to the Horned God."

The Wyve stopped speaking and turned to Betty. The giant lowered his burden, tore the bewildered man's clothes from his body and placed him on the altar stone. A Lord took up position at his head. The man, no more than a youth really, began to struggle. Betty pinned him down. Tobias noted the pleading look he cast at Tommy, the confusion and sense of betrayal. Tommy merely smiled. At that the young man stilled. It was a moment Tobias had often seen. The resignation at the inevitable, the closing down of awareness as if the mind had decided to flee before the body was harmed.

As the Wyve began to speak gain, the Lord dropped his sword across the man's throat, the force severing head from body.

"Through exsanguination we extract the essence of what gives us power," she said.

"Of what gives us power," repeated the congregation.

"And binds us to you, Cernunnos, through drinking of your holy offering. We become one."

"We become one," came the response.

Another Wyve had carried a bowl to the altar and was collecting the blood dripping from the corpse as the first Wyve continued to recite.

"Through the meat we extract the knowing
of what gives us power.
Through the harvesting of life,

do we honour the Mother and the Father."

As one, the crowd replied, "We honour the Mother and the Father."

This time, the blades of both Lords flashed down and carved the body into chunks before throwing the pieces into a nearby basket.

"Through blood," said the Wyve.

The first of the cattle was slaughtered, its carcass placed on the altar stone.

"Through blood," repeated Tobias and those around him.

"Through blood," said the Wyve.

The first of the herd was carved and a second sacrificed in its place.

"Through blood," repeated, again and again.

As the slaughter continued, the words became a steady chant, merging into each other until eventually, all that could be heard was the one word: blood. As the last of the sacrifices was made, Cernunnos spoke again.

"Beloved family, you have spoken the words and reaffirmed the bond between us. Eat and drink of the offering with my blessing. As the world Turned on that first night of our existence, so let it be as it was. Let us take back what was ours. Let the Festival of Blood be joyous. Let us have music and laughter, for this is our beginning!"

His voice was no longer a whisper, had become a clarion call across the night sky. His three mouths smiled with delight. An expression reflected by the faces of those who looked upon him.

"My cue, I think," said Fiddler, delightedly plucking the strings on his fiddle before turning to the bow. The notes flashed up into the heavens, shining brighter than they had done in a long time.

"Seems we're all on the same side," said Tommy to Tobias. "And we have a world to conquer."

Tobias laughed. He no longer felt there was any competition between them, the Father's words had given them the world. There was more than enough to go round.

CHAPTER THIRTY-FOUR

BETTY

Betty gazed around in delight. Fiddler's music was back, the notes dancing around his head, flicking on his skin, seeping into him. It eased the aches he had begun to feel, the weariness accompanying the pulse of the earth. Before, he had wanted to sleep, and whilst part of him still wanted to close his eyes, the other part of him responded in full to the exuberance of those around him.

There had been blood and meat, the appetiser to the main course still to come. He could sense his time nearing. He ran his hand over the cloth of his jacket. It was rough, caked in parts with dirt, soft and claggy at the cuffs where the blood had seeped in. He raised his wrist to his nose, sniffed its aroma. It was his favourite perfume, and the moon was wearing his favourite colour.

Imps chased each other amongst the crowd, squealing and shrieking, snatching up gobbets of meat as they fell. A few had already had their fill and were curled up in the arms of the Wyves, ready to be put to bed. Betty pondered his appetite. They could spare one or two possibly. One had even curled up at his own feet. He reached down and scooped it up. Its skin was soft, appeared hairless, due in part to its colour and the length of down. The creature rumbled at his touch, let out a satisfied sigh. Betty quickly looked around, everybody was busy, hacking away at the hide for treatment, sucking the marrow from the remaining bones, lapping up any splatterings of blood which had escaped attention.

Fiddler was playing his music to a group of Wyves and they were giggling like schoolgirls. Tommy was standing near Cernunnos, keeping careful watch on the Horned One. Nobody appeared to be paying him any mind. It was better to be cautious though. Stepping carefully over those who scavenged on the ground, weaving his way between chatting groups, he slipped behind one of the outer stones. The Imp continued to sleep in his arms, snuffling contentedly. Betty stroked it again, sang softly as Fiddler had taught him. The sound woke the Imp, its big eyes growing wider when they saw Betty. He continued to stroke the creature, gently at first, then pressing harder and harder. Bones gave a little beneath his fingers and the Imp gave out a shrill cry, swiftly muted by a broken jaw. It continued to struggle and gurgling sounds came from its throat. These too, were soon stopped.

Betty regarded the limp body, slit its skin with one of his jagged nails, peeled it away from the meat. He took another quick look round and moved closer to the stone. Lifted the carcass to his mouth and began to suck noisily. He had barely finished when a Wyve appeared at the entrance to the stone circle, scanning the ground as if looking for something. Betty swiftly hid the skin behind his back. It didn't matter he had blood and gore crusting his face and clothes. Everybody was in the same position. The Wyve gave him a curious look and seemed to be on the point of asking him something before changing her mind and returning to the gathering. She vanished, only to be replaced by Fiddler.

"Ah, there you are." The musician looked at the pelt Betty pulled out from behind his back and was now folding into his pocket. "I wouldn't take too many," he advised. "The Wyves can be vicious when roused. You wouldn't want to get on the wrong side of one of those." He shuddered.

"You've been in trouble with them?" asked Betty.

Fiddler's expression took on a faraway look. "You could say that." He was smiling.

"Aelfled," said Betty, recalling the one he had called Grandma. "You were in trouble with her more than once. Do you miss her?"

Fiddler sighed. "Yes. She was a good woman. Understood me better than any other, very forgiving."

"Her wolf wasn't though, was he?" said Betty, laughing.

"True," said Fiddler. "Couldn't blame him for eating them though, can you? I mean, he was protecting his mistress in some strange and twisted way."

"What now?" asked Betty.

"I think we rejoin the others and keep an eye on that other brother of ours. Things are taking a turn for the better and it would be a shame if

Tommy got into any bother, he does have a tendency to play games with people."

Betty felt the cooling pelt in his pocket. He would add it to the pack he'd left in the village. His worries were disappearing, his sense of protection growing. The world was righting itself at last and the beat of the land was pulling him on. All he had to do was follow.

CHAPTER THIRTY-FIVE

MEGAN

She could hear voices, a steady chant rising and falling. Like water, it washed over her, hypnotic, soothing. The Winchester beyond the walls faded from her mind. They had entered a place beyond any man's reach.

"Don't be fooled," said Sarah. "The truth is in the words."

Megan forced herself to remain alert as she strained to make them out, failed at every attempt. Each word merged into the next, almost as if hiding from her understanding.

They were in a chapel. *The* chapel from what she recalled. Her feet tapped on the hard, tiled floor, a noticeable echo in the absence of any sound from Sarah, who seemed to glide ahead. She looked towards the choir expecting to see those who sang, but the seats were empty. A small passageway ran off to the side, lit by the remaining sunlight shining through the stained-glass window.

Megan took in the multi-coloured image. The rippled glass, jewelled and brilliant. The woman who watched over those below, terrible in her stance. Behind her were fields filled with sheep, birds flew across the sky, a wreath of flowers circled her head. The pastoral idyll of the Mother, resplendent in her power, her arms raised out to her children at her feet. From up out of the abyss they crawled, demons whose forms slowly changed the nearer they drew to the light until they emerged, coated in unblemished skin with cherubic smiles. Beneath blades of grass, worms squirmed and beetles dug. Flies had settled on more than one infant, appearing to crawl into an open mouth. The woman's left hand hovered over the head of a child gazing up at her. Between her fingers could be seen the remnants of a butterfly wing—crushed. The Mother's smile was radiant. Megan shivered and averted her eyes.

"You should look upon her," said Sarah, pausing. "Nature is beautiful in so many ways. The interconnectedness of things, the web of life, each dependent on the other. Humans should accept what is and not judge because they deem it ugly or abnormal according to their own norms. The Wheelborns have evolved over the centuries to be what you now are. Who's to say you don't come from those dark places too?"

Megan again looked at the demons, thought back to the pit in Hweol's hall where bones were cast, of the place of that last Turn of the Wheel where her mother had died. The void into which she had gazed, where she had demanded to be taken. To have come from such a place? Surely not.

Sarah moved off again and Megan followed. In all this time, the chanting had continued without pause. Her companion pushed open a low door and they were in a dining room of sorts. A long table took up most of the room. Robed figures sat on either side. The left clad in maroon, the right clad in black. At the head of those singing monks sat the Master. His eyes locked onto Megan's and he smiled. It was an expression which soon faded as she felt something shift across her vision. Hweol was making his presence felt. It had the effect of wiping the smile from the Master's face.

She felt the skin on her neck burn at the site of that long ago bite. Despite Sarah's reassurances, she felt the connection.

"Daughter! Welcome!" The Master rose and advanced, arms wide like the Mother in the stained-glass window. Perhaps he looked upon them as butterflies to be crushed.

"It's been a long time, Father," said Sarah.

The two were stood in front of each other. Megan felt forgotten. The men at the table continued to chant. They appeared to have no awareness of their arrival.

"If you're searching for Tommy and company, you've missed them. They indulged in a bit of restringing and went on their way."

"I know," said Sarah. "We'll catch up with them soon enough. I have a little business to see to first."

"And what exactly would that be?" The Master's eyes narrowed as he studied them both, became crimson slits.

The chanting increased in volume, as if matching the tension of the atmosphere. Megan felt as if she was fading from the scene, watching the main actors on a distant stage.

"I came to give you a choice," said Sarah. "You come with us or—"

The Master fixed a red eye on the Wyve. Megan could tell nothing from her body language. The cowl hooded her face, kept everything hidden. Yet she sensed no fear, only quiet determination in her voice.

"You! Give me a choice! You forget yourself, daughter."

"No," said Sarah. "It is you who forgets. It is I who created you, and I who can destroy you."

He didn't miss a beat, dismissed the comment as if a fly, although Megan sensed the truth of her words. The chanting continued, started to invade her head. It felt as if her mind had become a hive of buzzing insects, an angry swarm stinging at every thought, sending them running for cover so she was unable to concentrate. And then—clarity. The meaning of their words became clear, a whisper from Hweol, who she understood was— had to be—on her side until they got to the village the Blodgitan had mentioned earlier. Their words were a trap and she had to stop them.

Side-stepping Sarah and the Master, she made her way to the table. Bowls and plates were empty. The serving dishes in the centre were filled with maggot-infested meat, bowls of rotting fruit. A sickly-sweet smell she had not noticed before hit her. The words of the chant had gone leaving behind an incessant buzzing, both in her head and in the air around her. Flies crawled over everything, a revolting moving blanket. Before her eyes, larvae transformed into their flying counterparts and more maggots emerged from the eggs. As the chant had transfixed her, so did the sight until she heard that voice from the depths of her. There was nothing she could see to stop it however. Then a flickering flame caught her eye. Fire.

Another guided her now, took control of her body. She didn't fight it, accepting the need in this instance to allow such an imposition. Megan moved to the wall and took down the candle and an old tapestry. She tossed the material over the corrupt food, smothering some of the insects in the process, poured the wine from a jug on a corner of the material and touched the flame to it. A small fire grew and it sent the flies into a fury. They blinded her as she tried to set another fire, sent her arm wide so the torch in her hand caught the robe of the figure nearest to her. In all this time, none of those present had appeared to pay her any attention despite her actions. Now the one who burned turned toward her. He, she assumed it was a he, showed no sign of panic, simply regarded her for a while as the fire took hold. Then he threw back his hood and she saw him properly. Hweol faded back into the darkness, forced her to confront the creatures on her own.

Megan stumbled back, the horror of the sight distracting her from the flies which continued to mass. It was a man. Or what had once been a man. Half his face was missing as if something had sliced the flesh. His mouth was open and still he continued to chant. She shook herself. Illusion. Had to be. And then the figure reached out to his companion, igniting him in the process. The fire jumped from arm to arm, each mimicking the movement of their neighbour, until the slow burn became fierce—and still with no sound of agony or desperation.

The company rose and the twin columns advanced towards her.

In trying to put an end to things, it seemed as if she had made the situation worse. Hweol had commanded the use of fire and she had stupidly obeyed, believing in his need for self-preservation. Would she ever learn?

"Megan." Sarah's voice cut through her thoughts. As she returned to Sarah's side, fire and flies continued to follow slow and steady. In no rush.

The Master laughed. "Seems things have gone a little awry."

"Really?"

Megan looked at Sarah, tried to get a sense of where this confidence came from.

"These are your creatures, naturally," said Sarah. "But ultimately, as I gave you what you demanded, they are also mine."

"You think they will obey you? A woman not seen in these walls for so long, their thread to you has weakened."

"That thread never weakens," said Sarah. "And only I can cut it."

The Master laughed, a mocking sound which echoed from the walls rising above the crackle of fire spreading from the grotesques to the wooden pews.

Megan began to cough. Her eyes stung and the buzz roared louder, holding her in place as the heat advanced. Then Sarah moved to the nearest victim, touched him. The fire did not jump to her, if anything it withered a little, blazing back when she stepped away.

"Father," she said. "Your sons would like to feel your embrace."

Still chuckling, he turned to the one nearest—and stopped. The man's arms were reaching out to him, reflecting the movements of Sarah's hands. Like a puppet master, she directed the impossibly burning corpse as it wrapped itself around the Master, joined by his brothers.

The Master was able to scream out once and then he was burning in the midst of them. The flies too, added to the conflagration, adding small pops as they died in the flame. The scene reminded Megan of the paintings of Hieronymous Bosch. It was a vision of Hell.

"Not quite how I expected things to end," mused Sarah as she guided Megan out of the chapel, somewhat too slowly for Megan's liking. "I was going more for a stake through his unbeating heart." She let out a soft chuckle.

Megan was silent. It didn't matter she had been brought up alongside creatures unknown to the wider world; blood-driven monsters who had fed on her family and friends for centuries. It was still hard to believe that something like the Blodgitan existed, behaved like the vampires of legend.

"Myths and legend have to come from some spark of truth," said Sarah as they travelled back through the city, quieter now as shops closed and tourists departed. "A mere glimpse of something can generate so many stories."

Megan looked back across the meadow, wondered that no smoke was rising, no orange light danced behind the windows.

"The fire will burn out," said Sarah. "The chapel will contain it. No innocents will be hurt."

Megan's mind had gone back to the moment the fire had revealed what lay beneath the robes.

"He chose his followers. Turned them. There was no one you would regard as simply 'human' in there. You have no need to feel guilt. If anything, you have stopped an evil in this world."

Walking across cobbles, onto more modern concrete slabs, past darkened shop fronts, seeing a few folk out for a late stroll, Megan felt some relief. A stain had been lifted from at least one corner of society. She felt better. Until they reached the neglected industrial estate once again and was reminded how close the borders between their worlds remained.

"Would you have these borders closed permanently?" asked Sarah as they stepped onto the murky track.

"It would be better, safer, for us," said Megan.

"Knowing it would bring about an end to such as me?"

Megan nodded.

"We are creatures of Nature as much as any other," said Sarah. "Would you destroy all that you fear? The sharks in the ocean, the snake in the grass, the wasp in the sky? These are all part of the chain of life, and you recognise that, live with it. Why should we not be accorded the same consideration?"

Megan could see the logic despite disagreeing with the reality. Ultimately, she understood, it was down to control. In Nature's web, man had been part of the food-chain, still was when in the wild, unprepared, vulnerable. A risk accepted. But with the creatures of Umbra, it was different. These had habits which inspired fear and loathing, although part of their makeup. And they had the power to assert control over humans. Man had taken himself out of Nature's cycles and put himself in charge. This position of Umbran superiority would not sit well if it became the norm.

"And we are a reasonable folk," continued Sarah. "It is why we inhabit small pockets of the world, live on the edge of a few communities. We do not seek to take over, take only what we need. Our appetites, if unleashed, would decimate mankind. We understand that, husband our resources, control ourselves."

It all sounded so reasonable. Her words showed a greater consideration for those weaker than anything green parties and conservationists were coming up with.

"But you cloak it all with cruel ritual," said Megan.

Sarah shrugged. "It keeps order, helps our folk retain a sense of who they are, although much has become distorted and twisted so that it is no longer a celebration of an offering given, and has instead become an assertion of the power to take and inflict suffering. I have been conflicted for so long. I do not give up my right to exist. Why should I? But how is it done, how we treat each other, that has to change."

Megan had no response. She agreed with everything said except their right to exist, and by thinking such a thing, it meant she was no better than anyone else. What sort of monster had she been turning into? Somewhere, in the darkness of her mind, she heard a chuckle.

They returned to the Ley path. Megan took a deep breath as they entered the Layerings.

"We'll be there soon," said Sarah, walking quickly.

Her speed surprised Megan. "You're in a hurry now?"

"The celebrations have started," said the Wyve. "I don't want to miss anything."

She had barely finished her sentence before they found themselves on a country lane, a village sign proclaiming the name Kinlet.

We're wanted here, said the voice, *the land brings those it desires.*

They had come to a fork in the road.

"We'll part here, for a little while," said Sarah. "Go into the village and wait for me. You'll be safe enough there."

"And where are you going?" asked Megan, distrust beginning to bubble up again.

"My family are here. I must greet them. Drink."

Megan remembered witnessing the Wyve drink from the remains tossed to her by the Blodgitan and shuddered. She had no wish to watch such a thing again. She made her way into the village, taking in the surface idyll whilst glimpsing the decay beneath. Nobody else seemed to be around, and she had no desire to seek anyone out. She needed time to gather her thoughts. She sat on a bench and stared into the surface of the nearby pond, allowed herself to ignore the dead eyes reflected back. Megan pulled the sword onto her lap and considered throwing it into the murk. She wanted rid of it—of her guilt. Hweol shifted inside. It felt as if he was just below the surface of her skin, was preparing to erupt. Both sensed freedom beckoning. She wondered what would come after.

CHAPTER THIRTY-SIX

AIDAN

When Aidan woke it was to silence. The initial relief at not being faced with the monsters he'd encountered gave way to worry. Whilst he had resigned himself to whatever end they had planned for him, he would still take a chance at escape. The sense of absence gave him hope. He slipped the photo of Chloe in his pocket and made his way downstairs.

Around him everything rippled, revealing at times an under layer of another world, a rotting and decomposing reflection of the one he currently inhabited. The harder he looked, the more he found himself slipping into the decaying vision and becoming part of it. He didn't fight it, better to deal with the truth than with illusion.

The stair risers felt spongy beneath his feet, causing him to reach out to the banister. The railings offered no support however, crumbling beneath his touch. He shifted his weight to the other side, preferring the security of the wall to the cavern beneath the bannister. It was a false security he found as a crack appeared in the plaster at the slightest touch, its dust sifting over his clothes. Moving as quickly as he could, he kept his focus on the bottom of the stairs, reaching it with a relieved exhalation of breath which immediately triggered a hacking cough as mould and spores invaded his lungs. Aiden pulled his T-shirt up over his mouth and nose and sped outside.

The air there wasn't much better, nor were his surroundings, until he saw something to lift his spirits a little. A young woman sat on a broken bench beside a miserable depression that once spoke of life as a pond. It had been full of pure clear water when he arrived, a family of ducks paddling across its surface. A beautiful lie.

He approached cautiously, took in the pale, anguished face, noted also a determination in the set of her jaw. Her clothes, jeans, cable sweater, and parka coat were filthy, looked too big for her, swamping her frame as they did. Her hair was pulled back into a straggly ponytail. It appeared as unwashed as the rest of her. And yet she did not resemble those he had met on the streets. This neglect was something born of other trials.

As he neared, she turned her face in his direction and he found himself looking into the grey eyes he had seen in Tobias and those like him. He paused, unsure as to whether he should speak to her. Had she been left as his guard?

"Don't worry," said the woman, "I'm not like the others. I'm human, pretty much." The sadness and despair in her voice matched her appearance.

"Pretty much?" He couldn't help repeating the question back at her. If she had even a small shared heritage with Tobias and his ilk, he felt it would be better to leave her be. Search for his escape on his own.

She was smiling at him. "You see a resemblance though, don't you?" she asked.

He nodded, disconcerted by her ability to guess his mind.

"I lied to myself for so long," she said, "pretending I wasn't who I was, that my parents were who I thought. But you can only fool yourself for a while. There is always a day of reckoning."

At her last words, her eyes clouded and he could see a storm of pain and conflict.

"Are you … are you alright? Can I help? Get you anything?" He almost laughed as he heard his voice come out with offers which, in another place, he would've been able to carry through. He couldn't do anything here.

She ignored his comments. "How did you come here?"

"Tobias," he said. "One minute I was sleeping in an abandoned industrial estate in Oldingham, the next everything's changed and there's Tobias, who I'd only known as a helper in a homeless shelter, and this … this thing he calls Cernunnos. And they make me follow them, make me drink—" He couldn't finish, and she appeared to understand.

"They take who they want, what they want, when they want," she said. "It's always been their way. I only really knew of those in my village and the Weald. I never knew there were those who lived in the cities."

"I think I've met some of those from your village," he said, knowing who she was referring to, realising as he said it how his understanding of the world around him was changing. "Where I'm from, those … things … don't really live in the city, they stay on the edge. Like those they mix with I suppose. We're the ones people won't miss or would rather weren't around. Seems we provided a good feeding ground for them." He disliked how his voice had taken on a tone of self-pity.

She looked at him with curiosity. "What led you to the streets?"

"Divorce, loss of job, no money, the usual."

She nodded. There was nothing she could really say, he supposed. Most people would be sorry but not mean it.

"I'm Megan," she said, as if coming to a decision. "Megan Wheelborn."

He had held off giving his name as it meant a relationship would be formed, that he would start to care. "Aidan."

Then he recalled her surname. "Wheelborn?"

"It's the family name," she sighed. "The name given to those who have blood links to those from the world Tobias and his kind come from. My parents were Wheelborns, but I found out only a year ago Tommy was my real father. He killed the man I thought was my dad, killed my mum, killed my unborn child, killed—almost killed—my husband."

The last drops of suspicion drained away. This was a woman who had suffered in a way beyond anything he had experienced. He could tell she spoke the truth by the way she held herself, the mist in the eyes, the sob of her voice, her whole appearance.

"But you are here," he said. "Why did you come?"

"My husband, there was a chance—I thought there was a chance—I might get him back. Somehow. Now I just want it all to stop, to let him rest."

Aidan gazed at the nearby houses. "Where is he?"

She gestured to the long thin bundle on her lap.

He stared at it in puzzlement. How could that possibly be a human? She unwrapped it and his confusion grew. A sword lay on her lap. Its steel surface was about three centimetres across and had the remnants of a wooden handle at each end. The metal itself had a strange sheen, a moving, drifting cloud.

"How? What?"

"We had planned to destroy them," she jerked her head back, as if those she referenced were behind her. "We took Tommy's swords to the forge, were going to throw them into the fire and stop the ritual. Instead, my husband fell into the flames. I saw him burn to death, but his spirit melded with this sword."

It sounded unbelievable. She had obviously had a huge shock. Perhaps this was a story her mind had created to protect her from the truth of whatever had happened.

"You don't believe me, do you? It was true though. His spirit was in the sword. He used to talk to me…"

"Couldn't that be something you told yourself?" he asked gently.

"No. It would've been so much simpler if it had. At first, they said there was a way to bring him back, that the Mother could return him to me but … he changed and the Wyves told me he could never return as the person I remembered."

"They could be lying to you."

"They could," she agreed, "but he changed, became a voice demanding blood, like they all do. Everything with these people revolves around blood and sacrifice. I need to free him from the blade to find peace for him."

"And for you," he said.

Something told him this still wasn't the full story, but he didn't press her on details. The whole concept was fantastical, unbelievable, yet so much had happened to him lately which was beyond his understanding. What he knew and could respond to was the little glimmer of hope she was clinging on to, the belief she could bring peace to herself and her husband. He sensed it was all she had left.

"I would've thought having that name offered some protection to you and your family," he said, wondering how someone so closely tied to these creatures could be forced to suffer so much. It was as if his words had flipped a switch and it all came tumbling out.

Megan told him of the villages of the Weald and their forced servitude to the folk of Umbra. She told of the creatures who lived there and the rituals the inhabitants of the villages were forced to undergo. She told him of the Five Turns of the Wheel in honour of the Mother. She told of the Mother's revocation of Hweol and Tommy's powers, and then she told him of Hweol and the spirit which resided in her. A parasite lurking, ready to take advantage. In another place, he would've thought her mad. Here, he found her horribly believable.

"The name," she finished, "is no protection, is nothing but a curse. And you? Do you know what they will do with you?"

"What they seem to do to every human they meet," he said. "When they first caught me, they called me their offering. They will kill me."

"They aren't here at the moment," said Megan.

"No, they've gone to Cernunnos. When we first arrived, I heard them talk, it's where I've assumed they've gone. They took another person with them. Didn't really get to know the poor bugger. I don't think you'll be seeing him though. Thought I'd take the chance and have a look around, see if I could escape." It sounded lame to his ears. How could someone like him escape a world like this?

Her response confirmed his worst fears. "If you've been marked for the role of honour, as they call it, they will make sure you cannot get away, despite appearances."

Aidan scanned the boundaries of the village, noticed how everything blurred at its edges. He could get up and walk straight out.

"Try it," said Megan, following his look. "They manipulate everything. The land, the air you breathe. They will make sure that whatever path you take, it will always lead back to them – unless they have let their guard down, and I think that highly unlikely. They used similar tricks in the Weald."

"It would mean leaving you alone," he said, suddenly reluctant to leave the vulnerable young woman. Vulnerable? He looked again and despite her appearance detected the strength beneath.

"I've been alone for some time now," she said. "I'm used to it. Go."

He rose and walked away, put his feet on the lane which had brought him into the village and followed it out. As the village sign neared, the landscape shifted and he found he was back at the start. He tried again, with the same result. He attempted the walk in the opposite direction.

Every road he took brought him back to the centre of the village. Again and again, he repeated the exercise until the frustration forced him back to the bench.

She looked at him sadly as he retook his seat beside her.

"They'll never let us go," she said.

He knew it was true. That was the moment Aidan gave up.

CHAPTER THIRTY-SEVEN

BETTY

The gathering had fed him well. Step by step, Betty was returning to his beginning. There would be more celebrations, more dancing, more blood. The land had quickened around him and carried him with its rhythms. The Father had welcomed him, the Mother had forgiven him. Nothing else mattered.

Betty saw the village church ahead. It was not his temple, he would leave that building of broken walls and rotting beams to his brothers. He preferred to be outdoors, amongst creatures kin to himself. The Mother and the Father had created him. Both had an all-seeing eye. They would know where he went and would call for him if needed. He didn't want prayers or songs—except the one song which turned the Wheel. For the present, he needed to listen to the land to which he was bound, the cycle of life, more so than Tommy and Fiddler.

From Tobias had come the news all was in place for his own rebirth. The heart had been brought and was his for the taking. He had seen its owner, Aidan. Felt no compassion or guilt for the man's suffering. He had what Betty needed. And a dress for the ceremony was waiting for him. He could even feel Megan's presence and with it, the possibility of another broken promise being resolved. That was enough.

A sense of excitement was bubbling up, the pressure of an energy which needed an escape. He had not felt like this since Megan had taken control of Umbra. It was time to run and hunt. Be who he was born to be.

Betty was across the green and moving round the back of the church before the others could say anything. A quick glance back revealed Tommy and Fiddler in quiet conversation, apparently not giving him a thought, but Tommy looked up at that moment and caught his eye, gave him a slight nod of the head. He had permission, not that he'd asked for it.

As he walked, Betty could see the layers which coated the land around him. Sister had painted a stage for them.

He headed down a path through an overgrown cemetery which came to an old track and then plunged into a wood. He noticed with surprise how this bit of land held no layers. A puzzle, but not one to concern him. The trees with their autumnal colours, the soft path with its dried, crumbly soil, the curled ferns and glistening fungi, were all real. He allowed himself a moment to touch, to dig into the earth, to ground himself once again into the creature he truly was.

A rustling up ahead caught his attention. Immediately, he was on its scent, trotting after it, light of foot despite his bulk. A faint hum caught his attention. It was coming from his left and he realised the path was running behind the church, joining up with a track leading from the cemetery. The hum was like an annoying wasp. It was a discordant noise, an irritant, it affected him no more than that, and soon the woods were carrying him far enough away for it to fade completely.

As he walked, he felt as if he was in two places at the same time. There was still the real, natural foliage of the human world, but something else was also creeping in. It had shades of Umbra and brought to mind the path which took them from one world to another. It did not feel dead and gloomy like the Old Ley they had walked. Instead, it felt as if this was a lived-in world. Could this be the other place Tommy had occasionally mentioned? The one often referred to in the old legends? Yet they had come upon it too quickly. He had expected days of travel to get there. The paths between worlds could remove the miles, but if they had been that close then the people would've known. There would've been a lot more toing and froing between places. The old stories did not give any sense of closeness of location. He didn't want to think about such things. Instead, he returned to his senses, allowed them to work on his surroundings rather than try to puzzle out the logistics.

There was laughter up ahead. A shout and a giggle. A scream. Imps! Betty began to run. He loved to play with the Imps. They had so much fun together. He moved quicker as their laughter grew. And then he was in a clearing where he saw them. A small group, young, they had a squirrel by the tail. They were playing catch-as-catch-can, or at least the child's version. This was their school. When they were older, they would chase bigger prey.

They stopped when they saw Betty and looked up at him in wonder. The one with the squirrel approached shyly, offered him the animal. Betty smiled and took it, worked quickly to free it of its pelt and threw the innards to the group. They squealed happily, fighting over fragments, which they devoured quickly. Their teeth were as sharp as those in Umbra.

They all crowded round him and Betty knelt down, offered them his hand to sniff. Cautiously they did so, then they stroked the hair on the back of his hands and on his arms, his legs. One reached up and gave his long hair an experimental tug. Betty noticed it no longer came away in clumps, that the hair on his skin had also thickened.

He lifted the Imp up in the palm of his hands and, smiling, opened his mouth as if to eat the creature who shrank back. Then he snapped his mouth shut with a laugh, showing he was merely pretending. The Imp giggled in delight and the others laughed. The Imp grabbed the hair again, and again Betty pretended to bite. They did this a few times, the Imp laughing more and more at each attempt. Then it tried again.

This time Betty was quicker and his teeth cut clean through the Imp's body. He chewed slowly, feeling the crunch of bone against his cheek, the dribble of blood down his chin. The other Imps had stopped playing at his feet and were watching. Then he spat out the remains. These Imps had a slightly more sour taste than back home in Umbra. They would require seasoning if he tried them again. The dead Imp's friends gazed at him for a moment and then burst out laughing. They started to run and beckon along another path. Betty followed.

The trees had changed and become a yew forest, similar to Soulsbury in the Weald. There would be a grove here, he was sure of it. Already, that transparent film was appearing, a layering of mist and fog through which wraiths and sprites moved. It added a chill to the air, although temperature was something which rarely affected him. His body had been made to adapt to any environment. The giggling continued further ahead and it brought back another memory. This one of Simon Wheelborn's last hours.

He had had to remain behind to entertain Megan, so Tommy had described the hunt to him. His stomach began to growl.

Whilst Tommy was hankering after new experiences, more power, Betty wanted nothing of this. For him, the land and the creatures in it was all he needed. If it hadn't been for his brothers, he would've stayed in the Weald even if his time was running out. It was his territory. He had marked it out long ago. He was looking forward to his return, reinvigorated to enjoy it all the more.

"Come, friend," called an Imp from up ahead.

They called him friend even though he had eaten one of their own. Who would they be taking him to? Hweol was not here. Sister was in the church. Who was here to greet him?

Another turn, down another path. This one narrower, lined with holly which reached out and pricked his skin, leaving small scratches, barely discernible beneath his fur.

As he walked, he imprinted his surroundings, its scent, its light, on his mind. He was drawing a map in his head and he would not get lost. Despite this being new ground, he would find his way here and back with ease.

Then, as he knew it would, the path stopped and led, not to a grove, but to a field. There were dwellings here. Several huts built from giant bones and with thatch woven between their ribs. In the centre of the circle, a fire burned and a pot hung over it. Cowled figures tended the cauldron.

He approached and one raised its face to his. A Wyve. How could that be when Hweol was elsewhere?

"Come, son," said the Wyve. "Come and sit at the fire and tell us your story."

Son? He had one mother, he belonged to no one else. Betty shrank back. He hated the Crones in Umbra. There was no meat on them and so he posed no threat. He never felt comfortable amongst such creatures.

"No? Perhaps another time!" She turned back to stirring the cauldron whilst the others cackled. The smell coming from whatever they were brewing was sharp and acidic, it held no attraction for him.

He moved swiftly across the open field, leaving the huts behind him. A hill rose up, bouldered and stony. Caves dotted its side. Beady eyes peered out from the darkness. One came out to get a closer look at Betty, and he was able to study the creature in return. This one was feathered and bone-bound, a cross between human and crow in form. They looked hungry. As if they were starving. It crossed his mind they might like to feed on him, and then he shrugged the thought off and moved on. If anything tried to attack him, he could more than handle it. Already he had the sensation he was one of the strongest creatures thereabouts, regardless of his weakened state. A condition which was already being reversed.

He trudged on, and rolling meadows lay before him. The space sang to him and he let himself go, pushed all his thoughts back into the darkness and let himself run and gambol as any child of Nature.

The Imps had reappeared and were laughing alongside him, forgetting the damage he had done to one of their kind—could still do. He noted the presence of others amongst them, darker colours, like those who lived in the soil and gathered blood.

He threw back his head and roared his presence. Wherever he was, the creatures who lived here knew Betty had arrived. He didn't care. Better to be in the open. To be honest in his murders.

The meadows ended at a river's edge with a bridge spanning its width. He didn't stop but ran straight over. The Imps fell back and he saw they remained on the far side. Immediately he sensed a change in the air. This was something different.

CHAPTER THIRTY-EIGHT

BETTY

The tree-lined field camouflaged a large dwelling. A hall made out of huge timbers. Somebody important lived here. A whinny came from behind it. Stables. The Lords did not live like this in Umbra. They only took their form for the hunt. Their home was one place he had never set foot inside. There was no one here to forbid him and he was curious.

He stooped his head beneath the high lintel and entered the hall. It was empty. No furnishings. No hearth. No tapestries. Merely the robes these Lords wore when they rode. At the far end was an open doorway, dark and forbidding. Betty headed towards it and found himself on a downward slope. Down and down it led, a spiral ramp, eating into the earth. Occasionally, he caught a glimmer in the tightly-packed soil walls, a flash of white, old bone long-buried. Something pink wriggled and he plucked it out, popped it in his mouth. At least the worms tasted the same.

Still he went down. The slope evened out onto a more level basis and he was walking through a tunnel, his head scraping its roof. His eyes had adjusted to the dark, sometimes spotting flickering lights where fiery torches had been set into the walls. Small shapes ran and scampered along the route, often passing him. Their forms were insubstantial and he found he could not touch them. The one time he tried to grasp one, his hand passed through. They paid no attention to his presence. Then it opened up into a high-roofed cavern. More light had been created in the circular chamber. The floor was covered with scattered bones. Rough benches and tables were dotted around but no one sat there. The air had thickened, rotten, rancid. Betty decided it was time to go back. Demons lived here, and he understood that was what the Lords really were. Devils in a different form. He turned and walked away. He didn't hurry, felt no fear. He was too much alive for their kind.

Tommy had often called them brothers. That meant he too was a demon or a devil. But Betty already knew that. He ignored the spectres drifting past and turned his feet back onto the slope which led him up and up, back to light. He came out by the cemetery. Betty laughed. Sometimes a person didn't need to be forced to take a particular route, sometimes they were set on it without them realising.

The hum had stopped and he could see the church emptying of its congregation. He watched them through his Umbran eyes. When they had arrived, the folk they saw were well-dressed, appeared affluent, healthy. Seen in their true light however, he saw those that wouldn't have been out of place on the industrial estate with Tobias. Tatty clothes and bloodshot eyes, stooped backs and shuffling gaits. The families too, looked ragged and wan. Skinny children clinging to the hands of weary mothers and reluctant fathers. They were heading over to the pub. The children staying outside to play whilst the adults went indoors. One of the men from the pub came out and handed bottles with straws in to the children. Some sort of soft drink. It too would carry whatever magic ingredient Sister had seen fit to add.

Betty preferred Cropsoe, the people there were solid, and so would these be in time, but it would take some conditioning to attain the same status. Sister had gathered them with abandon. Such a gathering did not speak well for their futures, if they had one.

He remained amongst the trees, camouflaged by the branches, and waited. He wanted to see the Mother. Her voice had been a constant in his head for most of his life but he could remember nothing of her appearance.

Then a creature appeared. Clad in green, adorned with flowers, and crowned with bone antlers, she was everything he had imagined. She shimmered as she moved and in her, he saw the birds flying, lambs playing, foxes killing. She carried nature itself within her. Not one being, she was everything. He continued to spy on her, a strangely shy feeling overwhelming him as he looked. There was no Tommy or Fiddler to talk for him, explain him.

She did not cross the green as he expected—he had assumed she would be seeking out her sons—and instead came towards him.

"So we meet again, Betty," she said softly. "So lovely to be face-to-face and to appear in my proper form."

Startled, he found himself looking directly into her eyes. How she had managed to move so swiftly shocked him.

"Mother?" he asked. He cast about in his mind but could remember nothing. He had tried to picture her often however, usually conjuring up a poor replica of Hweol.

She giggled and shook her head. "Try again."

He searched his memory but could recall no one who looked as beautiful as the creature in front of him. Then she put her hand on his chest and he felt his heart pound in response.

"Sister? You did not look like this before!" Anxiety prickled as her hand remained on his chest. Would she invade him as she had before? Who would rescue him this time?

She continued to smile, showing no sign of malice. "I was promised that one day I would be given a role more appropriate to my status, that I would be acknowledged as equal to my brothers. My reward has been a long time coming."

"You look like a queen," said Betty. He felt the need to offer her something, a gift to mark their newfound peace. He pulled the fox brush from his pocket and held it out. "A present," he said. "To say sorry."

She took the brush and stroked it. "It's beautiful."

"As are you," he replied, feeling even more shy.

"Thank you, Betty." She smiled at him. "Did you know that when you were a child in the womb, I often spoke to you. I would reach into the soil and stroke your bones, soothe your soul. When you were reborn, I watched and offered you a christening gift. Did Tommy never tell you I was your god mother as well as your sister?"

Betty shook his head. "I—forgot. I don't know how. The Mother told me it was all forgiven." The Mother's words had become a mantra, he repeated them as if they were a charm.

He noticed the slight tightening at her jaw, the hardening of her eyes. Some anger still remained, he hoped it wasn't directed at himself. She was pretty and he liked pretty things.

"They kept you from me," said Sister. "Made you forget. Tommy never saw things beyond himself. Another's feelings are of no concern. You know that."

He did.

"You see Kinlet for what it really is," said Sister. "And you saw it faster than your brothers. It shows how true to the soil and to the Mother you are. You can see we are trying to build a new world for our kind?"

"Yes," said Betty, and he thought of the dress waiting for him. "You left me a dress for the Dance."

"Yes," smiled Sister. "We need to bring our ways to the folk. We need to reset our calendar, offer the Mother what she expects."

"They are too few to Turn," said Betty.

"No," said Sister, "we have enough to make a new beginning. It is time for you to be baptised anew, given fresh life."

"And Fiddler and Tommy?" asked Betty.

A flicker ran across Sister's face, too swift for him to make out. She was one of those who wore a mask, unlike his brothers or the Wheelborn. He didn't like it when he couldn't read a person's face.

"I'm sure they won't be forgotten,," said Sister. There was an edge to her voice. "Cernunnos has commanded that what is past is past, and all is forgiven. Much as I would like to torment my brothers, I must obey the Father."

"And the Mother," said Betty. "She speaks to me."

Sister shrugged. "I do as I'm told and leave it at that."

"This place," said Betty. "Will you stay here, even though it's a dead place?"

She laughed. "The place of the dead is my world although I have been promised more. You'll understand soon enough and it is my hope that you will join me. We will have such fun, you and I. Now, you must excuse me a while. I have work to do."

Betty watched as she walked away and vanished into the trees. His eyes caught the sliding layers, their movement becoming hypnotic. Heavy lids lowered in response, sent the world fading until a rustling sound penetrated the sleep which had claimed him. He yawned and stretched amongst the ferns where he had been talking to Sister.

He wondered that Tommy and Fiddler had not yet come to find him. Did they miss him? They rarely let him off the leash and he was surprised to have been left alone this long. Then he heard the music. Fiddler was sending the notes to bring him home. He never could resist and found himself pulled in its direction. As he made his way back into the village, the true state of the buildings and its residents remained to the fore. The glamour of their arrival had worn off.

Tommy and Fiddler were sitting on the green. They looked up as Betty approached.

"Wondered where you'd got to, brother," said Tommy.

"Walk," said Betty. "Woods."

"Oh, find anything interesting?"

Betty smiled. "Imps, Lords. Sister again."

"Sister!"

Tommy looked worried.

"She was fine," he said. "We talked about things and she said bygones were bygones." He sat down next to Tommy and started poking at a beetle with a blade of grass.

"What *exactly* did she say?"

Betty scratched his chest. "Words," he said eventually. "A lot of words." His answer annoyed them. He could've given them more detail, except that he didn't like to hold information too long, it gave him a headache. He preferred to keep hold of the emotions. They felt better. Nor did he think Tommy would take kindly to the knowledge of her raised status or the hint that she intended to include Betty in her plans.

"I don't understand," said Fiddler, looking around. "This place is a dump, neglected, abandoned. They've filled it with folk from the streets— the drug users, the drunks, the sick, and the hopeless. Why all this show?"

"To impress the Mother and the Father," said Fiddler. "Show she's as capable as us."

"Ah, she wants a competition, wants to show me anything we can do, she can do better," said Tommy. "This is how the Weald was born. Do you not remember? A spell was cast over the mind until they became intertwined with our own people. They became Wheelborn."

Then Betty remembered and grinned at Tommy. "She said there would be a baptism!"

"The baptism! The First Dance!" said Tommy, clapping his hands with delight.

"But it is not the time of the Five Turns," said Betty, "and we have no swords."

"No," said Tommy. "This is the time of *the* Dance. The very first Dance. The Dance to begin them all."

"It's why the dress has been made ready," said Fiddler.

Betty wondered at the idea. "What is the Dance?"

Tommy smiled at him. "Something I can guarantee you will enjoy."

CHAPTER THIRTY-NINE

MEGAN

Behind them sat the villagers, a silent congregation for the moment. In the front pew, as befitted their status, sat Tommy, Betty, Fiddler, Sister, and Tobias. Hilda and her sister Blodgitan were seated in the choir whilst Sister Sarah sat with Megan on the opposite side of the aisle, Aidan between them. She could feel the fear coming off him in waves despite his resignation at his predicament. Whilst the congregation of villagers looked straight ahead at the altar, his eyes were fixed on a spot at his feet, taking him away from the service.

Megan, well-versed in the rites of the Umbrans, had no doubt he was to play a central role in the celebrations. Her heart wept for him. They wrapped their cruelty in the guise of religion and worship, when really it was a mere exercise in assertion of power. His ending would be unbearable, horrific—bloody. She felt responsible for him, the need to help growing, as was the awareness she could do nothing.

Cernunnos stood on the steps of the altar, the Mother at his side. Megan had still not come to terms with his appearance. His presence was overwhelming, one of his faces always focused on her. His red eyes a freezing burn, looking through—into—her. She could feel him talking to Hweol, an insistent murmur from which there was no escape. Her head ached. She wanted to rip her scalp away, release the pressure, the monster from within.

The Choir continued to chant, a rhythmic flow of words she could not understand for all her time spent with the Umbrans, it seemed a dialect from another age. Occasionally, she caught a sense of familiarity, then the brief glimpse of recognition floated away before she could determine its sense.

The globes of light, the Wyrd Walkers, danced along the aisle, growing brighter as they advanced on the altar. They dazzled, and Megan glanced at Betty, expecting him to snatch at one, but even he appeared awed by the occasion, sat wonderstruck.

Cernunnos reached out and touched them, a blessing which took away their glow, sent the spheres sinking into the ground. Megan watched, fascinated. With each eclipse, the floor had grown darker, blacker; appeared to twist and writhe, until gradually the strands separated into monstrous serpentine forms. Horned and red-eyed, they slithered around the congregation to form a reptilian barrier against any attempt to flee.

"This is their one day of life in this form," said Sarah. "Do not look into their eyes or you will be taken, by which I mean your mind, not your body. A human's casing, even a Wheelborn's, has no value to these. Even Cernunnos cannot prevent their choice. Cernunnos, the Mother, these serpents—they were all created in the same garden."

Created. By whom? Nobody had ever suggested at anything beyond the two creatures regarded as the parents of all. Megan considered whoever—whatever—it was, constituted the greatest evil. An absent presence deciding who should control and who should be controlled. There was no equality, only ever-growing cruelty as those who wielded the power sought to assert themselves more, became corrupt and distant. No Eden could have birthed such monsters.

"And the Mother?" Megan kept her voice low.

"She has some influence but chooses not to involve herself. In creating life—of whatever form—she does not favour one over the other."

"She favoured Hweol, allowed him to—"

"No," said Sarah. "What he did was because of who he was. It was *his* nature. Gifted by her. All she will ever do is restore balance. Pull back those who have gone too far. That is all she truly intended when she sent you to Umbra."

It was the confirmation of her growing suspicions. The people of the Weald had become toys to be used and manipulated on a whim. Anger and resentment surged through her. She thought of John and grieved anew. Megan's head throbbed as the chant grew louder and the serpents continued to circle. Hweol's presence, which had held itself back at the edges of her consciousness, had taken centre stage. She could feel him, pushing, pounding at her skull, the focus of Cernunnos tugging him forward. A prisoner demanding release. Pain rode her in waves and she cried out.

"Blodmanoth is upon us," said the Mother. "And it is time for family to be reunited and judgement made. Daughter."

The skull-masked face turned to her, and she felt the weight of the Mother's eyes. It forced her to her feet, move forward to stand before the horned couple. Hweol had intimidated her, but this was something else entirely. The power emanating from them made her understand exactly how insignificant she was, a vessel, that was all. A means to teach a lesson.

"My son's presence has caused you discomfort, but it has given all a chance to consider their paths in his absence. His penance would have lasted longer in its current form, yet the Father has chosen this moment to return—"

Here Megan detected a tone reminiscent of wives immemorial, the inconvenience of husbands affecting cherished plans, and almost smiled.

"—then so too must my plans change."

Megan looked up at Cernunnos. He appeared more terrible than the Mother, and whilst she dreaded to think what might happen, relief blossomed at the thought of her release from the monster inside her.

The choir had stopped its chant and one of its members drifted to the altar. From the table, she picked up a chalice and a knife. It was Hilda. Another followed, carrying an antlered skull. A third carried a wolf pelt with the head still attached. These had been the trappings of Hweol.

"Blodmanoth is the month of blood. Blood is family," said Hilda. "Now is the time of the Festival of Blood. The festival of family."

Sarah appeared at Megan's side. She remembered how the Wyve had drunk from the corpse on the track. How the Blodgitan survived.

"Have no fear," murmured Sarah. "You are safe."

Her words did not prevent Megan from mentally adding a 'for the moment' to that sentence.

"At this time," continued Hilda, "the Mother and the Father wish all their children to be present. It is time for Hweol to bleed."

Megan let out a scream as pain suddenly blossomed in her hand. Hilda had darted forward and sliced her palm open with the knife.

Sarah took her hand and held it over the chalice.

Megan's eyes watered as the burn of the cut deepened. She bit down on her lip to prevent herself crying out again, tasted blood in her mouth.

"Hold fast," said Sarah. "It is almost done."

"We take the blood," said Hilda. "We take the son. We water the bones of the dead and return them to life."

As Hilda turned away, Sarah quickly wrapped a cloth steeped in some vile-smelling liquid around her hand. The pain immediately faded. Not only that, she no longer had any sense of the monster in her head. Had it really been as simple as that?

One of the Blodgitan had draped the pelt over a chair, perched the antlers on the headrest.

"Blood to skin, let life return," said Hilda, sprinkling a few drops of Megan's blood onto the fur. "If the Mother wills it."

The Mother stared hard at Megan and then turned to Hilda. "The Mother wills it."

"Blood to bone, let life return," said Hilda, pouring the remaining drops in the chalice over the skull and antlers. "If the Mother wills it."

The silence in the church was absolute as they waited for her response. Megan noted Tommy's obvious anticipation, his eyes gleaming with excitement. After what seemed like an eternity, the Mother spoke.

"The Mother wills it."

The choir started to sing again, this time a gentle song. A tune Megan remembered from the nursery, though she had never understood the words.

"The babe swims in blood,
in the sea of the womb.
The youth swims in blood,
in the light of the moon.
The old swim in blood,
when their day is done,
and their dust swims in blood,

until a new Turn's begun."

The Mother caressed the pelt, stroked the skull, bent and kissed the bone, the blood staining her mouth. She ran her tongue over her lips and smiled.

At the same time, Megan felt the ground tremble. The walls of the church vanished, and she saw that where the altar had been there was now a mound. It reminded her of those small hills which dotted the English landscape, hiding as they did, the burials of ancient ancestors. She had seen images of excavations revealing whispered outlines of longboats holding the remnants of the dead. There was no boat here. A mouth into the mound gaped open.

"As the womb goes dark," said Sarah, "so does our world. It is by seeing our reflections, seeing ourselves as we truly are, that we can ever hope to be free."

That sense of continual rippling Megan had observed around her in Kinlet stopped. The veil had been stripped away.

"When the Layers are dissolved, we are all taken back to our beginning."

"This is my womb," said the Mother, standing at its rim. "Dry and barren, it needs to be filled."

At either side of the mound, a path wove its way to the top of the hillock.

Megan found herself closer to the structure, saw a dim light breaking into the darkness. She tracked its source and noticed a hole at the top of the earthen cavern. A third of the way beneath the hole was a metal grille creating a barrier between it and a depression in the ground directly beneath. The air felt dry and musty, a desiccated hollow which had been unable to breathe for a long time. It tickled her throat and she fought back a cough. She did not want to do anything which would draw attention to herself.

Movement behind her distracted her from this strange apparition. Hilda and her assistant moved between the villagers who seemed completely unaware of what was going on. Megan wondered what visions had been created to get this degree of compliance. The Blodgitan moved quickly, choosing men and women, apparently at random. The children they left behind seemed not to notice. Like sheepdogs, they herded the chosen forward until they reached the bottom of the path.

The serpents slithered forward, one for each side of the mound, coiled their bodies around the first at the front of each group. In response, those two people climbed the mound. A slow, reverential pace. Hilda leading one side, her assistant, the other. The remainder of the serpents formed a fluid barrier around the people, preventing their escape.

"Let the womb fill and the sea rise," said Sister. "This is my gift to the Mother."

At this cue, the Blodgitan at the top of the mound pulled out a knife. The blades cut across unwary throats and their bodies were sent toppling over the edge to land on the grille from which small spikes protruded to cut into the body, widen the gashes already there. Blood began to flow. There had been no sound, no screams or protests.

To Megan's horror, she noticed one of them was still alive and had started to struggle against their captivity. This served to enlarge their wounds and get the blood to flow faster. There was nowhere else she could look. People had died before because of her, and now it was happening again. If she hadn't brought Hweol back, they would still be living.

Small torches had been lit on the encircling inner walls, illuminating the scene. The blood dripped down into the depression beneath and the soil lapped it up.

The Mother gathered the pelt and the skull and took them to the edge of the hollow.

"In this womb will my son swim. When the sun rises, he will be born again." She dropped wolfskin and bone into the depression. "You will watch and you will learn how this will be."

The Blodgitan had moved deeper into the mound and were kneeling on the far side.

Megan touched the cloth bundle at her side. The Mother was bringing Hweol back. Would she do the same for John? All the misgivings, the feelings of revulsion towards the creature his spirit had become, vanished as hope flared up.

A small whimper nearby caught Megan's attention. Aidan. Terror had caught hold of mind and body, yet there was also a strange acceptance in his expression. The remaining villagers stood unblinking in their queues, guarded by the serpents, some of which had curled up in a monstrous resemblance of sleeping cats, their purring a disturbing rumbling.

"Ah, Sister," said Tommy. "Lovely to see the old place again. Wearing its real face. There's a lot to be said for going *au naturel.*"

Incongruous small talk as people died and blood flowed. Nor was it just the surroundings which had changed when the church had vanished and the truth of the village been revealed. Sister, whose appearance had been one of a middle-aged woman, of middle stature, of middle build, of everything which would usually render her invisible to the eyes of the world around her, had also shed her skin. The side Megan could see was of a beautiful woman, slim, supple, unblemished. Why would she choose to hide herself in that previous nondescript cloak? As Sister turned round to gaze upon the congregation, Megan gasped.

Here was something more akin to what she expected. This side of her face was the opposite to that first revealed. It was hideous. Decaying flesh, bone and tissue showing, hair like rat's tails on the shiny dome of her skull, her eye, bloodshot and weeping pus. Sister ignored Megan, continued chatting with her brother.

"Somebody had to look after it," said Sister, her smile a mix of the beatific and the demonic. "It is the place all come to in the end. Where you all will rest. The halls of Hel have a bed for everyone—even you brother."

Tommy laughed. "Not yet, Sister."

"That depends on the Mother," said Sister. "And I think it's time you started calling me by my proper name. Showed some respect. You are in my world now, *Brother.*"

"Children," said the Mother. "Now is not the time for squabbling. Whatever will our guests think? This is a time for rejoicing. My son will rise again, and you must prepare to receive him."

Megan suppressed a chuckle despite her predicament. To hear Tommy spoken to in such a manner, as if a wayward child, was amusing. It showed he could be put in his place, and Tommy was indeed looking chastened.

The choir continued to chant. The hypnotic words serving to keep the congregation quiet and biddable. Inside the mound, the stream of blood had slowed. Two Blodgitan moved to the grille and poked the bodies with spears, it did nothing to hasten the flow. They pushed the bodies up and off the grille. Megan heard a rush and then two more bodies tumbled onto the grille, both dead this time, and soon the rain of blood began again. The two which had been displaced were now being hung up against the back wall, and she could see the faint outlines of a narrow groove in the soil beneath running from the body to the hollow. Gullies to carry the last of their offering.

By now the contents of the hollow were crimson, its shade deepening as more dripped down from above. The smell turned her stomach. She forced herself to continue watching. There was a slight movement beneath the pelt. Megan thought it was Sister playing with the Layers again, but it was too slight, too exact to be that. The blood was wrapping itself around the pelt, turning it into an embryonic formation. Its similarity to what she herself had lost suddenly tore at her, threatened to rip an old wound wide open. Then she looked again and her anger grew. This was a bastardised version of her lost baby. Hweol was an abomination in so many ways and he was coming back. It wasn't right. It wasn't fair.

Sister Sarah had brought her here saying her husband's rebirth was in the Father's gift, and both Cernunnos and the Mother ignored her now they had released Hweol's spirit. Was that all she had been? His carrier? A suspicion took hold. She pulled the bundled sword close to her chest, cradling it with her renewed hope.

"What of John?" asked Megan, turning to the Wyve. "Couldn't he be revived too?"

The dark glitter of the Wyve's eyes gave her the answer she dreaded. "No," said Sarah. "I've told you. That was false hope given to help you endure your time in Umbra. You can only set him free to rest here, in Sister's—Hel's—halls. It is she you must see. When you are ready."

"But Hweol—"

"Is born of different matter, the bones of your husband are gone forever. There is nothing to gift him life."

Then Megan considered Aidan. A thought—unforgiveable and monstrous—occurred to her. "Could we not give him another body?"

How could she do what the Mother had done to her? Implant John's soul into another? She had been made to feel she as if she stood on the edge of madness. Yet it offered a solution. Which should she choose?

"No," said Sarah, sharply. "It is not for you to decide who lives and who dies. Have you learned nothing through your suffering? To ask such a thing of Hel, to consider it, shows you are becoming like them. And this one," she gestured to Aidan, "is needed for other things."

Fury bubbled up. The injustice of everything overwhelming her. Megan glared at Sarah. "Don't I deserve something? Some recompense for everything I have gone through in this twisted world of yours? I have been manipulated and abused, all because of some family issues between *them*."

"And you become them if you demand this. As corrupted as Tommy and the others."

Megan was furious. To be spoken of in the same manner as those monsters. She had suffered. She had lost everything. Deserved something.

"There are others we could find for what you desire. But don't they deserve their own lives?" asked Sarah, more gently now. "What right do you have to claim another in such a manner?"

"Seems to me like they've already been claimed," snapped Megan. "I'm merely suggesting an alternative."

"Then consider John. How do you think he would feel—if by some miracle such a request would be granted to you? Do you not think he would come to hate you for it?"

Would he hate her for giving him life? Or would the guilt at what she had forced upon another drive a wedge between them?

"The only way to know would be to ask him," said Sarah.

Megan stroked the blanket covering the sword. She had not unwrapped it for a long time, unable to listen to her husband's voice calling to her from within its blade.

CHAPTER FORTY

MEGAN

The line of villagers had dwindled as they were shepherded in turn to the top of the mound. Megan wondered at the thoughts inside their heads as they approached the summit, saw the fate of their predecessor, their own to come. Had the Mother emptied their minds or had Sister created another beautiful lie? Both were a means to the same end, and she dismissed the sacrificed from her mind. She had her own suffering to deal with and at least these people died unaware and, to a certain extent, happy. The last had fallen, and a tide of blood had risen to hide the pelt and bone, the beginnings of the creature beneath it.

The Mother spoke. "You have attended me, go now to the Father. Celebrate with him and renew your energies."

It was a dismissal obeyed immediately as the serpents, the Wyves, the Wheelborn, the Imps—all those vicious and cruel folk—turned away with renewed purpose. Megan watched them disappear but did not follow. Aidan remained close by. She knew he clung to her like a security blanket, his last hold on old realities, terrified at being swept away. Two of the Blodgitan remained beside the pit, watching, assessing—Midwyves.

"A mother's most anxious time is when the child is in the womb, so frail, so vulnerable."

Megan felt the stab of her words, the scars of her loss which had never healed properly, ripped open. Tommy's voice drifting through the air, his threat and his claim to her poor lost child. For the Mother to recognise this, yet have failed to protect her, roused her to anger.

"You took mine," she said.

The Mother took a step nearer to the pool of blood. It rippled slightly as if sensing her presence.

"No. That was Hweol and he has been punished."

"A year without form? A year tormenting me in my own head? And you reward him and bring him back, bring *your* child back, when you couldn't do the same for me? Or my husband?"

The Mother did not respond, had appeared to forget her. The surface of the crimson pool had shifted and Megan sensed something stirring beneath. The Blodgitan in attendance were crouching at the edge, watching with intense concentration.

"Hweol was my first born. In him are the laws of nature embodied, and in his cruelty is my balance. What is life after all but a continual cycle of life and death, a turning wheel of survival?"

The pool was bubbling, steady rhythmic waves crossing its surface. The ground beneath her feet and the walls of the cavern vibrated, keeping time with these movements. Their whole space felt as if it was pushing down, pushing out.

"Soon," said one of the Blodgitan, raising her eyes to the Mother. "His time is near."

The contractions attacked Megan and she gasped in shock.

"You are of his line," said the Mother. "You are tied to him, share his blood. This is why you feel his birth."

Megan didn't want to. Longed to do nothing more than rush forward, hold Hweol down, drown him, stab him. For a brief moment, her hand clasped the sword as she considered using the blade as the Mother had instructed her for that Sixth Turn, the one belonging to Umbra. But she couldn't. Whatever aspect of her husband's soul remained was held by that metal. She could not taint it—him. She pondered the spears on the grille, wondered if she had enough strength to pull it down. Not without help, she decided, and Aidan was too shocked to be of any use. She took in her companion and suddenly understood she could do nothing which would endanger him anymore than he was already.

Megan felt another pulse of anger as she realised she had become responsible for him. He hadn't asked for this but still she blamed him. She could do nothing but wait with the Mother for Hweol's rebirth.

What did it feel like to give birth and hold your child, living, breathing, in your arms? To feel soft skin, inhale the scent of another that was also a part of you? Waves of loss washed over her and she felt the tears on her cheeks.

A cold hand suddenly gripped hers. "Share this with me and know."

The Mother's touch took her spinning away from her surroundings. Everything vanished and she found herself spiralling into the darkness at the core of her being. There was no sound, only a dull roar in her ears as the contractions pulsed. A wave of pain and then a pause, another wave followed by a brief respite. She had no sense of anything except this blackness, firing its pain at her with an intensity she thought would tear her apart if it continued much longer.

"We give life with our agony," said the Mother, her voice penetrating Megan's blanket of unawareness. "Born of blood and pain, it is a microcosm of all that is to come."

Megan didn't want to be part of this birth, a subversion of all she understood of the process. To be a spectator, a participant, in the rebirth of Hweol was an additional horror. She did not have time to dwell on it further as another contraction came and pulled her back down into the dark. Faster and faster the waves came and she found herself gasping for breath. She wanted to break contact with the Mother, pull away, but the Mother continued to hold on to her. And then, just as she thought she couldn't take anymore, it stopped, leaving the faintest throb running through her body.

The Mother had let her go and the loss of contact set her swaying. Other hands caught and held her.

"Megan, Megan. You all right? What happened?"

She opened her eyes to find Aidan looking at her with concern, and then his gaze shifted over her shoulder and he froze. If she didn't turn, she could pretend a little while longer that Hweol had not come back, but her body betrayed her. Clasping Aidan's arm to anchor herself, she turned.

Blood sprayed in a fountain as a shape emerged from the pool, gobbets slithered over the creature's surface, some caught on his antlers hung in clots. The pelt clung to his outline, sodden through with the stolen ichor. She could barely make out his features as the blood of the womb clung to him in a scarlet caul. As he moved, the air shifted, bringing with it the stench of the dead. Aidan staggered back from her grasp, and she heard him retching behind her.

Hweol remained silent, his gaze fixed on the Mother. Something was passing between them, an unspoken communication, the formation of that bond between parent and child. Did he remember everything that had passed, or did he start again with no knowledge other than what the Mother decided he should have?

"This, this is the creature you tried to destroy?" whispered Aidan, returning to her side.

"Yes."

"You were brave," said Aidan.

"I was stupid," said Megan. "To think I had any power to change things was stupid, ignorant. After all I'd been taught, all I'd understood and witnessed, I thought I was strong enough to make a difference."

"You did," said the Mother. "You halted things, allowed balance to be reasserted, reminders to be given about what was tolerated. Most would not have attempted such a thing. Hweol will honour you for that."

As Megan took in the bone crown, the skeletal face beginning to appear, she wondered what he really thought. Did he share the Mother's opinion? Or would he seek his revenge for his public humiliation?

He was looking directly at her now but his eyes were unfathomable. She could read nothing there.

"He will speak to you when he has fed," said the Mother. "A newborn needs its food." She nodded at the Blodgitan. Both stepped into the remains of the blood pool and positioned themselves to support Hweol onto more solid ground. They didn't bring him to the Mother however, but guided him to the back of the cavern where the flesh remains of those who had been sacrificed were piled. They seated him on a ledge, and one pulled a limb from the nearest body, held it up to Hweol.

The creature sniffed and licked at the limb, started to bite. It was at that point Megan could bear no more and fled the mound, shaking off Aidan, wanting to be away from everyone and everything. Into the nearby trees, along paths strange to her, unknown territory, she continued to run. Should some beast appear, she didn't care. Better to die quickly and put an end to the swirling thoughts, the heartbreak of her losses. She ran until a gnarled tree root tripped her up and she tumbled to the ground, her fall broken by a dense growth of fern. As she lay there, she could see the stars through the canopy, the universe continuing as it had done and would forever. Like Hweol. Like the Wheel. She turned and curled up into a ball, allowed the last of her tears to fall until exhausted, she slept.

CHAPTER FORTY-ONE

MEGAN

She had nothing, nobody. Aidan still had Chloe, a chance to rebuild a relationship as well as his life. If there was something to live for then one had to do everything to survive—and she could help him. Her scalp prickled. There was no one nearby. Yet she could feel a presence, something pushing at her thoughts, trying to reach in. Megan pushed back, reset the barriers to stop the attempted incursions. Free of Hweol, she understood he and Tommy would still try to read her, ascertain her next actions. Months of mind games, of determined resistance, had made this much easier. It was almost enjoyable to allow them to come close, feel they were almost there and then slam down her defences. Decided at last, she felt comforted that the path she was taking was the same her mother had chosen.

She rose and picked her way through woods so similar and yet so different. The path had a tendency to lead the unwary astray should they lose concentration. Others drifted around her. The remaining lost souls from the village. There was little use for them now Hweol had been resurrected, and so they wandered, dazed and confused, not registering the dangers around them. One such was ahead of her and he suddenly veered off. She didn't call out to him, there was no point as she would be unable to help him, but she stopped at the place where he left the track.

Branches thrashed as unseen folk homed in on this lost sheep. Wood snapped and cracked, foliage waved back and forth as predators scented their prey, taking their time as it was evident the wanderer was going nowhere except into their midst. She wondered how long some of those creatures could keep their silence, so used to the giggling and making noise. One of them gave a low hiss, a sound which roused the man from his stupor, and then they were on him, and the night was filled with his screams. He would be one of many. An awful end, but better to finish the nightmares here than to go back with them to a society which wouldn't understand.

Would Aidan be able to cope? There would be no one, no one safe anyway, that he would be able to talk to about his experience. He would have to keep that part to himself. If he wanted to go back and make things right with Chloe, he would have to call on a strength she wasn't sure he had. The movement and shrieking ceased and her surroundings fell back to that sense of expectant quiet. Megan continued her walk, the path beneath her gradually accepting the weight of her tread, settling into a clear route leading to the grove. Just before it opened out into the clearing where their tormentors mingled and made ready, Aidan sat alone on a fallen trunk.

"They've left you unguarded," said Megan.

Aidan jumped at the sound of her voice and looked up. "It's not as if I can go anywhere is it? Whichever way I go, I'm pretty screwed."

"I've thought," he continued, "of killing myself. Denying them whatever it is they hope to gain from the manner of my passing. But I'm too much of a coward for that. A coward in life, it seems I'm to be a coward in death."

Megan sat beside him and took his hand. "No, you're not a coward. And now I must ask you to be as brave as you can. There is a chance, faint, I'll admit, but a chance I can help you and you can get back to Chloe."

"How?" There was disbelief in his voice. What was she but one young woman amongst a tribe of monsters?

"I don't – I'm not sure …"

"Don't try to feed me false hope-"

"No, please. Listen. It may seem as though it will never happen. I mean, once the ceremony starts—if the chance comes—you'll take it."

"Okay. I'll play your game for a little while if it helps the time pass. What then? If I do get away?"

"Find the village sign. It still exists somewhere amongst these ruins. The path out is there, you'll see it. Its shape cannot change. The Leys are part of the soil, imprinted by time, and neither the Mother nor the Father can destroy it or alter its route. But Sister can change its appearance, make you believe you are in danger. Ignore it all, ignore everything. Look straight ahead, picture Chloe at the end and run to her. You'll get there."

He gave a dry laugh. "I'm not the world's greatest runner."

"Doesn't matter. Every step away is a defeat to them." Megan nodded her head at the milling crowd, none of whom seemed the slightest bit interested in the conversation their prisoner was having with Megan. They assumed, no doubt, he wasn't going anywhere soon.

"And if I do get back. How am I supposed to talk about this? Come to terms with such knowledge? I couldn't tell Chloe or her mum any of this. They'd think I was nuts."

"You might not have to. The Weald and its folk have a habit of pulling a veil over this world, wiping the memory of outsiders who cross its path, and if it doesn't? Write it down, hey, turn it into a book!"

"That would be something," said Aidan. "Who'd believe such a story!"

They both laughed at that, and she left him musing on the actor he'd choose to play himself, anything to forget what might be coming. As Megan made her way through the many-robed figures—all had cloaked themselves in honour of the ceremony—she found Sister Sarah.

"Are you ready to say goodbye?" asked Sarah, nodding at the wrapped blade Megan still held.

"Yes," said Megan. She had finally accepted it would come to this and was ready to let go. She hoped it would be quick, painless.

The grove appeared to have increased in circumference, and as she looked up, it was as if they were cupped in the palms of cliffs rising high and around the ancient trees. The perspective was disorienting. Heightened further by the sight of the maelstrom at war above them. It reminded her of simulations of the beginning of the universe. Was this a fashioning of Sister's, a dramatic backdrop for the events to come?

The watchers formed a semi-circle, in front of which burned a small fire. Beyond this was a raised dais on which the Mother and the Father sat on thrones of bone. Beneath the dais, a doorway had been created, and through that, blazing up into the sky, roared an inferno. The crowd quieted as Cernunnos rose. An air of expectation hung over everything.

"Tell me, what is the First Turn?"

As one, all responded:

"The First Turn is the Turn of Beginning and Rebirth,

when blood runs freely and the moon turns red,

when the soil drowns in a river of death,

and we rise again."

The words chilled Megan as she listened. Whilst she had been wondering how to help Aidan, it suddenly occurred to her, they could, possibly would, take her too. The blood had been flowing in Kinlet. How much more could they need? The blade felt heavy in her arms, a burden she felt unable to bear much longer.

"Daughter." Cernunnos was looking directly at her. "You have an offering for me."

Offering? She had her husband's soul to free but not an offering, surely. Fearful at his intentions, she pulled the bundle tighter to her chest, reluctant now to deliver him into their hands.

"No," whispered Sarah. "You must give him up, release him."

"They won't harm him?" *A stupid question,* she told herself. He was beyond pain, wasn't he?

Tommy appeared in front of her. "This gift is needful. It is part of our rite."

"You said the Father would release him, let him rest in peace." She levelled her accusation at Sarah.

"I said he *might*," said Sarah, "though because of you, only one sword remains. It is enough. A sword to lead the Dance."

Megan was dumbfounded. She had allowed herself to trust one of the Folk and had been betrayed.

"You pretended to be on my side, understood," said Megan.

"All that was truth," said Sarah. "It made it easier to get you here. A willing pilgrimage carries value and honour."

Tommy took hold of the bundle as Sarah spoke. Megan let go. She had no choice. Despair took over as she considered how, once again, she had led her husband into an eternity of suffering.

"Not an eternity," said Tommy, to her unguarded thoughts. "Only a moment."

He made his way to the small fire in front of Cernunnos, unwrapping the sword as he went so that he held the blade in outstretched arms.

"The steel of the Father is fired in the flame. Let this offering, of steel and soul, feed him for eternity."

There was a long pause as if the Father was making a decision. Then he nodded and Tommy stepped through the small fire, passed through the doorway and entered into the inferno beyond. The flames wrapped themselves around him, colours a kaleidoscope of deep reds and dazzling orange. Tommy turned in its midst still holding the sword aloft which glowed brighter and brighter until a dazzling spark of brilliant white escaped, soared towards Cernunnos, who held out his hand in invitation.

Megan watched, listened for the voice of her husband which had faded to no more than a whisper of a murmur, stilled almost by her guilty neglect.

"I am the Father," said Cernunnos, holding his glowing palm aloft. "I am what was, what is, and what will be. This soul," he raised his hand higher, "has suffered greatly and deserves to be freed. One day he will walk again, in a new form, one of my choosing. Until then, be assured, I will guard him behind the shield of myself." With that, he raised the small, dancing sphere to his mouth and swallowed. Its light did not fade but dispersed along the skeletal scaffolding beneath the pelt so that Cernunnos became a beacon to all.

Megan watched the Mother's promise wither and die. She had finally been cut adrift from everything that had any meaning for her. She had nothing, and through her failure had become nothing. The thought ignited a spark of anger, roused her to consider her retribution. She would be the one to say what will be, if for a mere second.

Tommy, who had continued to stand in the fires, now stepped out and made his way back to the dais where he stood, head bowed in obedience to his parents. The Mother rose and stood beside Cernunnos. Then she raised her hand, let her breath roll over it and on to Tommy. It was the kiss of a Mother reclaiming her son, and as it touched his cheek, he raised his head.

All the years had fallen away, the lines and wrinkles, the touch of grey in both skin and hair. The frailty—in so far as there had been any—gone.

"Our son is reborn," said the Mother.

Then it was Fiddler's turn to step through the doors and into the flames, playing his wild music as he did so, sending the sparks whirling in delight at his melody. When he eventually returned to his place in front of the dais, he too was caressed by the Mother's kiss. That left Betty. A movement distracted Megan. She turned slightly to see Aidan being guided around the semi-circle and into the space beyond the dais, his captors keeping to the shadows so they were not seen.

More guilt clawed at her. To have let him go without any acknowledgement. He must've been feeling as abandoned as she had. She quickly looked at those nearest to her. It was as if she had become invisible.

Nobody paid any attention as she slipped away from the gathering and followed. Aidan was being manhandled by one guard, forced into the position of a penitent on the ground, kneeling with arms outstretched, hands bound to posts, bare skin of his back glowing in the fire. Then he was left alone. Megan had no idea how his end was to come, but come it would, his posture of supplication one she had seen so many times in past sacrifices. She took in their surroundings and determined they were alone on that side of the inferno which shielded them from view.

"Aidan!"

Dull eyes lifted to hers, recognition barely registering.

"Aidan. You have a chance. I can give you a way out but you will have to take it, no questions asked. Will you?"

His look continued to be uncomprehending.

"Chloe!"

At the mention of his daughter's name, a glimmer of intelligence returned.

"Go for Chloe!"

"How?"

"Let me take your place. Don't say anything. Don't waste time, keep in the shadows and run. I reckon all the danger is here in this circle at the moment, so you have a chance. Don't ask me to explain, just go. Will you?"

The reminder of his daughter roused him and brought him back to life. She could see a new energy and alertness. She took a small knife and cut the ties which bound his hands to the posts.

"Go," she said.

And Aidan ran into the shadows, in the dark, back towards life and his daughter.

"Good luck," she whispered after him.

Then she took his place, stripping off her shirt so her bare skin felt the heat of the fire, stretched her arms out to hold the posts to which Aidan had been tied. When whoever came through the fire next saw her, she hoped they would see merely the skin and not its owner.

The singing of the crowd, the buzz of their excitement and expectation filtered through to her and she shivered despite the cold. Suddenly she felt her mother with her again. That old connection through the darkness when they'd held on to each other as Liza had sacrificed herself in her daughter's place. They had given each other strength despite the terror both felt. *What had that felt like?* thought Megan. *How does the body cope with pain beyond anything a normal person would expect to suffer?* She wasn't sure she was strong enough. Then she felt another presence. Her husband, John. And another. Her father, Simon Wheelborn. Her family had come to her to help her across that barrier.

Knowing they were there gave her extra strength whilst the waiting was becoming unbearable. She hoped her end would be quick, that this death was not one of Hweol's extravagances. If Tommy knew it was her, he would certainly want to make an example of his daughter. Her stomach felt like ice and her body began to shake. She fought to hold on to the sense of family, she needed them to get her through this.

The flames behind her began to crackle and splutter, the heat moving in a different pattern as if something was travelling through them. The air had become warmer and felt as if it was dancing. Dancing. Betty was near. She knew his smell, his presence.

It was time for her to burn.

CHAPTER FORTY-TWO

BETTY

Drums. Their beat pulsed through the air, a rhythmic throb in echo of life. In the midst of the grove a fire had already sparked into being, flames beginning to leap higher at each vibration. Beyond the fire was the dais, the platform raised so the Father and the Mother could be witness to the rebirth of their wildest child. The grove itself was edged with a palisade of Folk, the followers of Sister, those who had come from the Layerings, the few from Umbra.

If they had brought gifts, there was no evidence of it. Gold could be seen in the fire, mistletoe hung in place of myrrh, whilst carrion flowers scented the air.

Above them, the stars glowed brightly. Betty clapped his hands in delight. This was all for him!

"Dance, brother," said Tommy, as Fiddler played his bow across newborn strings.

It was a song Betty had not heard since that first remembered time. He had worn a dress. Where was his baptismal gown? It would come. He had to wait.

Betty stilled. There was a strange calmness on his face as he allowed the flames to hypnotise him, revisiting his previous rebirths, preparing himself. He had recognised his time, understood from the magic of the Mother and the Father, this was his. They had given Tommy and Fiddler their span of years and now, he too would be reborn. With the steady rhythmic drumming behind him, lending its pulse to the night, the keening of those gathered, he felt as if he had returned to the womb. The contractions of this birth continued in response to his surroundings.

"The Wheel cannot Turn again without the most special of sons," said the Mother.

Her words, like music, washed over him, sinking into his skin, to his very core.

"He is the one who dances to the purity of Nature's rhythms. He is the one true to the very essence of survival. The one drive all creatures share, and which many are condemned for because of the perceived cruelty, is to be found in its purest of forms in this son. It is he who understands the beating heart of nature, it is he who understands it all as he honours it by devouring it. Let the heart be given and the heart be taken."

A heart waited for him.

Music continued to accompany the flames. Changed to notes gently plucked on Fiddler's strings. Almost a lullaby, the one from that long ago birthing.

"Dance," said Tommy, standing in front of him and slipping a new dress over his head.

He felt its texture, different to those previously worn. This one was made of so many skins, the young and the old, the sick and the healthy, all whose blood had restored Hweol to his rightful place. Little went to waste. If a living being was taken, every part of them was used, for that was the way to truly honour their gift. The skins were held together by stitches of ribboned veins and spider silk. The addition of butterfly wings and birds' feathers cast a dazzling sheen, a riot of colour over the grey of the death which held them. The gifted robe moulded itself to his form so it became a part of him, a dress gradually absorbed into his being so that he would wear it forever, even under more obvious garments.

As he ran his hands over the material, he felt the breeze as it drifted over the sacrificed, the caresses they had felt, the kisses shared, the work they had done. Every emotion was bound up in its fabric. In his dress was the wheel of life, and still something was missing.

"The heart is beating for you," said Cernunnos.

The drums pounded louder at this, became faster, contractions speeding up.

"The heart is calling for you, heart of my hearts," said the Mother.

Faster and the flames leapt with the music so the inferno beyond the dais revealed a little of what it had hidden.

Betty could see a kneeling figure, its back to him, bare skin glowing in the light. Beneath that skin was a heart, and it was his.

"The heart beats," said the Mother, "and you, my wildest and most special child, need a heart."

Betty's feet moved in time to the rhythm. It carried him through the smaller fire beneath those on the dais, and through the portal to the inferno. Without any thought, his mind and soul were one with the drums and the keening of the watchers, he stepped into the blaze. His family's words urging him on.

"We burn in the fire of the Mother's womb," said Tommy.

"We devour the ash of the roasted flesh," returned Tobias.

"We take into our souls the Mother's love,

And damn the mortal side to rest."

Betty became an inferno. He spun in its midst, not in pain, but in wonder, catching the flames and holding them, opening his mouth to taste their heat. The fire never dropped in size or intensity, continued to hold him in its palm. This was his cradle. The flames licked over him, not sparking, but settling on his body, laying claim to every part of him.

A beat.

Gradually, he became aware of it, a layer of sound below the drums and the chants continuing around him. This was the one heartbeat above all others calling to him. The one promised so long ago when he had danced beneath her bedroom window to the silver of Fiddler's song. It didn't surprise him to hear it in this place at this time. She had refused him before and she was making amends. Where the other had gone—Aidan, wasn't that his name—the one they had marked as his, didn't matter. None of it mattered. Her heart was his. The beat was roaring in his ears, demanding.

It was time to step out of the fire and take what was his.

Leaving the inferno behind him, there was only Betty and the offering on this side of the dais, a bubble which was theirs and theirs alone. Her back was to him, so clear and unblemished, a rippling white silk as the shadows of the fire danced over her.

His desire, his hunger, was unbearable. He plunged his hand into her back, ripping her flesh apart, ignoring the squelch of blood and air as his fist searched for his prize. If she had screamed, he did not hear it, if she groaned or continued to live as he searched, he did not notice. For him, only the heart called. His fingers probed, took care as the cavity cleared, found the jewel in its midst. A quick tug and he had pulled it out, held the organ in the palm of his hand. Like he had when he was a boy.

His Mother's words came back to him, telling him to look at it, feel it and then taste it. It had been so long time since he had eaten a heart offered in a manner such as this. Something which had barely stopped beating, could still be seen pulsing as Betty held and then devoured it.

He ate slowly, chewing every piece, ignoring the body twitching on the floor which stilled eventually. All that had gone before was done. This. This was what he had been born for. To be, to burn and to feast on the hearts of the world.

ABOUT THE AUTHOR

Stephanie Ellis' poetry has been published in the HWA Poetry Showcase Volumes VI, VII and VII, Black Spot Books Under Her Skin and online at Visual Verse. She has also co-written a collection of found poetry, Foundlings, with Cindy O'Quinn based on the work of Alessandro Manzetti and Linda D. Addison. A gathering of her dark twists on traditional nursery rhymes can be found in the collection, One, Two, I See You.

Stephanie Ellis writes dark speculative prose and poetry and has been published in a variety of magazines and anthologies, the most recent being Scott J. Moses' What One Wouldn't Do, Demain Publishing's A Silent Dystopia and Brigids Gate Press' Were Tales. Her longer work includes the novel, The Five Turns of the Wheel, and the novellas, Bottled and Paused. Her short stories can be found in the collections, The Reckoning, and As the Wheel Turns. She is co-editor of Trembling With Fear, http://HorrorTree.com's online magazine, and also co-edited the Daughters of Darkness anthologies. She is an active member of the HWA and can be found at http://stephanieellis.org and on twitter at @el_stevie

CONTENT WARNINGS

Ritual Death, Violence

Paperback ISBN: 978-1-957537=21-4

Welcome to the Weald.
The Five Turns of the Wheel has begun.
With each Turn, blood will be spilled,
and sacrifices will be made.
Pacts will be made...and broken.
Will you join the Dance?

In the Weald, the time has come for the Five Turns of the Wheel. Tommy, Betty and Fiddler, the sons of Hweol, Lord of Umbra, have arrived to oversee the sacred rituals...rituals brimming with sacrifice and dripping with blood.

Megan Wheelborn, daughter of Tom my, hatches a desperate plan to free the people of the Weald from the bloody and cruel grip of Umbra, and put an end to its murderous rituals. But success will require sacrifice and blood as well. Will Megan be able to pay the price?

Paperback ISBN: 978-1-957537-10-8

During the Spring Equinox underneath London, four people enter the caves, but only one will survive. Each trespasser must battle their own demons before facing the White Lady who rises each year to feed on human flesh.

Paperback ISBN: 978-1-957537-31-3

Stewartville. A town living in the shadow of the prisons that drive its economy. Haunted by the ghosts of its past. Cursed by the dark secrets hidden beneath. A town so entwined with the prisons waiting outside the city limits that it's impossible to imagine one without the other, or to ever imagine escaping either.

When a teenage boy digs into the history of the town, he discovers a tunnel system beneath Stewartville, passageways filled with dark secrets. Secrets leading not to freedom, but to unrelenting terror.

Stewartville. Where the convicts aren't the only prisoners.